VULCAN

VULCAN

CHUCK KIMBALL

Ordering Information:

For orders and inquiries, please contact:
1-888-404-1388
www.goldtouchpress.com
book.orders@goldtouchpress.com

Printed in the United States of America

To the love of my love, my wife. Without your help, guidance, and support, I could not have written yet another book. My dream of writing has become a reality once again because of your ideas, critiques, helpful advise and hard work.

Vulcan

Vulcan is the god of fire, and belongs to one of the most ancient stages of Roman Religion. Because of fire's destructive capacity the name was chosen for the covert operation depicted in this book.

PROLOGUE

Two days earlier

Two days ago, Hilda, Sargent Major Jenkins, Brett, and Lyle had stormed the Chateau du Bois in the vicinity of Bordeaux, France. The fierce attack had resulted in the assassination of a coveted drug kingpin named Renard. This individual was also known for having smuggled tons of illegal armory into the United States using a privately owned Russian submarine. On their last assignment, the four agents had been seriously wounded and were now recovering in the American hospital in Paris.

While hospitalized, Brett and Lyle received a phone call ordering them to attend a meeting at the American embassy in Paris the following morning. Lyle who had planned on getting married in four days was concerned this conference was about another pending black ops assignment.

The following day, the agent picked up Brett and headed to 2 Gabriel street in Paris. As they walked through the gated embassy, Patrick, a friend employed there, met the duo. The three of them were friends who had worked in Afghanistan. After a handshake and a hug that had to be aborted due to pain caused by fractured ribs damaged by the shock of bullets hitting their ceramic vests during the assault in Bordeaux, Patrick escorted Brett and Lyle to a secure room that had visual and audio communications with the National Security Agency at the White House. With a cup of coffee in hand, they sat down to await the connection with Colonel Jackson in Washington DC on the flat screen TV secured to the wall.

After a short thank you for a job well done in Bordeaux, the colonel advised Lyle and Brett that POTUS (The President of the United States) had reliable intel that more armory was being shipped by Aleksey, the Chechen, into the United States. Lyle who had invited Colonel Jackson to the wedding ceremony a month ago reminded him that he was getting married in four days. Immediately the colonel asked the date, time and location of the service. Colonel Jackson had become Lyle's godfather after Lyle's dad was killed on a secret mission when Lyle was only six years old.

After congratulations on the marriage, the colonel advised Lyle that the honeymoon would probably be cut short. As soon as definitive information on the shipment became available, he and Brett would be relied upon, once again, to do what they could to prevent the delivery.

The colonel saluted the men, and said, "I will see you at the wedding son." The screen went black.

CHAPTER 1

Paris

The next three days passed without incident. Lyle took a walk every day, worked out, and let his body recover. The wedding day was to take place in ninety-six hours. Sargent Major Jenkins and Brett spent their time sightseeing. Annie's mother, Marguerite, had arrived with two cousins to help with the last details of wedding and reception. Her father, a retired gendarme, was unable to join the rest of the family because of his poor state of health. Stephanie, Annie's friend, along with two of her colleagues from the American Hospital, were busy running errands and making final arrangements. Lyle gave them a hand by taking Jennie Anne for walks and to a local park where he introduced her to the swings and toboggan. On Monday the two of them attended a puppet show called Guignol, similar to Punch and Judy in the States.

Lyle was working in the kitchen when Annie came in with Stephanie, both talking a mile a minute. The other two nurses from the American Hospital were discussing the flower arrangements that would decorate the tables. Jacqueline, another surgical nurse who had met Lyle a few times, said to Annie, "Before he gets married, I want to hug your sexy man." Jacqueline was funny and a bit flirtatious. She hugged Lyle who was wondering when this excessive showing of affection would stop. She kissed him twice on both cheeks before releasing him. He had to get away, "It's time for me to take a short walk, relax and cool off. You ladies are overheating me; I cannot take all that attention."

Returning from his stroll, Lyle was somewhat red in the face due to the cold weather when he returned to the apartment. After closing the door gingerly, not to attract attention, he entered the bedroom where two mid-calf wedding gowns had been laid out on top of the bed, both of them were off-white. Many other things were hanging all over the bedroom. He was standing there when Annie came in and asked, "Which one do you prefer?" To please Annie, he studied the gowns, and rubbing his cheek, he said, "I know either one will look perfect on you. You look good with just a towel wrapped around you."

Lyle poured himself a glass of wine, warmed up a baguette, and cut slices of cheese and fruit. Isolating oneself in this small apartment was difficult. Soon, the helpers started leaving one by one, and the place was quiet again. With the returned silence, one could hear the characteristic musical two-note siren of an ambulance zooming in the distance.

It had been a long day. Lyle was now reading in bed, and Annie was getting ready to relax in a hot bath. When she reappeared in the bedroom, the bath towel accidentally or conveniently fell to the floor. She slipped between the flannel sheets and threw herself into Lyle's arms. Suddenly Annie reminded him that no one from his family, except for the Jenkins and Brett, would be present for the big day, "Your mother should be here, try to convince her it is not such a long trip after all. There is a non-stop flight from Atlanta to Paris. And remind her you will be meeting her the minute she will step off the plane." It was early morning in Atlanta, the best time to reach Monique. Annie kept on talking, "What about your aunt Anette and your uncle Remi? We need their company. They are all welcome, but I must know soon if they decide to attend our special day."

CHAPTER 2

Paris

Wedding day

The wedding was taking place in the Saint-Julien-le-Pauvre church which was built in the 13th century and is one of Paris's oldest churches. It is located on the left bank of the river Seine, in the 5th Arrondissement. The church had given comfort to many over the centuries. Today a marriage was going to be celebrated in this Roman Catholic place of worship dedicated to Julian of Le Mans who during his life fought for the cause of the poor. Amazingly, this church was built on the site of another church dating back to the 6th century.

As the bride and groom and their guests were getting ready for the service, a man of average height, about five foot eight, one hundred and seventy pounds, wearing an Irish flat cap pulled down over his eyes to cover a large scar across his forehead was stalking the building. Chekhov was the name of this uninvited individual. No one knew his full name except the police who had arrested him in the past, the first time when he was only sixteen.

The intruder's demeanor was suspicious. He slowly worked his way from chestnut tree to chestnut tree to reach around the back corner of the old church. Although his behavior was odd, one could not differentiate the man from the other Parisians coming and going. Chekhov continued advancing toward the back door of the building when a long black and shiny car approached; the vehicle bore embassy plates. Paying attention, he heard a man and a woman speaking in a foreign language. Being cautious, he slowly moved away until the couple disappeared. In the back of the church was the original eight hundred years old oak door. Earlier in the morning, at sunrise, he had picked the door lock and had entered the church. Inside the house of worship, he had climbed the winding stairs of the pulpit to hide an American 308 sniper rifle. Later, when all the guests would be present, Chekhov, at the top of this mirador, would get a perfect view to kill an American sniper named Lyle Mercer. Pulpits stand about eight feet above the floor and are no longer in use. Nowadays priests preach from the altar so they can face their flock.

Chekhov had been hired to assassinate Lyle, and his employer had provided him the type of gun that Lyle had used to kill Russians and cartel members. This execution would be worth two million euros, enough for this assassin to retire on.

An older gentleman in his fifties was walking toward the front of the building and suddenly stopped in his tracks. He remembered that the oldest tree in Paris, named "The Lucky Tree of Paris," was located in this neighborhood. He thought it would be a good idea to locate the famous locust tree that had been planted in 1602. Gently touching its bark was known to bring years of good luck. Doctor Leveque did not believe this myth, but for fun, he took the time to do it anyway. Dr. Alaire Leveque had taken care of Lyle in complete secrecy when the agent's life held by a thread due to critical injuries sustained during some difficult mission.

As the bright sun passed overhead, more guests arrived. Sitting in the first rows was a slender and charming looking woman, the mother of the bride, Marguerite, who was attending the marriage of her only child. She had been present at Annie's first wedding and had predicted it would end in divorce. In her heart, this one was different. She remembered feeling at ease the first time she met Lyle. He was calm and gentle, especially with grand-daughter. Marguerite was happy for her daughter, and also for the little girl from Bogota who would finally have a father.

There was another woman in the congregation who had made a long trip to attend this event. This woman, Lyle's mother, had remained single after the death of her husband. Even when surrounded by military officers who would have loved to know her better, she had declined any serious relationship. She spoke perfect French with a bit of a Cajun accent. Monique Mercer, the mother of the groom, was from the USA, from the state of Louisiana. She had also wanted grandchildren, even more than Marguerite did. Monique's son, Lyle, worked in Black Ops, for the Government. She did not know which branch. Her husband had been killed overseas while working on a similar type of operation when their son was only seven. This day had finally come, she had a little grand-daughter, Miss Jennie.

A Priest named "Father Daniel Chavet" came outside and beckoned the last guests enjoying the sun rays. The little rolly polly red-faced smiling priest closed the doors behind him.

The assassin calmly assembled his sniper rifle while he discreetly watched from the top of stairs leading to the pulpit. No one was aware of his presence. He laid the weapon down. The guests were noisy, conversing, introducing each other. Chekhov was waiting on the last stair at the top, right before the platform. Two men stood in plain view, just a few feet away in front of him. One was his target, Lyle Mercer, and the other, Brett Thompson. If he had time for a second shot, killing Brett would bring him another easy million euros. He smiled again, and his yellow, crooked, stained teeth reflected the ugliness of his soul.

Within minutes a beautiful woman, maybe five foot one or two, with long dark brown hair pulled up into a bun arrived from the rear of the church. Her dress was off-white, short and discreet. Annie knew that beauty was found in simplicity. A little girl with dark black curly hair, dressed in a pink smocked dress with a Peter Pan collar that Annie had ordered from a Cyrillus English catalog, held her mother's hand and tried to keep up the slow, steady pace. She was not yet two years old. Arm in arm with doctor Leveque, her godfather, they moved forward down the aisle between the pews as the wedding march was playing. While walking in the direction of the altar where she was going to be joined by her man, Annie was thinking about all the people, who, the past eight hundred years had attended mass, weddings, funerals, and baptisms here, and had sat in that old church.

She smiled, almost laughed, remembering something no one knew. Lyle had given her money to buy the wedding bands four days before this happy event took place. The day this purchase was made, she had been pulled over by the gendarmes for speeding. They had not given her a ticket when Annie told them she was on her way to buy her wedding rings. Instead, they had wished her happiness and had given her two warnings. One about speeding, and the other about picking the right man.

Once in front of the altar, the ceremony continued with the priest talking about marriage. He threw a few English words to amuse the foreign guests, told a few jokes, and got a laugh or two.

Father Chavet was about to say, "I pronounce you man and wife," when in the silence of the church, a shot rang out. Even with the use of a silencer, the sound was almost deafening. The bullet passed down through the right side of Lyle's neck, just below the ear, barely missing a major blood vessel, the carotid. The round continued and penetrated Annie's left lung. She sank to the ground. The last thing she saw was blood squirt from the neck area of the man she loved. The bullet continued and glanced off Jennie's head. There was only pain and blood as Annie's body was resting on the cold stone floor. Lyle had enough time to see blood on Annie's dress, and then he immediately collapsed to the floor, unconscious.

There were screaming and pandemonium. The people were running, wanting to get out. Not knowing where the fire had come from, Brett reacted a little slower than usual. He reached behind his back, withdrew his Sig Sauer 229 and chambered a round. The assassin was retreating down the stairs. Brett fired once, twice, and saw the murderer's rifle fall over the staircase railing. The hoodlum disappeared. Even with all the noise, one could hear the rear door slam as the hitman left the church. Brett was cautious as he approached the back door, he was not sure if someone would be waiting for him. As he came out, he could see the killer running down an alley. He followed him, but to no avail, Lyle's assassin was gone.

By the time Brett returned, Dr. Leveque had checked Annie and Lyle for a pulse. He immediately ripped off the injured agent's shirt and put it over Annie's wound and told Colonel Jackson to hold it and put pressure on the lesion. Sergeant Major Jenkins had covered Lyle's injury. Hilda leaned toward Patrick and told him to dial 18, the emergency number in France. Then, in one quick movement, Hilda was at the side of Jennie Anne. She stabilized the child she had called her grandchild the day she met her. Marguerite and Monique stepped away in tears. They did not want to get in the way. Some of the friends and guests had gathered around the victims, feeling useless. Dr. Leveque ordered everyone to give him room. At this time of day, the interior of the church was bright, full of sunshine, almost festive. Moments later the characteristic sounds of the French ambulance and police car interrupted the sobbing and crying; all the heads turned in the direction of the front door.

Chapter 3

Paris France

American Hospital

Late at night, the hall of the American hospital was silent, and the dim light that reflected on the walls gave the place a sinister feeling. A gendarme stood on the outside of Lyle's and Anne-Marie's rooms which were side by side. Dr. Alaire Leveque had arranged it that way. He also had Jennie Anne put in the same room as Annie's. The bullet which had passed through both Lyle and Anne-Marie had gone superficially through the left side of Jennie's head, near the coronal suture. The head surgeon who had taken over Jennie's medical treatment from Dr. Leveque said that Jennie Anne would be OK. Seizures could be a possible sequel to the trauma, no one at this time could predict. On the second day following the shooting incident, the little girl had regained consciousness but had no recollection of the terrible disturbance. In the afternoon, the nurses would lay her next to her mother during her nap.

The first twenty-four hours Marguerite and Monique were present at their children's bedside. Later they divided the day into shifts, taking turns. A third woman, Hilda, was splitting her time between the two rooms, relieving the two women while they left for food and breaks. Still unconscious, Lyle was not aware Annie lay wounded a few feet away. She had regained consciousness several hours after coming out of surgery, and her first words were, "How is Lyle?" Monique was about to answer, but there was a light tap on the door. It was Dr. Leveque and the Chief of Detectives. After a short discussion, Leveque informed the detective again that there was no progress in Lyle's condition, and he had no idea when the patient would come out of his coma. After some persuasion from doctor Leveque, the two women agreed to go for a walk while he looked after the patients. He did not hear them returning forty minutes later. Marguerite shook Leveque's shoulder to awaken him and to tell him to go rest.

Monique was worried about Lyle who had shown no improvement since his admission to the hospital. His coma was the result of the fall, not of any other injury. All the brain scans showed no damage, and the rest of the tests performed came back normal. To help her get some rest, she was provided with a cot.

Lyle was in a dream state. No one in the room noticed the rapid eye movement of his eyes. In his dream, Lyle was walking hand in hand with Annie. They were crossing through a green meadow covered in places with patches of yellow, white and purple flowers. Suddenly Annie stopped and gently placed her hands on his cheeks and said, "It is time to return Lyle. I need you to help me raise Jennie. We must love one another until it's time to leave the earth plane." Then a blinding bright light glared out, and in an instant, Annie was gone.

Lyle, with his eyes wide open, was staring and seemed to be in a state of panic. He extended his arms above the bed and yelled. "No, don't go, I want you to stay." Monique and Hilda watched and brought their hand in front of their mouth. Startled and scared, they pushed the emergency call light to report the event to the nurse on duty. Monique was in tears. She wrapped her arms around Lyle almost pulling out the IV in his arm. "Lyle, Lyle, my son, I am here. You are going to be OK."

The nurse checked the patient's eyes and talked to him. He appeared disoriented, in a state of confusion. He was looking with astonishment at all the persons in the room, jerking his head from one visitor to the other. Monique was reassured, the pupils were still responding normally to light. Dr. Leveque had just arrived, he asked Lyle a few questions that only required a yes or no answer. Then he asked him if he was thirsty.

After Lyle drank some water, he began asking, "Where is Annie? What happened? I saw blood, was she injured? Where is Jennie?" His speech was calm, coherent, and clear. Lyle's progress was remarkably good. His attending physician stopped by and was surprised to see the rapid change in his patient. He told Lyle, "I am going to check your head wound and the sutures first, then I am going to ask you questions. Don't talk until I tell you."

Twenty minutes later, the doctor addressed the three visitors present, "He might not be out of the woods yet, but so far his progress has been remarkable." Dr. Leveque suggested bringing Annie and Jennie to visit Lyle. The doctor replied, "Make it a short visit. As for Annie, she will probably be discharged from the hospital in four or five days. The drainage from her lung is clear and minute. The tubing will be removed in twenty-four hours. Her breathing is OK. As for the little girl, she should be fine. Sometimes head trauma can give place to seizures, but this is not an automatic development. Right now she is ready to go home."

Sitting up in bed, it was Lyle who spoke next. He was whispering to his mother, "I am not staying here too much longer, that assassin has to be tracked and taken down. When you get a chance, tell Brett I need to speak with him."

"Brett is meeting with someone at the embassy today. He left early this morning while you were still unconscious," Monique informed him, and she forcibly reminded him that his recovery had priority.

Lyle knew that the hospital needed to monitor him another week. Back to being his reasonable self, Lyle said, "Maybe Annie and Jennie can come to my room for a visit." Less than five minutes later they were together.

After a one hour reunion, the trio kissed, hugged, cried, and laughed. No one mentioned the wedding or the shooting. Instead, they made plans for their after discharge from the hospital.

That evening Brett showed up to speak with Lyle privately. He informed him that the bullets fired were from an American sniper rifle, the same weapon they had used in the past. Patrick was using the CIA network to gather intel. The CIA had been given orders by its headquarters to allow Patrick to work with Brett in acquiring intel. Then came the good news, "Operation Vulcan" was fully activated.

After Brett told Lyle that the scuttlebutt had it that the church shooting was pointing fingers at the Chechen, Lyle started to get out of bed. "Hold it, partner, you are in no shape to go hunting bad killers yet. Give yourself one more week, and maybe you can walk around with me some. By the way, you said you had a friend who had access to intel here in Paris. Could you contact him and see what you can find out?" Lyle became quiet thinking about Gabriel. Then he said, "I would tell you where to find him, but he made me promise not to give his address to anyone. This old man has helped me with many a situation. Leave me a burner phone, I will call him."

Brett reached into his pocket and handed Lyle a phone which he placed under his pillow. Lyle inquired about the colonel who had been at the church on that fatal day, "Did the Colonel go home?"

"He stayed two days, then got a call from Washington and left in a hurry. Colonel Jackson wants you to know that we are to work together to eliminate the Chechen and whoever is working with him. Also, he strongly encouraged me to utilize all resources available." One could see a smile on Lyle's face, in fact, his whole demeanor changed.

The following day, when Annie was alone with Lyle, she surprised him when she said, "Nowadays, a significant percentage of both young and older couples do not get married anymore."

"But, Annie I love you and..." Lyle could not get his sentence completed, Annie interrupted him. Raising her voice, she spoke, "Don't worry about getting a piece of paper and a ring. I want you to get well and finish what you were sent out to do. Go and catch the bastards who tried to kill us and the others you have been chasing. I know that keeping your commitment to your country is vital to your mental health. Now hush, get well, you have a job to do."

Lyle did not know what to say, he reached over and hugged Annie while placing his other arm around Jennie Anne. Lyle felt good to discover one more time how well she understood what was important to him, and that alone was proof of her love for him.

CHAPTER 4

Lyle was now being released from the hospital. Brett picked Lyle up and dropped him three blocks away from Annie's apartment. Lyle sauntered to her place, ears on full alert and eyeballs discreetly moving side to side, watching for something unusual. Lyle felt good being out of the hospital and appreciated the shy sunrays warming up his back as he was approaching the apartment. He gave a loud tap and two light ones on the door, the coded signal to let Annie know it was him at the door. Lyle had no more than entered when a familiar voice came from the small kitchen. He could smell the vanilla scent given off from the crêpes Annie was making. He walked over, lifted her long hair and placed little kisses from left to right on her exposed neck. She loved this attention.

He was back, and his return demanded a celebration of some sort. He poured some red vermouth into small glasses, and they had a toast to his complete recovery. Then Lyle raised his glass and said, "To the woman and daughter I love." Lyle walked over and sat down next to Jennie and gave her a strawberry. He resumed his talking, "I contacted my friend Gabriel, and he is going to call as soon as he gets any information about the assassin. Oh, by the way, Gab and I have a special announcement." Lyle knew it drove Annie mad when he turned partial revelation into a mystery. She had to know now. "You have always made me give in, not this time; you have to wait. That is final."

The following morning as most mornings, walking after breakfast had become a ritual that allowed Lyle to regain his health. In the courtyard of the apartment building, Lyle reached down to pick a daffodil that had grown along with tulips between some large rock.

Only the daffodils were in bloom at this time of year. As he turned to hand it to Annie, she said, "What about this announcement you mentioned last night?"

Lyle placed the flower in Annie's hair and admired her for a moment, then spoke, "I guess I have no choice, but to tell you. Gabriel wants to attend Jennie's baptism when it is time. He has no family, absolutely no one, and thinks I am his son. I know this invitation would bring him a lot of joy.

She was laughing when she said, "You were keeping that away from me? Yes, I would love that. I am not sure when and if this baptism should take place. We are in no hurry, and as you know, I am not a religious person. We will see."

Then Lyle's phone rang. He glanced at the number; it was Patrick. Annie who knew the routine, said, "Go ahead and answer it, Jennie and I will be up ahead, waiting for you."

Lyle looked both ways down the sidewalk, and it was on the sixth ring that he answered, "LM here." Then Lyle gave his code number. The news Patrick shared was important, "We have a hit on Aleksey the Chechen. His group of thugs is putting a load of arms together just outside of Moscow. I have no idea how long he will be there. Are you sure you are well enough to go after that bunch?"

Lyle did not hesitate, "I would crawl if I had to. Yes, I will be OK. I might be able to get more intel from my friend Gabriel tonight. If I can get a definite location for Aleksey, we will leave very soon. Can you get weapons within twenty-four hours?"

"Won't be a problem at all. As I told you, the COS is supposed to fill orders I request, if at all possible. He was not happy that I am running the op here, but the hammer came down on him. Just let me know what you need, and we will send it to the embassy. Maybe I can help with a flight or a ride?"

"I have a contact in Washington who will handle the flights, besides he never fails to get first class for us. Eat your heart out!"

"Lyle, I told you twice already, my retirement is close now, four months and counting. I might even use my four weeks vacation time to get out of here earlier. I need that job."

Lyle had been waiting to tell his longtime friend that the decision was final. He would be working with the black operations group under Colonel Jackson. "Are you sitting down?" There was a long pause, Lyle resumed, "You owe Brett and me a four-star dinner because you have been cleared to go to work as soon as your retirement is final. I am not sure with which group, that will be up to Colonel Jackson. We have only three groups." Lyle thought he heard an enthusiastic wow.

"Yes, dinner is on me. Bring Anne-Marie; I have not seen her since we were at the church."

"Sounds good. I will call you before we leave. Brett and I still have a diplomatic case that we will take with us. Thanks again."

Before he started to catch up with Annie, he decided to call Gabriel to see if he had an update. On the second ring, old Gab answered, and for a change, there was enthusiasm in his voice; he had news his friend would want to hear.

Breathing hard and talking fast, Gab said, "Aleksey the Chechen left. A friend of mine, a general in Moscow, says he is traveling through Ukraine and heading to Novorossiysk on the Black Sea where he owns a fishing boat. From there, he plans to take a load of weapons to Turkey, then overland to northern Syria or Iraq where he plans to turn the armory over to ISIS. Frankly, I wish you would not go after him, Lyle." Judging from the tremendous danger this undertaking posed, Gab was pleading Lyle not to interfere.

After saying goodbye, Lyle was so stunned he had almost forgotten he was to catch up with Annie who was now two blocks away. Soon they stopped for coffee, and Lyle called Brett to update him and inform him they would be leaving for Turkey the following day.

CHAPTER 5

Paris to Istanbul

It was early morning when Lyle woke up, not even four-thirty a.m. He quietly got out of bed, making sure not to awake Annie when he removed her arm wrapped around his neck. Lyle showered, brushed his teeth, and wrapped his robe around his tight body. In the kitchen, while sipping his coffee in semi-obscurity, he placed a call to Octo in the States to request two first class tickets to Moscow. Octo answered the phone on the second ring; then after almost five minutes of friendly chat, he told Lyle he would book his flights and call him back within the hour.

To pass time Lyle made chocolate milk. He tiptoed back to the bedroom to see if Annie was awake, she was, so he returned to the kitchen and poured her a cup of coffee. A hand reached out and tugged at the belt wrapped around Lyle's robe, and like a snake striking its prey, her hand grabbed his left wrist and pulled him onto the bed. He did not resist the amorous assault and ended up back in bed with his woman. She softly spoke into his ear, "Let me feel one more time your muscular shoulders. Her hands were all over his torso. She loved to palpate his firm muscles and would run her fingers over each bump, giving a name to the one she was caressing at the moment, pectoralis minor, pectoralis major, rectus abdominis. This tantalizing game drove him crazy, and before long the two lovers were in each other's arms making fiery lovemaking.

Soon, a little girl speaking from the other room brought them back to earth. At that instant, Lyle's phone rang, it was Octo relaying an essential message to Lyle. Intel had it that the Chechen had left Moscow and was heading for an unknown destination in Turkey. Lyle immediately advised Octo to get first class tickets to Istanbul for him and Brett.

With a gleaming smile, Annie looked at Lyle and said, "I heard, you are leaving today. Promise me you won't take chances."

"Brett and I will be flying out this afternoon. It will probably take a few days to gather intel before we can do anything. Don't worry; I have too much waiting for me at home to take risks. We will be extra careful, but I am going to get the bastard who attempted to kill the three of us." Lyle spent over an hour talking with Annie before he got up to get dressed, pack his bag, and make sure everything was ready and secure in the sensitive case. It was after eleven a.m. when he kissed his women and hugged them both. With a few parting words at the door and another quick kiss one last time, Lyle left.

It was just after noon when he pulled into the parking lot at Brett's hotel. He had called ahead; his partner was waiting for him in the lobby. Both men were now in operation mode as they were on their way to the car. They still had to meet Patrick to pick up another encrypted phone from him, and then head to the airport.

Patrick gave them two diplomatic passports with new names. He had made arrangements for his friends to meet a certain Ralph Kruger upon their arrival in Istanbul. The gentleman would be waiting for them after their going through customs. Patrick left, waving to them and, referring to their new identities, he shouted, "Have a safe trip, Mr. Johnston, and Mr. Thorton."

Lyle and Brett headed to the airport car rental at Charles de Gaulle airport to drop their vehicle. After going through the check-in without a hitch with their diplomatic pouches and passports, they were soon sitting down at one of the airport restaurants for lunch.

As they waited, Lyle said, "I know the colonel must have spoken to POTUS to get us those diplomatic passports, but his well-intended gesture does not make it a lot safer for us." They were finishing their beer when they heard the announcement for the boarding of their Turkish Airlines plane.

Once on board, Lyle turned his phone off and advised the cabin attendant not to awaken them. Within minutes both men were sound asleep. Three hours later both agents received a gentle tap on their shoulder. Once again they were face to face with the same tall, attractive, and slender lady who had welcomed them aboard hours earlier. Smiling, she said, "We will be landing in Istanbul in just under twenty minutes. May I get you a warm, wet towel and a cup of coffee?"

Both men accepted the offer. As Lyle was setting his coffee cup down, the jet banked and flew over the First bridge that crosses the Bosphorus strait in Istanbul, connecting Europe and Asia. Lyle could now see the Blue Mosque with its six minarets. The tall spires, resembling missiles and were almost menacing due to their size and suggestive shape. The plane flew over the bazaar, the huge indoor market, and soon leveled out, bouncing several times on the runway before taxiing to its assigned parking spot. Minutes later the two men disembarked and headed for customs.

With their diplomatic passports, going through customs was a breeze. A man moved up slowly toward them and said, "Welcome to Istanbul, Mr. Thorton, and Mr. Johnston. My name is Ralph Kruger from the American embassy in Istanbul. I will be taking you to a safe house. I imagine your flight was pleasant. Now on land, I recommend vigilance. As you know the walls have eyes and ears."

Lyle shook hands with the man and said, "We have been here before, thank you for the wise advice, I think we know the drill." As they were approaching Kruger's vehicle, they told him they would keep their diplomatic cases with them in the back seat.

"Fine with me, as long as you have room. I will be driving around for a while."

Immediately upon pulling out of the parking lot, Ralph Kruger and his passengers had spotted unwanted cars trailing theirs. It took almost an hour and a half before the driver could lose the two vehicles that had been following them since leaving the airport.

Suddenly Ralph Kruger entered the parking lot of a modest hotel near the Bosphorus Strait. "Here in Istanbul, you never know. You might be safe one moment and, when not expected, someone comes across wanting a piece of your ass. By the way, Pat told me you might be needing some weapons."

Lyle stated, " yes, among other things, we need a small drone."

"Ouch! As we speak, we have only two operational at the embassy. I am not sure the COS will want to depart with one." Lyle responded instantly, "Ask your boss to read the directive that came through from CIA. I am sure he will hand you one. The safety of many lives depends on us stopping illegal deliveries to the States, and to do that, some tools are essential, a drone is one of them."

I will see what I can do. Have your list ready for the items you want, and expect a call later tonight."

As Ralph was getting ready to leave, Lyle started to enumerate orally the weapons he needed: two Russian sniper rifles with extra clips and silencers, six bricks of C4 and electronic activating devices, six Russian grenades, and finally, six or more of the cheap ass flash-bangs. As he spoke, Lyle had been writing down a list that Kruger was now examining. He responded with a grin,

"What are you going to do, start a war on Turkish soil? I will leave you, gentlemen. Now I have to find my stalkers so they may accompany me back to the embassy."

CHAPTER 6

Istanbul

After Raph Kruger left, Lyle turned to Brett and said, "I have an idea. I am going to call Gab's friend, the old retired general who lives in Russia. Maybe he knows more about the weapons the Chechen is trafficking. On the seventh ring, a thick and rough voice answered the phone. Lyle, using the code Gabriel had given him, spoke in Russian. The gruff voice never introduced anyone. Instead, it asked for a phone number, promising to call back in five minutes.

Lyle filled Brett in with what had transpired on the phone. Five minutes went by and, almost to the second, the phone Lyle was still holding began to ring. Without any form of introduction, the old retired Russian general signaled that he was using a burner phone. Lyle asked if he had any intel on the comings and goings of Aleksey.

After coughing several times, General Naumov said,

"Aleksey left for Ukraine this morning with four truckloads of Russian military arms."

Lyle's hastened his questions, "Do you know where in Ukraine? How many men are with him?"

Once again, the general was interrupted by a coughing fit. Finally, the reply came, "Slow down my friend. According to my informants, Aleksey is accompanying the loads all the way to Kars, in Turkey, via Donetsk, a region that remains at war with Ukraine."

As the general continued to speak, Lyle cut him off, "Do you know if they are in Ukraine yet?"

"They left early this morning from their loading site, about one hundred and twenty miles southeast of Moscow. With the condition of the roads, I think they should be in the area of Donetsk sometime late tonight or early the next day." The general paused, then continued, "They will be there before noon tomorrow. It is only about eight hundred kilometers to Donetsk from where they left, but as I said earlier, the roads are difficult."

There was a sound of glass hitting glass over the phone. The communication was clear, Lyle heard the general swallow before resuming, "We know that after leaving Donetsk, they will go to Mariupol, a small city on the Black Sea. There the arms will be unloaded into a boat that will take the weapons across the Black Sea to either Batum or Zudg, Georgia. Once in Batum, you are almost in Turkey."

Lyle could hardly wait to ask another question, "Who is picking up the arms in Georgia?"

"You did not let me finish, my friend." Once again Lyle heard the old general take a drink. "After they dock, they will transfer the arms to Turkish trucks and take the goods south of Kars, in Turkey. ISIS will take over the convoy from there. I do not have any timelines other than they left about five a.m. this morning."

Brett could not hold back any longer, "Can the Georgian military or the police stop them at the border?"

The general laughed for several seconds which triggered another coughing spell. He managed to answer Lyle, "As in Russia, the Georgian police and the army are not paid well. I can attest to that. And of course, there is a lot of corruption. The old general laughed again before continuing, "Even the oligarchs are involved in crime, and they keep the honest cops at bay. I am tired now, and it is time for an old retired general to have his nap. When you see my old friend Gab, tell him I am whiter than the snow now." Then there was silence on the phone.

Lyle had just been confronted with significant logistics. Even though the Chechen's itinerary was not official as to places and times, the old general had given Brett and Lyle a good base to plan their next move. Brett who had remained quiet spoke, "We are most likely going to get only one chance at Aleksey, we better plan well and have a safe escape route out of this unfamiliar area." Brett left to get his coat, and Lyle called Ralph Kruger, the CIA agent from the embassy. He wanted Ralph to pick them up just outside the main entrance of the hotel and go over the equipment request.

Ralph opened the conversation, "Before you say anything, I am working on your request for a drone. My boss placed a call to the States. Whoever answered the call ripped him a new asshole for his expressing concern and hesitation supplying Operation Vulcan. However, we have the items you need; we are waiting for you to tell us where to send them."

Then Lyle gave Ralph a brief overview of his and Brett's plan. Ralph responded, "That is truly an audacious plan. As you know, I cannot give you any people for the operation. I can get more weapons brought in through the embassy or get computer help, but that's it. Under Vulcan, the COS has given me orders to help any way I can as long as I stay within limits outlined by the higher-ups." Ralph was very careful not to identify whoever was behind the restrictions.

"We appreciate. Thanks. I will need two copies of maps of Turkey and Georgia, both paper type." Lyle then went over the list again which this time included the maps. "What type of drone are we getting?" Ralph stuttered a couple of times before answering. After a deep breath, he said, "It will be one of our two small ones. I am sure you are aware they have limited battery life and are designed for visual information only. My COS was not too thrilled to let go of his drone,"

"We intend to get an overview of the loading and transfer areas of the arms before we try to shut down the operation. I expect you to send everything to the US embassy in Tbilisi, Georgia, today."

"Ah, here is a good place for a cup of coffee," Ralph said as he was pointing to a small cafe across the street.

Once inside the three men sipped Turkish coffee and talked for over an hour, then Ralph looked at his watch and said, "I will get back to you within an hour or two." He sucked in a deep breath of air through his lips and continued, "I know the COS is in the office today until four p.m. According to the coding on the directives, you are working for someone pretty high up." Soon Ralph shook hands with the two agents and left.

Brett and Lyle worked their way back to the hotel. Lyle called Gabriel and relayed the message from his old friend, the general. Nothing much was added to the information the Russian had provided. The conversation was brief.

While having a beer, Lyle's cell beeped. Ralph would meet them at the same small cafe at seven p.m. He suggested they order sucuk, a dried sausage made of ground beef with garlic and spices, pepper, cumin, and sumac. He also recommended the baklavas, his preference being the ones made with pistachios.

There was no new intel concerning Aleksey. Lyle turned to Brett and said, "Maybe we should consider trying to plant explosives on the trucks in Georgia, at Batum or the other fishing village when they reach their destination." He let the thought sink in before continuing, "Better yet, we could place tracking devices on the trucks in Georgia and follow them across the border into Turkey."

Before entering the cafe, Lyle looked the area over, making sure no one was tailing them. A few minutes later, Ralph showed up. The trio enjoyed their meal. Ralph picked up his wine glass and made a toast, "To your mission, my friends."

The rest of the evening they discussed each other's plans for retirement and their future. One hour later the trio left the cafe for a short walk.

Lyle mentioned that he was considering going after Aleksey's load in Georgia. Ralph stuttered just before he spoke. "I, I had no idea they were going to Georgia via Ukraine. How did you get that intel?"

Being cautious, as usual, Lyle thought for a moment and then said, "Someone from military intelligence passed the info to the colonel in charge of Vulcan. What do you think of us waiting for the tangos in Georgia?" Lyle now knew he had let the cat out of the bag. Ralph shared bits and pieces of information concerning the region, "I am sure you are aware, the CIA has less staff and resources in Georgia. But still, I think you would be a lot safer with more available ways to escape from there. Let me warn you, Georgia is unsettled, and you cannot tell the good guys from the bad guys there. As agreed, your weapons will be sent to Tbilisi, I can arrange it; we have staff flying there, back and forth, several times a week, they will be on their way this evening."

Brett was mindful of Lyle not wanting to give away too much information about their plan to anyone. As they walked in silence, only the sound of their shoes hitting the sidewalk could be heard. Brett broke the silence when he asked Ralph about his plans after his leaving Turkey. Lyle thanked Brett silently for getting the subject of the conversation away from the operation.

Back at the hotel, the agents packed, ready to leave within minutes. All three men left the room and walked to the embassy vehicle.

Ralph felt he was now part of the team. Once more, he reassured Lyle and Brett, "I will have your goods picked up by one of our agency men, and I will personally make sure everything is shipped out by plane tonight, to arrive in Tbilisi in the morning. I guess its time we head toward the airport."

While they were driving around the city, Lyle called Octo and had him reserve two first class tickets ASAP for first, a little detour in Gyandzhe, Azerbaijan, with a final stop in Tbilisi. Lyle had kept his conversation limited while on the phone. After saying goodbye to Octo, he turned around to face Brett and said, "We will fly to Azerbaijan at 4:40 a.m on Turkish Airlines. We better catch some sleep at the airport.

Once at the air terminal, they found a quiet, somewhat comfortable place to sit in one of the closed dining rooms.

Just as Brett started to doze off, Lyle said, "Open your eyes old buddy, I need to run an idea by you." Brett turned toward Lyle.

"What do you think about having Major Jenkins getting a Russian helicopter from either an American airbase in Turkey or Iraq, next door, so he may pick us up and maybe even save our ass in

Kers, Turkey? Remember, Kers is where ISIS takes over the convoy of weapons."

The empty dining room remained silent. Thirty seconds later Brett spoke, "Wow, that's a good one. I would have never thought of that, but am afraid we would be putting the Sargent Major in danger. Taking a Russian helicopter into Turkish airspace may not be wise. Otherwise, I agree, it's a good idea, especially if the shit hits the fan when we reach that convoy. We will have to extract fast. Are you going to call J tonight?"

Lyle looked at his watch again, then said, "We need to leave here by five a.m. That gives us less than four hours of sleep. Yah, I better call him now, as he will need time to get things organized if he agrees with our proposal."

CHAPTER 7

Istanbul to Tbilisi

While waiting for their flight to take off, Lyle dialed Jenkins's phone number. He knew that Sargent Major Jenkins would be ecstatic to hear from him. After the fourth ring, J started to announce the name of his tour company to the caller. Lyle stopped him, "It's me, Lyle." Jenkins was genuinely pleased to hear his friend, and his response reflected his pleasure, "You have blessed this old man with your call. Where in the hell are you? Tell me you are OK. How are Brett and the two little ladies?"

Lyle tried to answer J's questions briefly as they came in rapid succession, and then he presented J with an offer his friend would not refuse, "We need your services, but I must warn you, this project is not without danger. The last mission was perilous; this one will be even riskier. The odds are that one or all three of us may not be coming back in one piece."

"Where will this cataclysm be taking place? As you know, I can be ready in less than eight hours."

"Hold on Sargent Major, let me share our plan first. Take some time to reflect, and give me your answer later." Lyle took several minutes to tell him what Brett and himself had outlined in preparation for the mission. His account did not omit any of the significant obstacles they would be facing; it emphasized the hazards this operation would involve. A few seconds of silence followed, and J responded to Lyle's proposition, "That is almost the only way you can stop that convoy. Let me add a few things. You are much better off, as you said, taking out Aleksey on Turkish soil even though that agent in Istanbul favored Georgia. Give me an hour or two, as I need to make a few calls. I think that in Mosul, the military still has a few Russian choppers confiscated in Iraq. If I am right, I can have one, load it with extra fuel, set down somewhere close to where you expect to hijack that convoy, and wait for your call. Next, we could extract back to Iraq. That would be the safest approach."

Lyle was in disbelief when Jenkins not only accepted to participate but was already figuring logical ways to proceed. He ran thoughts through his head, then he spoke, "I am going to give you a code that will include numbers and letters. You will use the phone number I gave you on our last mission. When calling, mention 'Vulcan,' and give the code. The person on the line will be moving heaven and earth to provide you with whatever you request. By the way, don't forget to tell Hilda we miss and love her. But again J, talk it over with her, this Vulcan mission will be more grueling than the last one." J wanted to include Hilda in this assignment. He said, "We might need a medic again, maybe I should bring Hilda. You know she will want to come along."

"No can do J."

There was a pause, then Lyle closed the conversation. He relayed the discussion to Brett. Satisfied with the development, the two agents leaned back against their well-padded seats and fell asleep.

Three hours later both men awoke. They took turns into the bathroom to wash their face with cold water. Finally, they heard the boarding announcement for their flight. With their diplomatic cases in hand, they walked through boarding without a second glance. While waiting, Lyle turned his phone on and saw he had several messages, all from the same number. Sargent Major Jenkins had called three times. Lyle pushed in J's name on his cell phone.

"Jenkins here. Everything is under control, catching a flight to Bagdad in a few hours. I had a friend of mine make contact for me with Colonel Watkins in northern Iraq. Watkins used to be a young captain when I was on tour there, and he owes me a favor. We are lucky so far. I will need at least forty-eight hours, preferably seventy-two, to find us a Russian helicopter."

Lyle was so shocked with the ease and speed at which everything was falling into place. Lost for words, Lyle, at last, spoke, "Good God J—is there anyone who does not owe you favors?"

"You are the same way, Lyle. We serve our country and help others first before serving ourselves. I had to put my foot down at home. Hilda took me to task for not letting her come on this operation." Lyle could hear J coughing a little before he spoke again, "My Hilda needs some action."

"You know J; I will never be able to repay you."

"Would you stop that pay me back crap. Thanks to you, I'm living life to the full again. I have to head for Iraq." Then the line went dead.

As they were drinking coffee, the two agents heard their boarding call for their flight. Once on board, Lyle turned the phone off and advised the cabin attendant not to awaken them. Within minutes both men were sound asleep again. It was over two and a half hours later when both Lyle and Brett received a tap on their shoulder. As the two men opened their eyes, they saw a tall, attractive lady with long black hair and beautiful eyes once again. Smiling she said, "We will be landing in just under thirty minutes. May I get you a wet towel and a cup of coffee?"

While wiping their hands, they briefly went over suggestions made by both Lyle and Sargent Major Jenkins about their next operation. Lyle told Brett he had been in Turkey before, but not in the country of Georgia. He started to bring up a few facts that he had once read about the area. With a population of close to four million, this socialist-democratic country is very religious. Then Lyle laughed as he remembered reading about some 8000-year-old wine jars discovered there. His mind was now wandering. He was in a state of total confusion when, out of the blue, he mumbled something incoherent about the wedding, "That would make sense," he said out loud.

Brett who was dozing replied, "Sorry Lyle. What did you say." Lyle was prompt to answer his partner,

"You know Brett, nobody but a few knew I was getting married. Someone hired that assassin to terminate us while the wedding ceremony was underway. We can eliminate, the colonel, Patrick, Gabriel, Dr. Leveque, the Jenkins, Annie's mother and father. That only leaves Annie's two colleagues and her two friends who live just a few blocks away from her. Now here is what's funny, Stephanie's husband, Frederic, did not attend the wedding, but yet, her other friend's husband came."

"I've never met this Frederic. What does he do for a living?"

"He is a retired gendarme, a cop. He told me he retired early on a medical. He runs a small neighborhood epicerie (small grocery store) about five blocks from Annie's apartment."

Brett thought for a few seconds, then said, "Does he behave suspiciously when you are around him?"

"He is very nosy, always seems to be prying and even spying, and that's what is bothering me. Constantly asking questions about where I have been, what I have been doing. When and if I make it back, I think I will give old man Frederic a little CIA interrogation." Changing the subject, Lyle advised his partner, "Close your eyes old buddy. We might have a long drive from the capital to the Black Sea tonight." Lyle stopped thinking about his suspicions concerning Frederic. He started concentrating on Georgia again. There had been, and still was a lot of unrest in that country. He remembered reading that Georgia had a close affiliation with the West, and it wanted to become a full-fledged member of NATO. It had military connections with France, Germany, Israel, Japan, Turkey, and the USA. Lyle also knew that the country harbored significant Russian players involved in creating tension within Georgia. The state counted many seaports along Black Sea coast, and he hoped that the intel gathered from Gabriel's old friend was correct about the two ports Aleksey was considering to bring in his illegal hot load of armor.

Lyle's mind went blank; he was actually in a meditative state. The captain's loud announcement instantly brought him back to earth.

As the aircraft came in on its final approach, there were no visible signs of minarets. One could quickly tell the difference between Turkey and Georgia especially when the two men saw the people inside the terminal. They knew that this was not a Muslim country.

With no luggage to collect, they were now on their way to the car rental. All of a sudden Lyle said, "Damn! I forgot to turn on my cell phone. Hold it for a sec Brett." There were five messages from Octo, their loyal government geeky contact. Lyle pushed the button to replay the messages one at a time, "Urgent and critical, fresh news about the coastal armory unloading site. It has been changed." Lyle's face revealed his concern as he informed Brett, "Octo sent five identical urgent messages asking us to contact him. Let's find a quiet area where we can communicate with him without interruption." The two men found an airport bench. Lyle looked at his watch; it was three a.m. in Washington D.C., a bit early to wake up their loyal dispatcher. He decided to wait a while before calling. He looked at his watch again, and said, "We have almost an hour and a half. Let's get something to eat."

The men bought food and coffee from a food vending machine and sat at a table somewhat isolated from the few travelers present at the airport. They went over their plans for the day, plans that would probably have to be modified after talking to Octo. They briefly reviewed suggestions made by Sargent Major Jenkins. The time seemed to fly as the agents enjoyed their sandwich and cup of joe.

Chapter 8

Tbilisi, Georgia To Trabzon, Turkey

Lyle and Brett were getting anxious. Even though it was very early in D.C., they contacted Octo to find out what the emergency was all about. In an empty waiting room, secure enough to make a call, Lyle dialed the dispatcher.

He was surprised when the young man answered on the first ring, "Lyle, I was worried I would not reach you in time." Due to the eagerness to share his message, Octo's voice was high and squeaky, and he was slurring his words, "The-the delivery area has changed, the boat with the arms will be coming onshore in Turkey, near Trabzon."

"Take a couple of deep breaths. We just landed in Georgia. What's your source and what's the exact debarkation location in Turkey?"

Lyle could hear Octo breathing deeply, then he spoke, "Colonel Jackson contacted me, just in case he could not get ahold of you. Aleksey will be arriving somewhere near Trabzon, in Turkey, in sixty-nine hours from my time. Give me a minute to figure your time." Lyle was getting impatient, he quickly replied, "I can do that. Where did the intel come from?"

"Colonel Jackson said it came from a gentleman in Paris, an older man named Gabriel who claims to know you."

"Well, I'll be damned. Old Gab is a miracle worker. Hold on." Lyle turned to Brett to let him know that Aleksey's load was on its way to Turkey. Now grinning, he added, "We will have to check airlines for a ticket back to Turkey after we pick up the goods that were sent here from Istanbul. "Lyle put his phone back to his ear, "Octo, you are a godsend. Get some rest, and I will make contact back with you in about four hours, give or take. Advise the colonel we got his message. Thanks again, my friend."

They were on their way to Turkish Airlines where they hoped to get a direct flight to Trabzon later that evening.

The Turkish Airline reservation clerk checked her computer, then said, "I have a flight that leaves at 6:10 p.m. and arrives in Trabzon just after 1:00 a.m."

They still had to pick up the other sensitive cases at the US Embassy in Tbilisi. Lyle asked the clerk, "If we reserve the flight and miss our plane, can you put us on an early flight tomorrow?"

"That would be no problem. However, there will be a $300.00 US charge to change flights."

To avoid any complication, Lyle bought two first class tickets on the next morning flight and headed to the car rental where the employee gave him the address of the closest hotel to the airport. Within the hour they were in their room where they showered and changed into their last set of clean clothes. They decided to rest a while before driving to the embassy.

Lyle's phone rang. It was Jenkins letting them know that he had found a chopper in Iraq. Lyle said, "How in the hell did you do that, and where is it?"

"I had a colonel who owed me a few favors. He is getting one ready for me as I speak. The US confiscated several Russian helicopters when we invaded Iraq. When it is time, I will take it to Fallujah, about 70 miles west of Bagdad."

The two men then briefly discussed their plans. After hanging up, Lyle, chuckling, told Brett, "I don't know how he does some of the things he does. I guess we better hit the sack; I'm exhausted."

Up after a few hours of sleep, they had several cups of strong coffee and a hearty meal, and they headed for the US embassy in Tbilisi. There, at the gate, a staff sergeant checked their identity and took them to the waiting center inside the building. Ten minutes later an older man came over to meet them. He led them to a small locked room where the two sensitive cases were sitting on a large walnut table. The man looked at Lyle and Brett, then said, "You must have some pull somewhere. I will step out of the room so you can check your cases. I am sure you know the codes. When done, knock twice, I need you to sign a form before you go."

Within minutes Lyle knocked on the door, and the older man handed him a release form to sign. An hour later, the two agents were back at the airport where they turned their car in and headed for Turkish Airlines once again. They still had two hours to make calls and grab a beer. Brett spoke first, "It's tiring and hard getting around with three cases. Maybe I should rearrange their contents and fit the smallest one inside one of the other two."

"We are flying first class, let me go back over to Turkish Airlines and see if we can pay an extra fee and take the cases on board with us." At the ticket counter, they were told that there was no way they would allow the more significant case in the first class cabin. The clerk did say the diplomatic packages would be unloaded first in Trabzon. Feeling relieved, the two men had two more beers while time slowly passed. Before boarding, Lyle sent a text to both Octo and J, then keyed in his iPad and read what Wikipedia had to reveal about the City. Tbilisi, the capital of Georgia, has a population of 1.5 million. It lies on the banks of the Kura river. Due to its location, it had been an essential east-west trade route throughout history. With its multiple cultural backgrounds and its rich past, the city is a tourist destination. As he perused the pictures of the historical sites, he noted that conifer trees often surrounded ancient structures. After a while, he leaned back in his chair and closed his eyes. It was not long before they heard the announcement to board their flight.

Once on board, Lyle began to reason why Aleksey would change his destination. The new choice made sense to Lyle. Unloading his arms on Turkish soil, not far from his final delivery site was more rational. On Google maps, he briefly looked up the city of Bratzon. Lyle made a mental note to buy street maps once there. He looked at his watch; it was almost one a.m.

After landing, Lyle and Brett rented two SUVs for two weeks. They took out additional insurance for they were ninety-eight percent sure they would not be returning either car. Both agents gave the clerk a false passport and other IDs to match, and paid with matching credit cards. It was nice and even comforting to have the number one forger in the world supporting you, Uncle Sam. With their sensitive cases sitting in the back seats of their vehicles, a blue SUV for Lyle and a white one for Brett, they headed into downtown Trabzon, or Trebizond as the people would say in English. Guided by their GPS, it did not take long for the two vehicles to reach the Ramada Plaza Trabzon hotel on the water's edge.

It was somewhat of a struggle to pack the cases, two bell boys came to the rescue and carried them to the check-in counter. Lyle gave the men a generous tip and said good night; it was almost two-thirty a.m. In their room, Brett cleaned the armory while Lyle showered. Neither man said another word as they hit the sack, and neither man heard the heavy snoring of the other. It had been a very long forty plus hours since they had a decent night sleep.

No one was up at five a.m. It was way after six when Lyle extracted his tired body from the bed. He made coffee in their room while Brett was taking a cold shower to wake up. They knew they had a difficult job before them, and not much time. Aleksey's weapons were due to arrive in the area within the next eight to ten hours, or earlier. Brett and Lyle, using unconfirmed information, were expected to spot a small boat bringing in the contraband and two or more empty trucks to pick up this same contraband destined to ISIS.

Once Lyle and Brett had taken in enough caffeine, they headed to the restaurant downstairs. While eating a hearty Turkish breakfast composed of an omelet, white bread, feta-like cheese, honey, and jam, Lyle glanced at the city map and noticed that all the streets led to the seashore. Lyle, with his index finger on the map, suggested they drive down the main road until it hits the Yolo road leading to a to a small cove between Trabzon and the town of Rize. With a pen, he traced the itinerary on the map and handed it to Brett. This small sheltered bay where only a few local fishing boats came and went would be an ideal place for Aleksey to conduct his business without attracting attention. As of now, the two partners would have to keep a lookout at all times for trucks waiting by the water. Having two SUVs to cruise along the coast allowed better surveillance. They were still unsure where the transfer from boat to trucks would take place. Brett suggested they mix with the locals around the Trabzon busy harbor, "If we greased a few hands maybe someone's tongue will loosen. This method has always brought result before, but bribery may not work here." Brett then leaned over and took another piece of toast, smothered it with butter and preserves. Lyle looked at his watch, and said, "Seven or eight hours. If I don't find anything in the dock area, I will go about twenty klicks to the east. We'll find them."

Both men finished their breakfast, went to their room and took out the tracking devices, two flash-bangs, and several grenades each. They placed the sensitive cases under their beds, and as they left their room, Lyle put the "Do not disturb sign" on the doorknob.

The two agents walked the wharf area of several sites where a small boat could easily anchor. Late in the afternoon, just outside of the seaside town of Rize, east of Trabzon, Brett noticed four old Turkish REO military trucks without any military markings or plates. They had been assembled in

Turkey by Turk Otomotiv Endustrileri A.s., trademarks visible on the lower part of the front doors. He nonchalantly walked around the vehicles, they all had new tires, and their back loading doors were locked. Looking at the area over, he spotted a hotel and a restaurant not far from the parked trucks. Using the stalking techniques taught by the CIA, Brett soon observed six rather large, sturdy looking mid-aged men with beards. Sitting together in the restaurant, the gentlemen were having dinner. Brett continued to watch. One man left the table to go to the restroom. There was something martial about him in the way he walked with an air of dominance. His soldierly looks suggested he had received military training.

Brett took out his binoculars to get a clear view of the cases that had been placed between the men's legs, underneath the table. He was not shocked, and not even surprised by his findings. On two of the cases were red squares with heraldic shields and in the center was a double eagle, the National Symbolics of Russia. Brett now knew they had their men. After putting away his field glasses, he slipped away to make a phone call to Lyle who welcomed Brett's news.

"Man, am I glad you found those killers. I have had no success all day. Were you able to put on the tracking devices?" Brett could detect the relief in Lyle's voice.

"As for me, the only intel I could get here was from an old man who spoke broken English. He said that Rize harbor was where the fishing boats from Ukraine docked. The old geezer said that fish and other items are brought into Rize continually. At least this is what I grasped." Brett spoke next,

"I am walking back toward the trucks. Once I plant the tracking devices, what's next?"

There was a long pause on the phone before Lyle answered. "I had a chance to study the road maps this afternoon. There are only two main routes out of here to the southeast leading to Bayburt, a city north-east of Turkey. Activate the devices as you plant them on the vehicles. We will still have about six hours. Call me back with the name of a place to meet you for dinner. I am heading to the hotel to get all of our stuff; then I will meet you."

"Oh, before I forget, those trucks each had eight Jerry cans of fuel mounted on their sides. They have to be our boys." Both men closed their phone conversation.

Less than hours later, Lyle parked on a side street just around the corner from where he was to meet Brett. Before joining his friend, he made some crucial calls, to Octo and Colonel Jackson. He wanted to know if the CIA or the Military satellite could monitor the area of Siirt, a town south-east of Turkey and close to the Iraqi border. His last call was to connect with Sargent Major Jenkins, the man who would provide a quick ride out of Dodge. Being in the same time zone it was convenient, J answered on the second ring.

Lyle wasted no time in getting to the point after they said hello. "Right now, we are in Trabzon, on the Black Sea, north of Turkey. Our bandits are loading tonight, and we expect them to work their way southeast, toward Siirt, not far from the Turkey-Iraq border. Tracking devices are in place."

J's voice took on a higher pitch due to excitement, "The CIA and the military were able to get me a Russian Karmovka-60 helicopter. It was one brought down during the Iran-Iraq war. It lacks air agility but is airworthy. The aircraft mechanics are still working on it as we speak. Oh, I will have it loaded with enough extra fuel for a real vacation."

Lyle started laughing. After regaining his composure, he said, "We will monitor the convoy and keep you updated. I will call you back in four to six hours unless there is a drastic change. I repeat we should be heading for Siirt." Lyle spelled the name of the city for Jenkins.

"I will have the chopper in the Mosul area by morning. Once you have a good idea where they are heading, I will take it about ten miles from the Turkish border." Lyle heard J's voice go up another notch, "I will have three Ah-64 Apache helicopters escorting me. Yahoo!"

Lyle was speechless. Old man J had pulled it off again. He was sure the mention of 'Operation Vulcan' had officers somewhere giving orders, but it still took contacts on the ground to get things done. Lyle's last words to Jenkins were "Godspeed J."

CHAPTER 9

Trabzon Turkey

Neither man was up at five a.m., their usual wake-up call. It was way after six when Lyle pushed his tired body from the bed. He made coffee in their room while Brett was taking a cold shower. The two men knew they had a long and arduous day before them. A load of the armory was due somewhere in the general area in less than twenty-four hours. They headed to the restaurant downstairs for breakfast.

While eating a hearty Turkish breakfast consisting of an omelet, different cheeses, and white bread, Lyle glanced over at a detailed city street map he had spread out on the empty half of the table. He was especially interested in the wharf area. Studying the streets of Trabzon, he said, "We will drive down the main road until it hits Yolo road, then we will turn right and go to a small cove between Trabzon and Rize." Using his index finger, he pointed at a small sheltered bay that looked like an excellent spot to discreetly transfer illegal weapons from boat to trucks; very few fishermen did business there. Lyle handed Brett the map. All day they would keep on the lookout for several Russian or Turkish trucks while cruising along the water in their separate cars. Both agents knew that some vehicles had to meet with the boat to pick up the merchandise. They would find them.

Brett had a suggestion, "We should mix in with the locals around the docks. We could grease a few hands, and maybe someone's tongue would loosen." He then leaned over and took another piece of toast, smothered it with butter and preserves. "It has worked for us many times before. But, of course, people in this part of the world may not react to bribery the same way." Lyle looked at his watch and said, "It's now almost eight a.m., that means we have seventeen or eighteen hours."

Brett was perusing his map, he turned to Lyle, "If we don't find anything in the Trabzon dock area, I will drive about twenty klicks to the east. We'll find them."

Both men finished their breakfast, went to their room and took out the tracking devices, two flash-bangs, and a few grenades each, and placed the sensitive cases under their beds. As they left their room, Lyle hung the "Do not disturb sign" on the doorknob.

They went their separate way walking the streets leading to the dock and methodically cruising along the waterfront and in parking lots adjacent to hotels and restaurants. So engrossed in their search and so dedicated to the cause, they forwent lunch. In the afternoon, outside of the town of Rize, Brett noticed four older looking Turkish REO military trucks without any military markings or plates. The vehicles had been assembled in Turkey by Turk Otomotiv Endustrileri A.s. Under a thick coat of dust, painted trademarks could hardly be seen at the bottom of the front doors. As Brett walked nonchalantly around the trucks, he noted that all had new tires and their back loading doors were locked. Looking the area over, he found a two-story hotel just around from where the trucks were parked. Using the stalking techniques taught by the CIA, Brett soon spotted six rather large and sturdy looking bearded mid-aged men sitting together around a table in a restaurant. Brett continued to watch. One man got up to go to the restroom. He had a martial demeanor, he looked hawkish and very energetic; one could tell he was a soldier.

Brett continued to observe. He took out his binoculars and focused on the cases that had been placed between the men's legs, under the table. He was not shocked, actually not even surprised when he discovered painted on the cases, red squares with heraldic shields with a double eagle in the center that represented the National Symbolics of Russia. Brett now knew he had their men. After putting away his field glasses, he slipped away to make a phone call. Lyle immediately rejoiced and felt relieved hearing the news.

"Man, am I glad you found those killers. As for me, I have had no success all day. Were you able to put on the tracking devices?"

"Not yet. I wanted to share the good news first."

"The only intel I could get came from an old man who spoke broken English. He mentioned that just outside Rize was where the fishing boat from Ukraine dock. The old geezer said that imported goods are brought in Rize."

Brett who was now ready to go plant the tracking devices had a question for his partner, "What's next?"

There was a long pause on the phone before Lyle spoke. "I had a chance to study the road maps this afternoon. There are only two main routes out of here. Activate the devices as you plant them on the vehicles. We will still have about six hours. Now, give me the name of a place in Rize to meet you for dinner. I am heading to the Hotel to get all of our stuff then I will join you." Brett had more to say, "Those trucks, each had eight Jerry cans of fuel mounted on their sides. They have to be our boys." Both men closed their phone conversation.

Two hours later Lyle parked on a side street, just around the corner from where he was to meet Brett. He needed to make an important call to Colonel Jackson to find out if the CIA or the Military satellite could be used to monitor the area of Siirt, a city south-east of Turkey. Next, he dialed Sargent Major Jenkins. Being in the same time zone, J answered on the second ring.

Lyle wasted no time in getting to the point after they said hello. "We are north of Trabzon, Turkey. Our bandits will be loading tonight. We expect them to work their way to the southeast toward Siirt, a city not far from the Turkey-Iraq border. Tracking devices are in place on their trucks."

As J spoke, once again his voice took on a higher pitch indicating excitement, "The CIA and the military were able to get me a Russian Karmovka-60 helicopter. It was one brought down during the Iran-Iraq war. They lack air agility but are airworthy. The aircraft mechanics are working on it as we speak. Oh, I have it loaded with enough extra fuel for a real vacation."

Lyle could not help laughing. He replied, "We will monitor the convoy and keep you updated. Both Brett and I believe the trucks will be heading for Siirt." Lyle spelled the name of the Turkish city for Jenkins.

"I will have the chopper in Mosul by morning. After we know for sure about Siirt, I will take the helicopter closer to the border, to Amadiya, Iraq." Lyle heard J's voice go up another notch when he said, "I will have three Ah-64 Apache helicopters escorting me to Amadiya. Yahoo!"

Lyle was speechless. Old man J had pulled it off again. Sure, Operation Ares had the man at the top giving orders, but it still took contacts on the ground to be successful. "Godspeed J." was Lyle's last word.

CHAPTER 10

Clouds had partially obscured most of what little moonlight there was, and now smoke, coming from somewhere was creating a dirty looking conversion layer over their heads. The two agents had been following the convoy at a safe distance when suddenly the trucks' lights could no longer be seen as they disappeared behind a small ridge. Brett and Lyle suspected the men had stopped the convoy and were taking time off for the night. To find out what had caused this new development, the partners decided to approach the caravan on foot, quietly of course. It was after eleven p.m. Brett was leading his partner on foot walking less than a hundred feet ahead of Lyle who was driving his partner's SUV. The other SUV had been left behind. They were operating with no headlights, and Brett had to depend on what little moonlight there was to drive through dry brush and rocky terrain. In this arid region, the vegetation was almost absent. It took them a long time to find a secure hiding place to park the SUV. Lyle made sure the vehicle was turned around and pointing back down the trail. They both carried car keys fitting each other's vehicle.

It was after midnight. Surprisingly, Major Jenkins answered almost immediately when Lyle called him to relay their latitude and longitude, and the GPS coordinates. Jenkins said, "I am sitting with my Russian chopper about forty klicks to the northwest of Mardin in Turkey. Your rental escape helicopter has been fueled and awaits your commands." J was sure this would get a laugh.

Lyle chuckled, and said, "The trucks are not going anywhere right now, I think the men are eating and resting. If all goes well, we are going to hit the enemy at daylight. We have explosives on three of their four vehicles. They left Trabzon with extra help, and now there must be a total of twenty men in this convoy."

Brett and Lyle were now just a few yards away from the group of men who were busy smoking and warming up food on a small campfire. From their Mirador, the two agents were staring at a big 50 mounted on a four by four pickup. If all went according to their plans, they hoped to take out Aleksey first, blow the trucks, kill as many men as possible, head back to their SUV, and get out of Dodge. Once the battle was underway, they would have Jenkins land and pick them up in a secure area. The agents did not want J to take chances should the bandits get the upper arm. If that happened, J was to turn the chopper around, Lyle and Brett would depend on their vehicles to save their skin.

Time was dragging. The site was now plunged in complete silence and darkness. Only the contour of the trucks was vaguely visible. The surveillance of the improvised camp continued. It was time to get the cases open and prepare for the assault.

An hour before dawn, most of the stagnant smoke had dissipated. Jenkins contacted the two partners to give last-minute recommendations. On the second ring, Lyle answered and listened to J, "Give me a ring before you begin the carnage so I can start the blades turning. That will save us several minutes of warm-up time. I can be there in twenty-five to thirty minutes, maybe less. Again, make sure you call me before your first shot."

"Roger. All systems are a go. We will contact you when we are ready to fire." Lyle placed his phone in his chest pocket. Both men attached grenades and flash-bangs to their belts. They filled their spare ammo pockets, chambered a round in their Dragunov sniper rifles after setting the safety and checking their scope, they hung them over their back. Both men chambered a bullet in their automatics and their Hecker and Koch semi-automatic guns. They placed other explosives in a pack with the timers. After stuffing pockets with energy bars, they put the rest of their armor in their small backpacks. Last, Lyle and Brett made sure that if their opponents seized anything of theirs, nothing would be traced back to them or the homeland.

Should anyone try to open the sensitive cases, they would blow up immediately. Inside each car, they had placed half a block of C4 with a timer switch allowing either man to blow the vehicles if needed. The two agents looked at each other, gave a thumbs up, pulled their night vision goggles over their eyes, and headed out.

It took them almost an hour to work their way around the ridge and down toward the camp. They stopped about four hundred meters from the Mercedes SUV next to which, they thought, Aleksey was sleeping. Creeping forward, they found themselves staring at the pickup on which a big 50 had been mounted. There was no way one could crawl farther and plant an explosive under the rig equipped with the big 50 or under Aleksey's SUV, as six guards were patrolling around the two vehicles, and Lyle was well aware they were not asleep. He studied the trucks that were parked in a single file and spotted the dents on the three trucks where Brett had planted explosives. Now he knew which trucks needed attention. Lyle tapped Brett on the shoulder and whispered in his ear, "I am going to place bombs on the rest of the trucks." At this time, they checked their earbuds, and com-link." Then Lyle spoke into his throat mike, "Testing, one, two, three." The drill was over. Lyle spoke, "You see those boulders about two-hundred yards up the hill, I am going to see if I can get behind them for safety after I plant the explosives." After Brett acknowledged, Lyle continued, "No matter what happens to me, you are to take out Aleksey, blow the trucks, and leave." Brett responded firmly, "We can fight together as we always do, terminate Aleksey, blow the trucks, I will cover you why you make it to the boulders. Two guns can do a hell of a lot of damage; you know that." There was a long silent pause before Brett spoke, "Come on old buddy; you know that."

"Stand down Brett, take no risks, if I get hit, you go, OK?"

Before answering, Brett knew damn well he would not leave his friend unless he, himself, went down. Brett pretended he would follow the order, but as always, he would stand by his partner. Then jokingly, he said, "I agree with that, old friend. One of us has to be present in D.C. for the de-brief and let them know about the suitcase nuke."

Lyle looked at his watch and took out his cell phone; it was time to give Jenkins the signal to warm up his helicopter as the warfare was about to begin. At that moment, J walked in the direction of his Russian chopper. He would be there in twenty, twenty-five minutes.

Lyle quietly worked his way down through the short and scanty brush, then spoke calmly into his mike, "Is the coast clear to proceed?"

Once more, Brett studied the area with his infrared unit. "No Tangos around the first truck, but there are guards by the other trucks."

"OK, thanks. Our ride home will be here in twenty-five minutes. You take out Aleksey if you spot him. I wanted to be the one eliminating this evil man, but you are the better sniper."

"Will do. You will owe me a twelve pack for my services, sir." There was a quiet chuckle in both earbuds.

Like a snake in the grass, Lyle worked his way to the truck parked near some dry bushes. Once he was less than twenty feet from the vehicle, he clicked his throat mike twice. Lyle was in place. He then slid slowly under the truck. Within two minutes a block of C54 was in place with its electronic device activated, awaiting a command to send a charge into the high explosives.

CHAPTER 11

Hell on earth

When Lyle slid back across the open space, the night was over, the black sky was now taking a dark turquoise tint, and the horizon was turning orange with a beautiful pinkish hue. It was not quite daylight. Crawling, Lyle was cautiously advancing through rocks and brush as quickly as he could.

Brett spotted his partner and at this precise moment noticed something else. In the distance, one could see a few men moving toward the ridge where Aleksey's Mercedes SUV was parked. With his binoculars, Brett observed two men coming out of one of the three small pup tents. He cooed into his mike, "Hurry up my friend, Sir Aleksey and his suite are among the living. His staff is probably going to fix coffee for their boss."

Lyle did not verbally reply. Instead, he pushed his voice mike twice to acknowledge that he had heard the transmission. His focus was on the fifty feet of steep climbing ahead of him. Several times he slid backward, caught a bush, and then continued upward toward the boulders. Lyle heard Brett speaking in his earbud, " Aleksey is walking toward the campfire. Tangos are adding wood to the fire, looks like they are going to make coffee." Lyle was now almost to the big rocks; he asked Brett to be ready to get the inferno underway.

"Give me two minutes, no more, take Aleksey out, blow the trucks, and head for our SUV. Can you still see me?"

Lyle had found shelter behind large rocks for protection; the firefight could start.

"He is drinking coffee. Are you ready to party?"

"Yes, let's do it. Let's get it done. I will blow the first truck, Aleksey will freeze when he hears the blast; you take him out at that precise moment. Then you start taking out as many tangos as you can. After I blow the first vehicle, Aleksey's men will rush and take cover under the other trucks; this is when I will blow trucks and men.

Lyle activated his sender, and there was an immediate response as the blocks of C54 blew the vehicles, reducing them to small and large pieces of metal. Some men fell to the ground, hit by the shrapnel, others were desiccated, cut into pieces, large and small. The screaming was sickening, and the scene was horrifying. In the tents, stunned guards awakened by the deafening noise of the blast were now running erratically like rabbits, aimlessly going in all directions with nowhere to hide while explosives went off, and bullets were flying everywhere. As the site was turning into a war zone, Brett had hit Aleksey high in the chest, ripping out his throat, almost severing his head as his soul left for hell. Another followed that well-aimed shot, and another, as men fell to the ground already dead, or soon to be. They were exposed, having no place to hide from the bullets that were flying nonstop. Two vehicles had been spared, the pick up on which a big 50 was mounted and Aleksey's SUV.

As both Lyle and Brett were pulling down on another man, the big 50 opened up from the back of the pickup truck sitting about a hundred feet from where Aleksey was killed. The rocks and dirt around Lyle were turning to powder as the 50 caliber machine gun tore up everything in its way. To make matters worse, Lyle knew it was the sound of an American model machine gun, most likely one left behind by the US troops in Iraq. Brett tried a shot at the man behind the weapon, but the round bounced off the armor plating used to protect the stationary operator. The gun switched to Brett's location and opened up with hundreds of rounds, tearing up the dry shrubs around his hiding place. The bullets were flying, and the noise was deafening. He needed to move behind some boulders to his left, and fast.

Lyle could see his old friend was in trouble. To help him, he opened with three round bursts; this maneuver produced loud piercing screams, Lyle had hit the gunner in his leg. The gun pivoted toward Lyle, again pinning him down, making him hug the dirt. Then the two agents heard the savage yelling of a few men as they began to work themselves into a trance. "Allahu akbar, Allahu akbar" they continued to yell as they started running up the hill where Brett and Lyle were. Many of the terrorists hiding under the trucks had disintegrated instantly, only a handful of fighters were left standing, but the odds were still against Lyle and Brett. There was almost no chance they could make it over the ridge to safety. The big 50 had them pinned down. There were six men now working their way up the hill toward them. A bullet hit Lyle in the leg; he bit his lip, knowing the pain was coming. Lyle looked in the direction the shot had come from and saw two men advancing toward him.

Lyle spoke into his mike, "Two men, by the dead trees, two hundred yards to your right. Can you get a shot?" Brett who had worked his way behind some boulders for better coverage took a peek, lined up his scope and fired, killing one man. The 50 was being reloaded with another belt of ammo protruding from a large military ammo box. Brett fired, one man was hit and fell off the back of the pickup. As he recycled another round, he heard Lyle in his com unit, "I took a bullet in the leg, no way I can make it out. Go now as they reload, I will use three rounds burst to keep them occupied."

There was no way Brett would leave. As long as he could pull a trigger, retreating was not an option. He threw a grenade with all his might; loud and harsh screaming accompanied the explosion. Then he fired again at the second man running toward Lyle but missed. The terrorist had reached the hill and was now moving toward both agents who were trapped.

Suddenly out of the blue, loud music could be heard, someone was playing the national anthem, yes, the Star-Spangled Banner. I am losing it, thought Lyle, I must be comatose. Approaching from the east, they spotted a helicopter with the sun at its back. The sound got louder and louder. As the chopper was approaching, they spotted the

ISIS's black flag sticking out from the chopper pads. As the helicopter banked to make a run, they also saw the flag of Russia painted on the doors of the chopper. The aircraft made a three hundred and sixty-degree turn. Brett spoke into his throat mike again, "This is it; we are dead. We stand no chance against a helicopter." Brett screamed when a sharp rock hit him with force in the neck, and his wound was bleeding profusely. He applied pressure to the lesion the best he could. In the meantime, the deafening sound of the Star Spangled Banner kept on playing.

Lyle and Brett had no idea that Sargent Major Jenkins had the men in Iraq not only paint on the Russian emblems and install the flags, he also had them mount four loudspeakers rescued from a mosque that had been destroyed in Mosul. The ruse did not fool the man with the 50; he turned his gun toward the Kamov Kd-60 chopper as a 9MI7 Skorpion missile tore into the pickup. There was nothing left of the small truck. As the Russian helicopter turned, the Yak-B machine guns opened up toward the last live terrorists who were finishing their climb. The music kept on playing while the screaming maimed men continued their fight. Just then, a thick and blinding dust cloud could be seen in the far distance, a convoy of trucks and men was approaching the camp at high speed.

Jenkins stopped the blaring music from playing and spoke into his loudspeaker, "More men approaching from the south." At this time, several bullets passed through the cowling of the chopper; another survivor of the carnage, equipped with an AK47, was firing at the helicopter. He was now collapsing on the ground with blood gushing out from his neck. Lyle had taken him down with his sniper rifle.

Then J spoke into his comm unit, "I am going to hover over and let my helper down on a line to give aide, what is your status?"

Lyle spoke first. "Shot in the leg, probably could walk using my gun as a crutch." Brett spoke next, "Just a minimal wound, you take care of the family man." Both Lyle and J knew Brett well enough to know he was minimizing his condition. J moved the chopper above Brett, then a corpsman dressed in camo was lowered down from the helicopter. The medic opened his Red Cross bag and started to assist the wounded casualty. J turned the chopper outward and headed toward the rising dust that was rapidly approaching.

When the medic leaned over to check his lesion, Brett brought his hand to his mouth; he was unable to speak. It was Hilda giving him first aid. He mumbled something, then passed out from the loss of blood. Hilda knew she had to work fast to save Brett. She immediately injected him with morphine. She did not want him to be moving or even wake up while working on him. Hilda opened up the wound to find the bleeder and compress it with a hemostat. She cleaned the site and put on a sterile dressing. Brett was in severe shock due to the loss of blood. He was pale, cold and clammy. Hilda started an IV. She had no more than hung the bag on the branch of a dead tree when the firing started again. The attack was coming from where Aleksey's SUV was parked. With Brett's sniper rifle she started shooting back at her aggressor, hitting him in the high chest. She turned her sights toward the second shooter who was running for cover behind what was left of the SUV.

Soon they heard the sound of another Skorpion missile blow up in the distance and saw flames shooting upward.

Lyle dragged his injured leg behind him. Blood was still oozing unsafely, even though he had applied a tight pressure bandage. His pulse was rapid, his face pale. Before he passed out, he had tied on a tourniquet the best he could.

Within minutes the big Kamov returned. There was no more firing as J hovered above Brett and lowered the rescue basket from a winch that he had hooked on before leaving Iraq. With adrenalin at a peak, Hilda placed Brett into the Stokes stretcher, laid in the guns, and grabbed the cable. She knew she would have to pull the basket into the chopper and be lifted back down again as she needed the basket for Lyle. Within minutes she was back in the basket, ready to be let down over Lyle.

As J pulled the chopper back toward Lyle, he was letting it down as close as he could. J looked back to the south, the dust storm created by the ISIS fighters was approaching, it reminded Jenkins of the dust storms produced by the haboob winds of Egypt. He knew that the approaching pickups were equipped with 50 caliber machine guns. By now, Jenkins had no more Skorpion missiles left, and only a few rounds in the Yak-B machine gun. J spoke into his mouthpiece, "We have company coming."

Hilda let go of the line about five feet from the ground. Blood was leaking through the bandage Lyle had applied earlier. She immediately tightened the tourniquet, drug Lyle into the basket, grabbed the Stokes line and yelled, "Go" into her comm unit. After pulling the stokes basket into the chopper, the medic immediately opened the wound to expose the bleeder and stop the hemorrhage. As she worked, she told J to head over the hill to the north-east. They needed to locate the two vehicles the agents had rented earlier. Before passing out, Brett had told Hilda about a switch he kept in his pocket that was to be used to blow up those SUVs.

As the chopper pulled over the ridge, Hilda clamped on the hemostat in Lyle's leg, then reached into Brett's pocket and as the helicopter approached the cars, she pushed the button on a small black device. Immediately there were two massive explosions as the C4 disintegrated the vehicles. Hilda hooked up an IV and started cleansing Lyle's wounds before she spoke again, "Time is critical dear, these two men might not make it if we don't get them to a field hospital like yesterday."

"Roger that," J said as he almost red lined the RPM with the throttle. "I will be in Mosul in under an hour. I am going to contact the field office now." Little did J know that after calling the field unit, J's old friend, Colonel Watkins, had ordered two black hawks helicopters in Turkey to escort J's chopper back into Iraq airspace and to a field hospital.

No one questioned or stopped either Hilda or Sargent Major Jenkins as they accompanied Brett and Lyle to the temporary hospital. Almost six hours later, a doctor told Hilda and J that the two men had come within minutes of losing their lives and that without the work of the two retired field medics, both men would not have made it. For the next forty-eight hours Hilda and J stayed at the bedside of the injured agents. Later a captain came in and told them that they were being transferred by helicopter to Bagdad. Just as their chopper was getting ready to take off, Colonel Watkins came by to shake their hand with J and Hilda, and thank them.

After arriving in Bagdad, the four spent three more days at the hospital. Five days later a private aircraft picked the four of them up and flew them to Paris, France, to the American Hospital.

The following day Lyle's mother, Monique, flew from Atlanta to France as soon as she could to be at Lyle's bedside. While recuperating, Annie, Monique, Hilda, and J visited the two patients every day. On the morning of the third day, Patrick, Lyle's friend from the US embassy visited them and announced POTUS had sent orders to fly Lyle, Brett, Hilda, and J First Class to Washington DC. in ten days. The government would provide a hotel room, a driver, and car for a week in DC.

CHAPTER 12

Paris

Three days later

Brett and Lyle were recovering faster than expected. To regain some strength they walked together around the hospital halls, increasing the distance each day. They were on their tenth lap when the head RN informed them of their release the following day.

The next morning, the Jenkins visited for a while and announced they were returning to Curacao. Later the two men were discharged from the hospital. They took a cab to the hotel where Brett had stayed once before. Brett felt so much better, he wanted to take a walk and wander in Paris, hoping to come across a lovely Parisian lady. Since Monique was staying in the same hotel, Lyle stopped by to say hello before heading to Annie's place. Monique wanted to spend time in Paris to visit the major sites. She also wanted to enjoy the new grand-daughter she hardly knew. Lyle called Annie, said goodbye to his mom, and left. He still had to rent a vehicle.

The following days Lyle enjoyed both Annie and Jennie. He worked out and ate well. On the third day, Annie asked Lyle to watch Jennie so she could visit with Monique for the day.

Annie and Monique enjoyed a full day shopping at Le Bon Marche, the first department store in the world which opened in 1838 and was designed by Gustave Eiffel, the man who built the Eiffel Tower. Monique found the Galeries Lafayette, another luxury world, magnificent with its gorgeous Byzantine glass dome. The two women enjoyed lunch and a view of Paris from the rooftop cafe of this huge store. Annie who knew her city well had all sorts of interesting bits of information that Monique enjoyed.

Lyle decided it was time to get into a lengthy discussion with Frederic Girard, a retired gendarme and now the owner of the neighborhood grocery store. He suspected this man of spying on him, and he knew he could trap him into saying something that would disclose facts that someone, most likely the Russians or drug cartel, was paying him to keep them informed of Lyle's location and movement. He dressed Jennie in a warm coat and left the apartment.

It had just been over an hour and three glasses of wine later when Frederic disclosed something that only Lyle or the Chechen's close associates would have known. Using the interrogation techniques taught by the CIA, Lyle trapped Frederic two more times into divulging compromising information. Now Lyle knew the man was a spy. Showing no adversity, remaining cagey, he finished his wine, bought a few things for the evening meal, and headed home with Jennie Anne. Annie was not back; she had not returned from her shopping escapade with Lyle's mother.

Having confirmed his suspicions about Frederic, Lyle had to prepare the traitor's elimination. With no witness present, he went into the bathroom, pushed the small two foot by two-foot cover on the ceiling. The small area that allowed workers to work on electrical or plumbing pipes if needed. Just inside the space, and under the insulation, wrapped carefully in a small towel, was a half-empty bottle of Succinylcholine and two syringes. The same container that he had used in Carcassonne and again in the Yucatan sometime ago to put two old men to sleep permanently. Now it was time to put another old man to sleep, a gendarme in his late fifties, an unscrupulous and greedy man, a traitor. Lyle filled two syringes and carefully placed the vial back in the towel and hid it. Before leaving the bathroom, he made sure there was no debris on the floor and checked for boot tracks on the toilet seat cover. A bit tense, Lyle went into the bedroom, opened his case and placed each syringe in a secure wrapper. He took his automatic, chambered a round. After putting the locked case away, the agent laid his dark coat, gloves, and hat on a small chair in the corner of the room. This assassination did not worry Lyle, he was confident there would be no autopsy as the old man had a history of heart problems, in fact, recently, he had been admitted to the IC unit, and for a time he was not expected to live.

Upon the shoppers' return, Lyle started to reheat some leftovers and brought out the delicacies bought earlier. The trio talked for a while, watched TV, and talked some more. Lyle got up, he decided to go for a walk, " I am going to go breathe some fresh air, relax, and cool off." Lyle walked into the bedroom, plugged in the numbers to open the case, took out his holster and gun, grabbed the wrapped syringes, and slid them into his empty coat pocket. After giving Annie a peck on the cheeks, he gave Monique a quick kiss on the forehead and left in the cold and dark evening. It was nine thirty at night.

Lyle walked over several blocks from Annie's before heading south toward the grocery store. Every Friday, Frederic Girard's wife went to visit and spend the evening with their daughter and granddaughters. When Lyle slipped down through the alley where Frederic kept his trash cans, it was pitch dark. There was no moon, and the clouds had rolled in early, plunging the street in gloomy darkness. Lyle looked around carefully to see if the second floor had an escape ladder, there was none. He studied the granite rock building further and found a cast iron drain pipe on the corner of the structure. It was firmly attached to the building, so he climbed the old pipe quickly. His leather gloved hands found many metal ties used to hold the tube in place all the way to the top. Within a minute he was on the roof. Lyle knew which room was Frederic's room because the light was on. This bedroom had double French doors which opened out onto a small balcony which overlooked the street below. Before sliding off the roof onto the balcony, the agent studied the area and alley as he had to make sure no one was present in the street. The fog was moving in thicker now. Like a cat, he slid down the metal rod holding the terrace. Quietly the agent pushed his body against the side of the wall. As he moved, he observed the street which was quiet. Lyle gently tried the door; it was locked. He reached into a small square leather pack attached to his belt and took out a set of lock picking tools. Within thirty seconds the French door opened. The light in the room was now off.

Gingerly, Lyle slipped along the wall toward the head of the bed. He could smell the heavy scent of cigarette smoke. Frederic was a chain smoker, and his Gitane cigarettes stunk. Lyle reached inside his coat and took out the holder with the pre-filled syringe from inside his pocket. He pulled the cap from the needle of death. Lyle leaned forward to find the carotid artery visually. Standing motionless, he could smell the foul breath of cigarette smoke mixed with liquor. Frederic was also an alcoholic. As Lyle injected the potent relaxant, his free hand covered the mouth and nose of Frederic Girard forcefully. In less than a minute the overdose of succinylcholine had done the trick, the traitor was no longer a threat to Lyle, Annie, and others.

Due to the cold, Lyle was red in the face when he returned to the apartment. After closing the door, Lyle caught Annie and his mother admiring the purchases made earlier.

Lyle had not lost his appetite over Frederic's death, he poured himself a glass of wine, sliced a baguette lengthwise and prepared a well-garnished sandwich. As he was sipping his wine and enjoying his late meal, he suddenly heard the characteristic 'nee eu nee eu nee eu,' the sound of the French ambulance, a little more musical than the 'you ooo you ooo' of the American siren. Lyle looked at his watch, Frederic's wife was back, she had just discovered the body.

He was reading in bed when Annie appeared in the doorway. Pretending to be part of a vaudevillian performance, she started twirling around Lyle's side of the bed on her beautiful and firm naked legs and dancing with a sexually provocative hip movement. This burlesque show was designed to get his attention. She spoke, "You said you were back to normal. Let's test your level of wellness. I think that when I get through with you tonight, you are going to wish you were back in the hospital." She was all words. Annie was not aggressive at all; she preferred her man to be the initiator of their sexual frolics. Of course, she ignored what Lyle had been doing less than two hours ago, and she had no clue the ambulance had made a racket on the street because a man she never suspected of having malevolent intentions had just been killed by Lyle, the man she loved.

By then he had laid his book on the nightstand and was now applauding the prancing and the speech. He was quick to reply, "I had only a leg wound, just a little scratch that has nothing to do with my sexual ability. That part of me cannot fail when I have a floozy prancing by my bed. By then, he had grabbed her by the wrist with firmness. She was now against him. In her arms, he could temporarily forget the execution of Frederic.

THREE WEEKS LATTER

CHAPTER 13

Paris

On the horizon, the sun was timidly filtering through the light fog that was lingering over the city. Lyle closed the shade and rolled over in bed. It was just past six-thirty a.m. Feeling tired, he was beginning to believe that Annie was right, his last injury had affected his overall performance. He was worn out. Carefully he slipped from the bed, put on his robe, and headed to the kitchen. While preparing some coffee, his busy mind was erratically running dozens of thoughts and ideas. Before leaving on his trip to DC, he had to contact Gab and pick up his mother and Brett at their hotel. Later he would drop Jennie Anne at her maternal grandmother's hotel. The toddler was going to spend a week at Marguerite's while Annie would be in Washington D.C. with the rest of the clan at the invitation of Colonel Jackson. Lyle sighed, "Ah! the coffee is ready." He poured himself a cup as Annie entered the kitchen wrapped up in a cozy robe.

It was just after eight a.m. when Lyle contacted Gab on his cell phone. With the usual chit-chat over, Lyle shared what had transpired in Turkey. He was careful not to reveal any locations and to avoid pronouncing the participants' names on the phone. Gab could not let him continue talking; he had to interrupt the caller who was just about to tell the elderly gentleman that he was heading to the States for a while. Gabriel needed to be heard, so he spoke firmly, "You better sit down, son."

"I am sitting, go ahead. What's so bad?"

"I spoke with two of my friends in the motherland. They both say, and affirm, that the Chechen, Aleksey is alive. Lyle who was not alarmed by the news, never let Gabriel finish and calmly declared,

"No way, I saw him standing next to a vehicle we blew up. Brett shot him, and the killer's body flew everywhere, his neck was sliced off, he was decapitated."

Gabriel insisted, "My Moscow friend, the general, is reliable. He said that on several occasions, Aleksey had used a double whenever he thought there was a threat to his life. He has become overly cautious, especially after being shot at in Dublin." The agent was not convinced but started to doubt himself.

"Brett and I saw his beard, and he limped on the right side, it was Aleksey." Gabriel detected the distress the news had produced. Disappointed, in disbelief, Lyle was slowly getting uncertain about Aleksey's death. He thanked Gab and asked him to continue investigating this unbelievable development and announced he would be leaving today for Washington D.C. and would be returning in about ten days to two weeks.

"While you are gone, old Gab will put out feelers everywhere. You must be careful, Lyle. My old friend, the general, he is not one to start rumors. The old man concluded the dialogue on a happy note, "Don't forget to invite me to the baptism of the little one when you get back, eh?"

"You will be invited. If anything comes up, use that phone I gave you, or the one hidden inside the wall, outside your shop. Thank you again for getting ahold of the Russian colonel. See you soon."

Staring straight ahead and standing motionless following the alarming news, Lyle remained stationary for a full minute. There was still much to do before going to the airport at nine-thirty a.m. and turning in the car.

Annie was dressed and had put her hair up in a bun. Lyle walked into the bedroom to pick up her suitcase and Jennie's. After returning from his rented vehicle, he called his mother and Brett to be sure they were ready to go. Lyle loaded his pack and case, and within minutes the five of them were on their way to Marguerite's hotel to drop the little girl, Jennie. Then Lyle brought the travelers to the airport and drove the car back to the rental agency which was adjacent to the terminal.

In the comfort of the United Airlines First Class club room, they waited for the announcement to embark at ten-thirty five a.m. On the plane, they took their seats. Annie let Monique take the window seat so she could see the sights from the sky as they gained altitude after taking off. Because Lyle needed to relay to Brett the fiasco concerning Aleksey's fake death, the two men sat together.

As the big Airbus sped down the tarmac, the wheels soon lifted off the pavement, the nose of the jet rose, and the people were pushed back against their backrest. As the plane banked, Monique was trying to see if she could spot some of the monuments she had visited earlier. She was reminiscing her visit in France, and with some regret in her voice, she said, "Lyle's father and I, we had planned to spend our honeymoon in Paris, but due to circumstances, we never did. Every time we scheduled a trip, his country needed him, his homeland had priority! Monique had a bitter smile on her face. Shaking her index finger, she added, "Don't let that happen to you."

To cheer Monique, Annie was making plans for her next visit to France. They would spend their time touring the south, from the Pyrenees mountains to the Riviera, and from the Atlantic to the Alps.

The stewardess was cruising in the aisle serving a glass of champagne to the First Class travelers. The four friends made a toast to their upcoming adventure in Washington DC.

Lyle had filled in Brett on the news from Gab. Like his partner, Brett was shocked and angry. He did not like to be fooled, and revenge was on his mind. Then the men talked about what they would be doing in Washington. Their trip in the capital had been offered, more or less ordered, by the colonel, no information had been forwarded. They were wondering what festivities, dinners, and excursions were in store. What was the reason for this invitation that included Annie and Monique?

After one stop in the States to go through customs, the plane took off again, and landed at Ronald Reagan International Airport in DC at 6:11 P.M. As the four stepped off the plane, a man from the State Department met them and escorted the guests to a black vehicle outside the terminal. He told them their luggage would be sent to the hotel. The sergeant saluted, even though Lyle and Brett were not in uniform. The driver gave his name and asked everyone to buckle up. They would be staying at the Hilton Crystal City at Washington Reagan National Airport. All that attention was puzzling the two women.

Once at the hotel, the same State Department representative handed them three hotel key cards, one for Monique, one for Brett, and one for Annie and Lyle. As Lyle was holding the plastic card, he looked at his mom and Annie and said, "Colonel Jackson had to have his hand in the reservations. There is no way some bureaucrat would know Annie and I share the same bed." Everyone laughed. Monique had known the colonel when he was a young lieutenant assigned to work under her husband who was a captain at the time.

Just before the young sergeant left, he turned to Lyle and said, "Tomorrow, I will be picking you up at 10:30 a.m. for a guided tour of the city. Your lunch will be on your own. When you get tired, call me, I can bring anyone of you, or all of you back to the hotel. Tonight, enjoy your dinner at the hotel, you have a prepaid reservation for four at La Rotonde restaurant, and the wine is included. Rest well, I will see you in the morning." Before leaving, the young man handed a business card with a phone number to Brett, saluted, and drove off.

To regain some vitality after this busy day which had been a mixture of pleasure shattered by dismay, Lyle decided to take a shower and relax before going to the elegant restaurant located at the very top of the hotel. Annie gave him a languishing look as he was getting undressed to change into something more fancy for the restaurant. In her sensual voice, she said, "Are you inviting your floozy; she can help you get rid of the germs you came in contact on the flight. People were sneezing and coughing. Besides something else very pleasant might happen if I scrub you vigorously enough."

After a short laugh, Lyle answered, "You don't have to ask twice; it is flu season. People on the plane and at the airport were hacking.

I detected some wet, nasty, greenish sputum productive coughs. It might have been whooping cough, pneumonia, and maybe even TB. I agree with you; a thorough cleansing is in order. I think we better scrub each other since we were both exposed to the same contagious bugs.

Annie adjusted the water temperature, then Lyle followed her into the shower. At first, the back scrubbing with soap was genuine, but soon the situation degenerated and the potential victims of respiratory diseases were all over each other. Lyle washed Annie's breasts gently while he kissed the sensitive nape of her neck, a spot she loved him to brush lightly with his lips. His hands began to explore her well-proportioned body tenderly. She diligently gave him the same loving and playful caresses. From the warmth of the running water, their bodies were turning pink. The all-consuming passion they had for each other intensified and soon they found themselves on the floor of the spacious shower. Accidentally Annie's buttocks closed off the drain, and the water began to rise in the shower stall. The two lovers were so intensely engaged in their lovemaking that soon water was running over the side of the shower berm onto the tiled bathroom floor. It was Lyle who noticed the flood. Laughing, Annie who was already throwing towels on the floor offered a suggestion,

"Maybe we should slow down, dry the floor, and finish what we started in our king-size bed."

CHAPTER 14

Washington DC

Over the next four days, the group enjoyed the history and architecture of Washington DC. They took a day trip to the White House with their military guide. The group of four spent a day at the Smithsonian space museum, planning to come back another day to spend time at the museum of natural history. Taking advantage of this visit to Washington DC, Monique went to see her husband's headstone at the impressive Arlington cemetery where some 400,000 servicemen were laid to rest. Even though her husband's body was not buried there, mother and son could feel his presence during this moving visit. According to the government, Lyle's father's body was never recovered, and Monique never accepted the shady and questionable explanation given to her by the government. Lyle stood there silently, mentally communicating with his dad, regretting not having had the opportunity to spend more time with his father as a child.

Annie and Monique enjoyed the guided tour of George Washington's elegant Mount Vernon Estate and Gardens. This bus trip to the plantation south of Alexandria, Virginia, took the entire day. On the evening of the fourth day, the same gentleman who had met them at the airport was waiting for them in the lobby of their hotel. He informed the group that a vehicle would pick them up at eleven a.m. the next morning. They would be attending a special meeting in the White House which would be followed by lunch. The man turned slowly and said in a very stern voice, "You men are to be in your military dress uniform when I take you to the white house. If you go to the concierge, he has your attires waiting for you, as for the ladies, I suggest semi-formal dress." Then he turned and left through the lobby door.

There was a lot of speculation, but Lyle and Brett still ignored the reason for the hoopla. So far they had been kept in the dark, and no one would reveal the real purpose of their visit. They had not worn a military uniform in several years, in fact not since being assigned to the unique covert black operations detail. They reported to the registrar in the hall to receive their impeccable uniforms, wondering if they would fit. The shirts were so heavily starched; they could stand on their own. Monique had seen her son frown; she said, "I can't wait to see you in your dress uniform. It's been a long time since I've seen a man as handsome as your father in uniform. The two women were also in the dark; they had no idea they would attend some function requiring a semi-formal dress. What they had brought would do.

The next morning, at 11:00 a.m., the four friends gathered in the reception hall of the hotel. Slim and tall, Brett and Lyle looked very handsome. They appeared to have gained five inches in their uniforms. Their healthy tan stood out against the white shirts, and their hair had been trimmed to perfection.

The escort came into the lobby and invited them to the car that would take them to the White House. Annie was wondering what she was doing there. She was humbled thinking she was on her way to the White House, not as a tourist but as a guest. Monique seemed to go with the flow, looking at ease. When they approached the security, each guest was handed special badges to wear. No words were exchanged. After the guard returned from a small sentry box where he had made a call, he waved the vehicle through. The same procedure followed as they entered into the wing of the White House. Brett leaned over toward Lyle and said, "We've been here before, I wonder if this time it's going to be for a court marshal, an ass chewing, or just a plain old thank you."

A master sergeant who stood next to a closed door said a few words to the escort who turned to the four guests and said, "I will be leaving you for now. At about 1430 hours I will take you back to your vehicle. "Good day." The master sergeant opened the door and said, "Follow me please."

As they stepped into the small, warm, beautiful room with oak floors and mahogany paneling, they spotted a couple they knew, Sergeant Major Jenkins and First Sergeant Hilda Jenkins, also wearing their dress uniforms. The Jenkins had been informed of the ceremony in their honor. Lyle said, "I did not expect to see you here. I think I have an idea, they are going to de-brief us, and they did not want us to compare notes." Jenkins replied, "They picked us up earlier and drove us around through the city. I am sure you are right, no comparing notes." The men continued to talk as well as the woman. Then a door on the left front side of the room opened.

A staff sergeant entered the room, then as another man stepped through the door behind him, he said, "Attention." The three men and Hilda stood immediately. Monique who was once married to a Major rose in a smooth movement. Annie was left sitting; hesitant, she slowly stood up.

Colonel Jackson entered the room with all his ribbons, medal of honor, Bronze Star, Silver Star, Purple Heart, and others US military decorations. The four in dress uniforms immediately saluted. The colonel returned the salute and said, "At ease, please, sit down." Then he walked over to Monique sitting in a soft, comfortable, leather chair next to the aisle. Colonel Jackson stood firmly erect, then slowly saluted Monique, and said, "I thank you and your husband for serving our county. I miss the major and you, Monique. If it had not been for your husband, I would not be here today. I thank you once again."

Monique stepped forward, wrapped her arms around the Colonel, and they both shared a silent moment. Monique's husband was ten years older than her, and a he was a captain when young Lieutenant Jackson was assigned to work with him in covert operations work. Later her husband was promoted to major and left on assignments for extended periods. The young lieutenant who was stationed close by became a surrogate father to Lyle and taught him how to defend himself. A few years later Jackson was promoted to captain. Monique saw less of Captain Jackson.

After Monique and Colonel Jackson ended their hug, she sat down, and the colonel moved to the front of the room. He studied the three men and one woman sitting with their backs straight in front of him. He took a deep breath and began the procedure ordered by POTUS. The door opened on the left once again, a well-dressed man in civilian clothes came in and introduced himself as an aide to the president. From his podium, he briefly explained the secretive act laws and passed around several printed forms for everyone to sign. The man went over to the sergeant by the door and spoke into his ear. The Sergeant left, and in about five minutes he returned, stepped into the room and said, "Ladies and gentlemen, the President of the United States."

You could hear a pin drop in the room after everyone stood up. POTUS asked them to sit down. Instead of reading from a prepared script, he thanked the four sitting in the front for what they had done over the years and especially on their last mission. Then he told the four dressed in military attire to stand. POTUS sent Colonel Jackson to pin on the Army Distinguished Service Military Medal on each of the four members of the service. After the colonel was through, POTUS said, "Since these four risked their lives to save our country and ensure our security, it gives me great pleasure to award each one the Presidential Medal Of Freedom. I hope you know that you saved millions of lives by stopping that illegal traffic in Turkey. I thank you again, and your country thanks you also. God bless you, and God bless America." POTUS turned and waved as he left the room.

Then the colonel spoke. "You will now be taken to a special dining room to have lunch in the company of some behind-the-scenes characters who participated in the heroic success we are celebrating today; they are Octo, Willie, Colonel Thompson, and myself."

While walking to the dining room, Lyle approached Colonel Jackson and said, "If it had not been for Gabriel, my old friend in

Paris, sir, we would not have stopped that load in time. Is there anything you can do to show him some recognition?"

"Stand down, son. Patrick had lunch with Gabriel earlier today in a secret location. I am well aware of this man's contribution to our war against drugs and arms trafficking that poisons us. Patrick awarded Gabriel the Presidential Medal Of Freedom on behalf of POTUS. I will tell you all about it later.

The lunch was spectacular as POTUS had his chef cook for the group. Annie enjoyed the delicious and elegant meal. All the guests were friendly, and the ambiance was pleasant, not intimidating. After lunch, two black Tahoes drove the guests around Washington DC to see more of the sites.

In the evening, Brett said he was meeting a lady in the bar of their hotel that he had met the night before. Monique, the Jenkins, Annie, and Lyle went to a well-known fish restaurant congress members frequented.

Back in their room, Annie told Lyle how proud of him she was and how privileged she felt for having attended this special ceremony. She suggested they continue the celebration right here in their room. Lyle ordered some champagne. They looked at the pictures taken throughout the day, and Lyle brought up some anecdotes, funny stories, about the people she had met. They went over the well-kept secret surrounding the rewards and the presence of the Jenkins.

The evening was not over, the two lovers laughed and pulled off clothes as they talked, played and rolled around on the king size bed.

It was almost six a.m. when there was a knock on the door. Lyle opened, it was room service, "Here is your coffee and breakfast your wife ordered."

CHAPTER 15

Washington DC

To airport

It was a gloomy day. The sun was absent due to a smog layer which was hanging over muggy Washington D.C. The Jenkins were leaving the capital in two hours, on their way back to Curaçao. At ten thirty a.m. J and his wife Hilda invited Monique, Annie, Brett, and Lyle for coffee at the airport. Monique would be flying back to Atlanta Georgia one hour later, and Annie's flight back to Paris was scheduled to depart at one p.m. Lyle was spending every last minute with both his mother and Annie.

The previous evening, he had informed them that following the luncheon at the white house, the Colonel had given him his next assignment. Annie had attempted several times to find out where Lyle and Brett would be going into harm's way next. As skillful and judicious as she was, she failed to get any details about the whereabouts of the mission. She thought Lyle had not been himself since his return from the Middle East, even though he was continually assuring her that he was feeling good. Lyle's mother always worried she would lose her son the same way she had lost her husband.

They walked to the gate to see Monique off. She promised she would come back to visit Annie and little Jennie. Finally, it was Brett's turn to say goodbye to Monique. She had wanted to meet the young man for many years. Annie, Lyle, and Brett returned to the waiting area. By then everybody was quiet and sad.

Once Annie was out of sight, Lyle turned to his partner and said, "The colonel wants to meet with us when we go pick up our passports and supplies. Let's get a cab and head over there now. I will give him a call and let him know we are on our way."

An hour later, in a small room at CIA headquarters, three men sat down to discuss the final details of their mission named Vulcan. Colonel Jackson informed the two men that Patrick, presently stationed at the embassy in Paris, had been assigned to their team. He went on to explain that his involvement would be required only if conditions warranted it. Lyle and Brett could place a call to him at any time at their discretion. All US embassies and military, as well as the DEA, CIA, NSA and homeland security, were given orders by POTUS to assist the agents with intel. As usual, the colonel advised them that they were on their own, that POTUS needed complete deniability for their actions. Then he reached into his briefcase and brought out a brown folder with a seal printed on the cover. He opened it slowly and brought out a piece of paper. The colonel went through the written words on the document line by line. Questions were asked, and answers were given for about twenty minutes. Then Colonel Jackson got out of his chair, stretched his arms, and said, "You can pick up the weapons you need, here, from the CIA. They have your four passports, credit cards and other support documents ready. I think you better get another refill on your coffee before I tell you where you are heading to." This imposed delay in naming the next place where they would be facing fire was a bit nerve-wracking.

The men talked about good and bad times, the wedding that did not happen and of course about their visit to D.C. At last, Colonel Jackson said, "I don't have much intel for you, but you know how to find the problems and how to eradicate them." Pulling his chair up closer to the table, the colonel opened a file marked "Top Secret." As he looked at the two men across the table, he pushed a copy of part of a map toward them. "Look at the area in yellow in both the states of Louisiana and Mississippi. In your previous briefs, you had seen action there. The CIA has gathered unconfirmed intel regarding a load of arms brought on a Russian cargo ship named the Anakriyain2. These weapons may be smuggled in the marked area in Mississippi where, I remember, Brett had killed some men on swamp boats during Operation Ares. The ship arrived over twenty-four hours ago. That is why I had to cut your visit short. POTUS wants you to go back into the swamp ASAP, kill as many gunrunners as you can, and stop that shipment from ending up on our streets."

The partners looked at each other. Lyle knew he needed to let Brett take the lead as he was the one who had found out where the locals received the deliveries, on Skip and Horn Island, off Gulfport, Mississippi.

Brett said, "We have two possible leads, sir. The first one is an area just off the coast, in the vicinity of Gulfport. When I was there, the Cajuns and red necks were talking about this site, and one of the old men I wounded did mention Horn Island before a gator devoured him. That is all the intel I could get as they were planning to kill me. About the other lead, I will let Lyle explain, sir." Lyle shared what he knew, "Same thing, sir, Cajuns in the Louisiana swamps were armed with AK's and were hired for receiving and delivering weapons. As we mentioned in our brief before, we have killed several of the Babineaux family members. I believe it would be wise for us to head to Mississippi first and see what we can stir up. As usual, we will keep you informed through Octo."

"Sounds good to me. Just don't get wounded again, I can't help you. If any members of the House or Senate found out about troops activities on American soil, they would raise hell. Here is a copy of the intel I have. When you're done, use the shredder." Colonel Jackson stood up, shook the men's hand, saluted, and left through the door connecting to another hallway.

The agents sat at the table for a while and discussed the intel listed on the paper handed to them. Brett laid the document back on the table, then said, "As usual we are on our own. It's after two p.m., do you feel like heading out today?"

"Beats sitting here. When we get there, what do you think about going back to that bar where you spent time before? I'll stay back in the woods until you get info."

"My beard is not long enough, to remain unnoticed, I need to look scroungy to go there. I will have to let my hair and beard grow for a while. They would be suspicious if I showed up today, they would all hush up. I think we should go to New Orleans and pay a visit to that cargo ship, the Anakriyain2. Lyle approved the plans, "you hit it right on. You call Octo for tickets to New Orleans, and I will get the Sergeant outside the door to get our car and driver ready to take us to our hotel."

As the two men walked out through the halls of CIA headquarters, Brett dialed Octo. As usual, the clerk was glad to hear from his friends. After some chit-chat, Brett asked Octo to reserve two seats to New Orleans ASAP. The two men continued to talk as Octo worked his magic with his girls (computers). Brett could hear the clerk talking to himself as he punched the keys on his computer keyboard. All of a sudden, he said, "I have them. Two tickets, first class on Delta, leaving at 5:45 p.m. arriving at 9:15 p.m. Anything else you will need?"

"We will need two SUV"s, different colors, with GPS, Brett answered."

Within ten minutes Octo had everything set up. They could use their regular names for tickets and charge their car rental to a different identity upon arrival. "Anything else the girls can do for you?"

Brett said, "Give me a minute." He turned toward Lyle. "Where do you think we should stay?"

"Have him get us two rooms on Bourbon St. Brett spoke with Octo for a few more minutes, and turned to Lyle, "He has two rooms for us at the Royal Sonesta Hotel, at 300 Bourbon St." Lyle who spoke Russian was hoping to pick up a rumor or two from Russian sailors in one of the many bars along the dock. Chances are they would be on furlough, getting drunk and laid. Brett closed the cell phone conversation at looked at Lyle. There was a knock on the door. The marine Sergeant saluted and said, "Your car and driver are waiting for you."

The agents shredded the documents, grabbed their cases containing the weapons provided by the CIA, and followed the Sergeant. During the drive to their hotel, the discussion centered around the good times they had had in the military. Brett shared a story of a night to remember he had out in Paris. The two men had a few good laughs.

Once at their hotel, Lyle told their driver to wait as they would be back in fifteen minutes. Within ten minutes both men met their ride in front of the hotel.

CHAPTER 16

Washington DC to
New Orleans

At the Ronald Reagan National airport, people flying in economy class were lining up to register their luggage. Two men standing in a first class line at the Delta desk waited only a few minutes before they were greeted with a smile and handed their tickets. As they were having a beer in the exclusive first class lounge, awaiting their boarding announcement, Lyle looked at Brett and said, "I had time to think about involving Patrick. We could send him to Moscow to meet up with James Rockford, the guy in charge of agents working in the field? Maybe the two of them could make CIA Intel available to find out where slippery one-legged Aleksey is hiding out. I would like to know where in the hell he is, and how he is getting Russian arms."

Brett spoke, "Not a bad suggestion. I don't think Patrick is ready just yet to be back in action again. Let him get his feet wet in Moscow. We might be able to obtain more intel too, and eventually go back to Moscow or Chechnya to take out that bastard." The two men heard their boarding announcement. They had no more than sat down in their first class roomy seats when a woman with black hair and beautiful light brown complexion addressed the agents, "My name is Armance, may I get you a pre-departure drink?"

Brett smiled, and said, "I would like a glass of champagne, thank you." There was a pause as she was pouring the wine. Brett thanked her and said, "I wish I could also offer you a drink once we get to New Orleans." Brett was not very polished when approaching women, a nice guy, but far from being accomplished in the courting domain. This precipitate invitation did not perturb Armance who leaned over and whispered into Brett's ear, "Meet me at ten p.m. at the Galatoires, 209 Bourbon St. I usually go there to relax after my last flight." Then she gracefully stood back up, looked at Lyle and asked if she could get him a drink.

When Armance walked toward the galley, Lyle leaned toward Brett and asked him what the lady had whispered. Grinning, he replied, "I have a date at ten p.m. at a century-old Creole restaurant on Bourbon St." Beaming, he added, "Don't wait up for me tonight, my friend." Brett had been surprised by the favorable reply; he had not expected the response he received. The flight attendant handed both men a small plate of hors-d'oeuvre. As she turned around to return to the galley, her hips moved slightly in a flirtatious way.

"You are a lucky, man. You will be able to practice what that woman in the Paris bordello introduced you to."

Brett smiled at his friend, "Do I detect a bit of envy, and maybe even jealousy? The woman in that brothel introduced me to things you can't imagine, and it was not all sex either. She shared with me her philosophical views on life which left me thinking. Yes, I enjoyed my time with her." After a few sips of champagne, Brett remained on the same topic and said,

"I want to have what you have, a woman who loves me and who is willing to wait for me like Annie does for you." Brett leaned back in his leather seat and closed his eyes.

There was a forty minute stop in Atlanta Georgia.

It was 9:14 p.m. when their aircraft made its first bounce on the tarmac at Louis Armstrong airport in New Orleans. It bounced slightly once again and taxied slowly to its unloading zone. Lyle followed Brett toward the exit door of the plane and saw Armance lean forward, and he heard her say, "Thanks for flying Delta." Her eyes sparkled when the two agents went by, Lyle noticed her fingers lightly brushing against Brett's firm muscled arm as he stepped through the door. Armance thanked him also for flying with Delta as he reached the door. Lyle was thrilled Brett had been given some attention from a lady. The man had many good qualities and deserved to find someone as kind and understanding as his Annie.

Without any luggage to collect, the two men headed straight for the Hertz car rental to pick up their two SUV's. While at the counter Brett asked the clerk if he could exchange his SUV for a Mercedes. Brett turned to Lyle and said, "We might have to look like wealthy drug dealers around town when we come across the Russians gunrunners. I was going to mention that to you earlier, but meeting Armance stirred me." Brett never even broke a smile when he spoke.

As the two men walked toward their rental cars, Lyle spoke first, "I thought the humidity in DC was terrible. It is far worse here, and that smell of Aircraft fumes is overwhelming, thank God Bourbon St. is far enough from the airport." Lyle laughed softly, then said, "By the way, what will you wear to go to that dinner tonight? you must leave a good impression."

"All I have in my pack is my dark clothes to board the ship."

"As soon as we get to the hotel, why don't you ask the desk clerk where to go shopping for something decent."

Brett without hesitation replied, "I must not look overdone."

Forty-five minutes later, the two vehicles parked at the Royal Sonesta Hotel. As the two men walked into the lobby, Lyle said, "I will take care of the rooms. Ask the female clerk where to go for garments, ladies always know best where to send a man to buy clothes." Lyle rushed over and handed him his key card and smiled, "If you have time, come to my room before you head out to dinner."

Just under an hour and a half later there was a knock on Lyle's door. It was Brett who had given the knock procedure that they had used for years. When Brett stepped into the room, his partner did not know what to say. Brett looked handsome, he had gotten a shave and a haircut and was wearing a Tom Ford dark navy blue blazer, khaki pants, and a white shirt. To complete his looks he had purchased an expensive pair of Ferragamo Italian shoes.

"Now I understand why Armance noticed you; she knew that with her special touch, she could transform you into a handsome partner."

Brett looked at his watch, then said, "I better hurry, I have to take a shower and be at the restaurant in forty minutes. It's only a few blocks from here. Should I take the Mercedes?"

Lyle thought for a moment, then said, "No. After a long dinner, a lady like Armance would love to walk up and down Bourbon Street. I guess we will meet downstairs for breakfast at six a.m. Have fun and be wise!"

CHAPTER 17

New Orleans

Brett walked into the Galatoire, a restaurant known for its traditional New Orleans cuisine. Looking for his date, he gave a circular glance at the crowded room. Suddenly, out of nowhere, Armance walked up to him and, after a few welcoming words, took him to her table, the table where she had enjoyed many meals in the past.

They would have champagne to celebrate their first date. The waiter handed the wine list to Brett who studied it for over a minute, "Please, bring us a bottle of Veuve Cliquot." Armance spoke to express her appreciation, "I like your selection and I am impressed. Do you know that this champagne was featured in movies such as Casablanca, Babette's Feast, also in series such as Downtown Abbey, and in several novels?"

This date was their first encounter; the conversation was a bit awkward, but after their first glass of champagne, the atmosphere became jovial and warm.

In her line of work, Armance had been approached by several gentlemen wanting to take her out, but she had been so devastated by her divorce two years earlier that she had lost interest in men and romance. She quietly watched and listened to Brett who seemed charming, kind, down to earth, and who did not overplay his hand and mind.

They looked at the menu. Many of the dishes where foreign to Brett. Armance who was accustomed to the local cuisine took time to advise him, "We should have a Jambalaya, this restaurant serves the very best." She described the dish, and Brett approved, "Sounds great to me. We must have a good Zinfandel to go along with the dinner." Brett ordered a Seghesio Home Ranch Zinfandel. After the food arrived, and their wine glasses were filled, Brett made a toast to Armance, "To a friendly lady who accepted to dine in my company." Then he said, "By the way, why did you decide to have dinner with me?" She started to giggle, and replied,

"On the flight, I spotted the US seals on your cases, and I somehow figured you had to be fairly respectable. I found you pleasant and reserved; I mean not loud, and not aggressive." She tasted the wine and said, "Oh, this is a great Zinfandel. Where did you learn about wine? You knew exactly the one to get."

"That was an easy selection. My friend, the one you met on the plane, had purchased that wine the last time we had dinner at his aunt's."

It was close to ten when they left the restaurant. The city was alive at this time of day, so Brett suggested they walk down Bourbon Street to enjoy the music coming from the popular spots, bars, and strip clubs. Soon Armance said, "I have a seven a.m. flight tomorrow, I need to go home. This evening was very special; I want to see you again, and next time, I will have you discover this old city on foot."

Brett hailed a cab. Before she got in, she took a pen from her purse and wrote her phone number on the palm of Brett's hand. Then she leaned forward, furtively kissed Brett on the cheek, and murmured, "Thank you, I enjoyed your company."

CHAPTER 18

New Orleans

It was after six a.m. Lyle had been sitting at a small table in the hotel dining room since 5:45 a.m. Brett nonchalantly walked in wearing Levis, a black polo shirt, and his brown hiking boots. With his four day stubble, his short, thick, and coarse hair, he looked masculine and sexy. He had the sort of muscular physique women never fail to notice.

As Brett was sitting down, Lyle picked up the coffee pot and filled Brett's cup and topped off his own. He was curious to find out if the date with the flight attendant had been a one night fling or the beginning of a happy and long-lasting relationship. He would not mention the romantic meeting; it would be up to his partner to share his evening. After a sip of coffee, Brett asked about the plans for the day. Lyle had decided that they would take the two vehicles and head to the Port of New Orleans.

Brett downed half a glass of orange juice, and said, "Are you thinking about boarding the Anakriya in daylight?"

"No. Today I intend to sneak around the containers the men are unloading and later, mix with the Russians. Maybe I can pick up some information while they are taking a break at one of the taverns outside the main gate. I perused the dock area on the iPad last night; there are several bars close by, just outside the dock. I will have to sip a few beers there and listen. What I want you to do is check out the exterior hull of the ship, all sides, and find us a safe way to board it during the night."

Brett took a few bites of scrambled eggs and pancake, finished his orange juice, then said, "I think we can board from the dock using the tie ropes. Also, I want to see if there are small boats to borrow so I can get around the back of the vessel. We might have to climb the ship side using a rope and hook. Before leaving, let's check our burner phone numbers."

After the two men finished breakfast, they wrote the numbers directly on the back of their phones and checked out their earbuds and throat mikes. Lyle said, "Remember, the ship may be leaving in two days." After their third cup of coffee, they headed for the parking garage where they set their GPS and left for the docks. There, they parked the two vehicles several hundred feet apart. Both agreed to meet for lunch at one p.m. at a cafe, half-mile away.

Throughout the morning, Lyle who had been observing the dockers' comings and goings could find nothing out of the ordinary. The cargo containers looked legit, and all the workers seemed busy with their assigned tasks. He left and walked to the first bar just outside of the gate. After getting a draft beer, Lyle took his mug and slowly worked his way toward a group of large scraggly men in the back of the room. He could hear two of them yelling at each other in Russian. Lyle was slowly sipping his beer while keeping an eye on the men. Suddenly, just a few feet away, there was an uproar. A man about six feet eight inches tall hit another fellow in the chest and yelled, "трахающие Чеченец ленивы." (Fucking lazy Chechens). Ah, Lyle thought, there are Chechens on-board. Lyle finished his drink and left the bar. Outside, he instinctively wiped his brow with the back of his hand as the humidity was rapidly climbing to the point that it was almost unbearable to work outdoors. He looked at his watch; it was time to meet Brett for lunch.

When he drove into the parking lot of the small cafe, Brett's black Mercedes was already there. Getting out of his SUV, Lyle spotted his partner drinking coffee while sitting in the shade of a bald cypress. He sat down next to his friend on the exposed buttress roots of the enormous conifer, and said, "Well, it is now confirmed, we have Chechens aboard the ship. I could not find out anything unusual all morning. The Russians at the bar were complaining about how lazy the Chechens are; I wonder if those men are the drug and weaponry delivery guys. What did you find out this morning?"

"Before I tell you about the ship, I am sure you are dying to hear about last night," Brett gave a silly laugh as he spoke. Lyle did not comment. "Just kidding." He chuckled some more, tapped Lyle on the shoulder, and continued talking,

"As I vaguely mentioned earlier, there are only two ways we can get on board. One is to use the tie line ropes that extend from the stern to a dark area at the edge of the pier. Another possibility would be to borrow one of the small fishing boats tied up about one hundred feet away and go around the bow, throw a lineup up and over the side of the hull, and climb aboard in complete darkness. Either way, I don't see much of a problem. I spotted only one guard on duty on the deck during the entire three hours I spent watching the ship."

Lyle asked his partner, "Do you feel like going aboard tonight?" Brett approved,

"I think it would be a good idea since the dock crew has finished unloading the ship and time is running out. During my watch, I noticed that one container had been left behind on the deck. It is stored against the railing on the west side of the ship and is not of average size, much smaller. From the dock, it seems to be built of wood or plastic that has been painted silver to look like metal. Both wood and plastic can float. We have to investigate."

Just as Lyle started to speak, one of Brett's burner phones rang. He was fumbling through the pack he had taken off his back, the phone continued to ring. At last, he found the right one. "Brett here." It was Armance calling,

"Hi, I hope I did not disturb something important. I will be leaving Atlanta in just under an hour. Would you like to meet me at five in front of the restaurant where we ate last night and go walking around town?"

"Give me a second or two; I need to check with my boss, we are on assignment." Brett put his hand on the phone, looked at Lyle with a grin, then spoke, "Do you think I have enough time to walk around town before we head out tonight?"

"Absolutely. Ask Armance if she would like to have dinner at my aunt's at six-thirty p.m."

Brett took his hand off the cell phone. "I would love to meet you at five. What about having dinner with my partner and his aunt at six-thirty p.m.?"

"I would love that. May I bring the wine?"

"Thanks, but no, Lyle always picks the wine, it's like a ritual with him," and laughing, he added," He thinks he is a connoisseur. Lyle's aunt lives just off Bourbon St. She is unique. I hope you don't mind Jambalaya again, that is what is on the menu."

"It will be a real pleasure seeing you again and meeting your friends. We will walk up a good appetite first." Lyle could not help noticing Brett's joyful demeanor, but he was quick at returning to reality, "We need to find out about that small container you spotted."

"Fine with me. By the way, when I was working with the DEA, here in New Orleans, while you were in France, I found out they had available several instruments we could use. I saw small x-ray devices, gunpowder detectors, and Geiger counters. Maybe we should head over there and equip ourselves."

"Super idea. Let's go."

The supervisor at the DEA checked their IDs, asked Lyle and Brett many questions. Being tired of the inquisition, Brett became cocky, he handed the clerk a business card and asked him to call the number listed on it, which he did. Minutes later the man was offering to load the devices. No longer suspicious, he asked if the agents needed support or backup. The two men walked out to their vehicle where they stored their new gadgets. It was almost four p.m., time to stop for a beer. Lyle called his Uncle Remy. After chit-chatting back and forth, Lyle finally said to his uncle, "There is a good possibility that Brett and I will have to return to the Babineaux's watering hole. Could we borrow your airboat and canoe?"

"Yes, you may, if you let me go along. Those people are dangerous bastards; they have been killing fish and destroying the gator population using grenades and automatic weapons. Yes, I will damn sure be ready. When are you two coming?"

"We are going to search a ship tonight, and in the coming days we might have to go into the Mississippi swamps, not sure yet."

"I know those swamps along the Mississippi waters and also the islands. I'm sure as hell you could use my help."

Lyle did not say anything for five seconds, "You know it could be a one-way trip. I will take you along only if you promise to follow orders. Can you do that?"

"Hell yes, son. But if I do have to see my maker, you make sure you take care of all my friend on my hummocks." Remi was referring to his chickens and swamp creatures.

"Will do. I will give you a call tomorrow with an update." The two said goodbye, and Lyle put his phone back in his pocket. Both men returned to their hotel where Brett showered. Wearing only a towel wrapped around his trim abdomen, he entered Lyle's room and told him he was leaving in ten minutes and would join him at his aunt Annette's at six thirty. Now alone, Lyle called Octo to ask him to find the itinerary of the Anakriya from the Russian port of St. Petersburg on the Baltic sea to New Orleans. He wanted to know if there had been any intermediate stops anywhere on her sailing journey. Octo would get satellite photos of the ship before reaching and after leaving each port of call. Before hanging up, he requested the exact departure date and time of the Anakriya from New Orleans.

Being out of clean and decent clothes, Lyle left the hotel to go shopping for two pairs of pants and two shirts. He wanted to be presentable for dinner at his aunt Annette's place and meet Brett's lady friend.

CHAPTER 19

New Orleans

Same day

The weather was humid and hot over New Orleans. Brett was on his way to meet Armance whom he spotted a block away; he waved at her and picked up his pace.

When he was close, Armance extended her arms and held both his hands. They stood there a few minutes chatting and deciding which way to go. Brett asked her about her day and told her about his own without much enthusiasm, "We walked around the port, inspected one of the vessels, and later we picked up some devices we needed to step up our investigation. Oh, before I forget, dinner is at six-thirty. We should pick out a bouquet of flowers for Lyle's aunt. Annette, you will see, is a wonderful lady, warm, pleasant, and very hospitable. She is the sister of Lyle's mother. Both women are from New Orleans. His mother, Monique, lives in Atlanta, Georgia, where she teaches High School. Lyle's father was killed overseas while on special operations for the Army. I think Lyle was five or six at the time. His mom never remarried. That's enough. Tell me about yourself."

"I fly up to DC and then back here most of the time. Working First class is by far the best section for a flight attendant; travelers in First class are usually more civilized compared to the ones in Economy class. I was assigned to the back of the plane for several years until I got enough seniority to move where I am presently working. Now I will tell you a few personal things; I hope I don't bother you, stop me if I do. My nickname in Fran which derives from Francine, my middle name, and my last name, as I told you last night, is Ancelet. I was married once for two years. Having been deceived by my husband, I lost any desire to meet men after my divorce over a year ago. I no longer trust anyone. At this instant, Brett grabbed Fran by the shoulders and brought her closer as they continued walking on Bourbon street. Both were so intensely talking and listening; they never noticed the animation around them.

It was Brett's turn to pour out the details of his past. "I was never married, and this is a plus in my favor. When I settle down, I will not be bringing along the enormous problems created by cantankerous and expensive ex-wives, and the heavy burden children add to a divorce. Those two handicaps can wreck a new relationship presto. I am single and free. I met several women, and most of the time their views on life were opposite to mine. I like mature people who are mellow and kind, individuals who enjoy simple pleasures and are not obsessively ambitious. All my relationships have been brief, and none left an impact on my life. As a child, I grew up in two foster homes after the sudden death of my parents. At eighteen, I joined the military. When you saw the symbol on the briefcases, you knew I worked for Uncle Sam. This job demands that I be absent a lot. Lyle, my best friend and partner, is engaged to a cute French girl named Anne-Marie, she lives in Paris. She saved his life a couple of times when he was near death. Recently she adopted a little girl from Bogota, Colombia. I hope you get to meet her and Lyle's mother; both are lovely people. I hope I did not disappoint you too much with my biography."

"You did not. I like your simple approach to life and your honesty. You could have pretended to be a prolific lover with a multitude of bimbos wanting you, I would have believed it, but you did the opposite, and I like that."

A few blocks down the street, they found a flower shop where Fran chose an arrangement called Floral Garden, a mixture of roses and white lilies. After picking up the bouquet, they retraced their steps in the direction of Annette's house. Fran suggested they take a detour across a small park that was just a little off their route. In the semi-obscurity brought by the luxuriant vegetation, mostly bald cypress trees and sycamores, Brett stopped, hugged and kissed Fran. They stood there for a full minute, just holding each other in the deserted alley of the park.

Soon after, the duo reached Lyle's aunt's small psychic/voodoo shop. Just as Brett started to knock on the door, Fran noticed the sign advertising Psychic Readings/Voodoo. "Wow, how interesting! I can't wait to meet the lady. My grandma dabbled in the occult, but she was seldom accurate in her predictions."

Lyle answered the door and invited Fran and her beau to come in. He shook the girlfriend's hand, and said, "Come in, my aunt can't wait to meet you." Annette who had been preparing a feast for her guests joined the trio. She was still wrapped in her butcher's apron that was almost reaching the floor, and her hair was disheveled. Fran presented the host with the flowers, and the four of them sat down to talk while sipping an aperitif. Lyle offered them a Kir Royale, a mixture of champagne and crème de cassis (blackcurrant liquor.)

The conversation was so enjoyable that Annette temporarily forgot the food on the stove. A sounding buzzer alerted her that the dinner was ready to be served. Soon the foursome gathered at the table that had been set with good taste.

It was almost midnight when Lyle noticed the time, he said, "Brett, we have to finish our inspection, I suggest we get going." Brett and Fran thanked Annette for a beautiful evening and a tasty dinner.

As Fran started to walk toward the door, Annette said, "Lyle, you and Brett, hold up for a minute or two, I need to take Fran into my little shop and show her something." When the two women were alone in the dim light of the voodoo shop, Annette asked her guest to sit down and to turn over the palms of her hands. "I want to do a reading." Fran had shown some interest in the host's so-called gift during the visit.

As part of the ritual, Annette had lit incense. She systematically shuffled the tarot cards, had Fran pull out five cards which she laid in a line on the table. She intensely looked at the palms, turned over one card at a time, silently studied each one, and then looked at Fran's palms again. She leaned back, and said, "If you are ready I would like to share something with you." Even though she was not a total believer, Fran could hardly wait for the predictions.

"You were married once, unhappy, and divorced. You have met someone who can bring you joy. You will find lasting love real soon." Then she looked Fran in the eyes, squeezed her fingers snuggly and solemnly said, "There is something called time, this will bother you at first, you must overcome this time element if you want the happiness you deserve and desire. If you can accept this, you will have a family and will become four. That is all I can tell you for now." Annette looked tired, and almost struggled as she stood up to see her friends at the front door.

Everyone kissed twice on the cheeks before leaving.

CHAPTER 20

New Orleans

Next day

Brett walked around the Mercedes and sat down behind the steering wheel. While driving Fran back to her apartment, they talked about their evening, and of course about Fran's little detour in the voodoo shop was brought up. She shared very little, "I did not expect Annette to do that reading, but I am glad she did."

They got out of the car. Brett walked her to the door, gave her a passionate kiss, and wished her good night. As he drove back toward Bourbon Street, he pushed Lyle's cell number.

"Lyle here. I have everything loaded, meet me in back of that cafe where we had lunch, I think I have a plan worked out for us."

"Roger that, I just turned onto Bourbon Street, I should be there in a few minutes."

The two cars were parked in the dark behind the fast food restaurant which was closed. Brett got out of his Mercedes and joined his partner on the front seat of the SUV. Lyle went over the last minute briefing, "I cleaned the guns and screwed on the suppressor on the sniper rifle. The two gauges are in my backpack." The inventory done, he reviewed how they were to proceed to board the ship, "As I shuttle across the tie downline line, you can watch for tangos. Your night goggles are in the back seat with the sniper rifle and your black pants and shirt. Once on the deck, I will let you know

I made it, and then I will cover your ascent. Why don't you change while I check a couple of things?"

Brett asked, "Are we going to try and open up the container if the meters detect something?"

"Yes, if there is a way we can do it without leaving any evidence someone broke in, but of course it will depend on the nature of the substance we will encounter. I think we should. Also, I would like to recon the hold of that ship; we might pick up something of interest. Are you feeling dangerous tonight?" Brett shook his head and changed the subject,

"We all had a good time at Annette's; she is a nice and generous lady. Fran found your aunt very charming. I hope that someday she will meet the rest of your family."

"Annie is going to bring Jennie Anne over to my mom's for a visit in a few weeks. If we don't get bogged down, maybe we can get together for another big dinner. What else did Fran say?" Giggling, Brett added, "She would not tell me anything about the tarot card reading. Well, let's go to work."

The two men had backed their vehicles in two separate places outside of the fenced-in parking area, ready for a quick exit if needed. After working their way through the maze of containers, and being careful not to get caught by security, they soon met at the aft of the ship. There was a quarter moon, but black clouds were playing hide-and-seek with the source of light coming from the sky. Brett chambered a round in his sniper rifle and pushed on the safety. He climbed on top of a container box and laid down. From his mirador, and with his night goggles on, the agent had a perfect view of Lyle who was tightening the straps of the pack on his back before slowly let his body hang from the thick ship tie rope. His feet were over the line, and his gloved hands were pulling his body slowly toward the deck of the Russian ship, the Anakriya2. When he reached the hull of the vessel, Lyle spoke softly into his throat mike, "Is it clear to climb on board?"

"No tangos in sight, go."

Once standing on the deck, he pulled out his Glock and looked around. Seeing no one, he spoke into his mike once more, "Clear to come aboard."

Together now, the two men headed toward the spot where Brett had seen the odd size cargo container earlier in the day. The box that had been left behind on the deck was carefully examined. Tapping it, Lyle claimed it most likely was made of plastic, a material which would allow it to float. He took out one the meters to see if he could detect the presence of black powder, nitro, or other explosives on the box and the deck around it. The device did record a light trace of hazardous substance where the two leaves of the locked door met. Lyle walked along the adjacent area where, according to dusty linear marks on the floor, another small container had been stored at one time. The needle of the dial of the explosive detector was picking up the presence something like nitro or black powder.

Lyle took out the twelve inch by fourteen X-ray machine and returned to the container. He tested all four sides, turned to Brett, and said, "They must have applied some shielding material to the interior walls, I get no picture. Is there any way you can break in without leaving a trace?" Faced with the unknown, Brett was cautious, he said, "Could be hazardous. Let's see what we can pick up with the radiation detector." Lyle got his partner's attention, "Brett, look at this." Brett came over and kneeled down, the needle of the radiation counter was erratic. "It is alarming if the missing box was dropped off on the US coastal water with such a hazardous load. We need to go to Mississippi and find that container, and if safe, rescue or destroy whatever is inside."

Due to the full attention given to their troubling findings, the two agents had lost touch with their surrounding. Just as Brett started to stand up, a man stepped around a bulkhead and spoke in Chechen, "What the hell are you doing here?" As he began to unstrap his rifle, Brett pulled his Glock 40 with the silencer screwed on it and fired. Hardly a sound, no louder than a BB gun, was heard as the two rounds hit the guard. One in the forehead, and another high in the chest. The man fell to the deck with only a slight noise caused by his gun barrel hitting the floor.

With his finger pointed, Lyle signaled Brett to go to the corner from where the guard had soundlessly emerged. In the meantime, Lyle grabbed a folded black tarp stored against the railing. He leaned over the bleeding man, wrapped him up inside the plastic sheet, along with two metal pipes. Some strings found inserted between the folds of the tarp came handy. Five minutes later there was a muffled splash followed by whitish bubbles appearing on the surface of the water as the corpse sank into the deep, dark oily looking waters of the port.

Both men, with their gun in hand, walked to the end of the bulkhead, then back. Lyle was puzzled by the missing container, he said, "I wonder where they dropped off that box. I bet it is heading to the Babineaux command post. It may already be in their hands. I will call Octo in the morning and have him find out exactly when this ship is scheduled to leave. Do you know how long a drive from here to where you shot those rednecks on the airboat?"

"I would say a good six to seven hours. We can drive up highway ninety and cut over to Biloxi. I know of a small town where we can stop at a motel less than one hour from the bar where the locals gather. We don't want to go into that area until it's dark, and if we do not want to look out of place and raise suspicion, we better wear something more scruffy."

Lyle paused, then said, "Maybe we should wait to hear from Octo. I am trying to find out if the ship made other stops before reaching New Orleans. Let's go clean up, rest some, and head out about nine or ten. Does that fit your schedule?"

"Not a problem. I will call Fran and tell her we have been sent on an assignment."

Even though Brett was ecstatic to have met Fran, he was unsure about this relationship and was almost worked up at the thought of being committed to one person. To him, marriage suggested captivity and heavy responsibility. So far he had enjoyed a carefree, untroubled, and laid back life, and he was afraid to lose these privileges. He occasionally asked Lyle his views about living with a woman, about children, marriage, and all the responsibilities linked to each situation. Lyle always reminded his friend that he was no expert, and each time he would advise him to take it one day at a time. "You don't know Fran, you have just met her. My advice is for you to enjoy each other and not to rush things, not until you are sure, undoubtedly sure."

Back in their room, the men packed, showered, and cleaned their gear before going to bed. They had agreed to meet for breakfast downstairs at six a.m.

Chapter 21

New Orleans

Lyle stretched his arms as he was walking across his room. Looking out the window, he could see threatening clouds moving in over New Orleans. There was no reason to rush, so he showered and went down to the hotel restaurant. After finding a table with a good view of people coming and going, Lyle glanced at his watch; it was just after seven a.m.

Something had been bothering him ever since Brett and himself had discovered the suspicious space on the deck where there might have been one more container like the one they had found and probed. He wondered if this missing box had been dropped overboard somewhere along the coast of Mississippi or in the waters of another country, or worse if it had been unloaded right here in New Orleans. He needed to call Octo to find out if the military or NSA had a satellite picture of the ship docked elsewhere while on its way from Russia to the States. He stood up and walked to the breakfast buffet where the display of dishes was overwhelming. One had a choice of six egg dishes, sausages, waffles, meats, cheeses, four kinds of bread, a variety of soups, tempting buns, fruits, and cakes. Lyle chose a few items and returned to his table. After laying his tray down, he placed his plates of beignets, his spicy Louisiana sausage called boudin, and his glass of orange juice directly on the starched white tablecloth. Brett had not arrived yet, so Lyle called Octo and asked him to check if the military had a picture of the Anakriya leaving Russia and images of it docking and departing from other harbors, on its way stateside. He insisted on getting photos of the ship taken over the past week while in US waters and especially while anchoring in the port of New Orleans. Lyle ended the conversation as Brett walked to the table, "Good morning! Wait until you see the buffet. You better grab two trays."

Brett returned with a tray in each hand. Besides the breakfast basics, he had selected oysters, stuffed tomatoes, and turtle soup. As the two men ate and sipped coffee, they went over what they had discovered aboard the Anakriya. The core of their discussion remained centered on the radioactive readings and their coming trip to Mississippi.

As Brett noisily sucked down a big bay oyster, Lyle told his partner about the call and conversation he had with Octo. Grenades, flash-bangs, smoke grenades, explosives, and switches, all the items they needed had been ordered and would be arriving late that day at the airport. I am going to call uncle Remi to come in and pick me up. I know you don't care for snakes and gators so the two of us will go and find out what the Babineaux clan is stealing and dealing in these days."

"Thanks. Glad to pass up that excursion, but we still might have to go deep into the swamps of Mississippi sooner or later. What do you have planned for me today?"

"Before I tell you. There has been something bothering me about those containers. I want you to go to the DEA office and inform the asshole, supervisor Garcia, that we are extending our rental of the equipment a full week. If he gives you any trouble, remind him what phone number to call.

"That's not a full day's work."

"There is more. Go down to the harbor master's office, and find out the depth of the waters a few miles away from the port, especially in the vicinity of the islands. Also, find a store where one can rent scuba gear and a pontoon boat with both a conventional and an electric motors. I don't expect to be back until late tonight, or until tomorrow morning. Call if anything significant comes up, otherwise breakfast between six and seven a.m. tomorrow, right here."

Fran had the day off; Brett calculated that his agenda would not keep him busy all day.

Lyle had pushed in the numbers of his uncle's cell phone. On the tenth ring, as he was about to give up, he heard, "I guess you are ready to go sailing. Glad to hear from you, go ahead, Lyle."

"Yes, I need your help. Could you come in and pick me up as soon as possible at the dock?"

"I have a couple of shrimp traps to check, and I can be on my way. Give me an hour." Remi glanced at his watch. "I will be there between nine-thirty and ten." Brett who had heard the exchange between Lyle and his uncle said, "I hope you are not going to that drinking spot to face the Babineaux clan. Promise me you won't try to take them on, not until I join you. Do you remember what happened the last time we confronted them, the three of us ended up trapped; we almost did not make it out, and I repeat, there were three of us. I am wondering if we should get Patrick to help this time."

"Don't worry; uncle Remi is going to spend a few dollars on free liquor for the boys. Once drunk, they will become harmless and will be eager to talk. Remi has never failed to find out the information we need. While there, I will check out their airboats for hazardous chemicals, and I will call you as soon as I know anything. We have a lot to do, let's head out. Don't forget; you also have to go to the airport and pick up the box of goods later tonight."

Lyle pushed his plate, shook Brett's hand, and headed for his SUV. In his car, he took out his encrypted phone and called Octo. On the second ring, he heard the anxious and excited voice of his friend.

"Octo, I forgot to ask you to call Colonel Jackson. He may be able to help you get the pictures of the Anakriya. Remember, I must have a satellite photo of the ship as it docked in New Orleans."

Both men went over the request, then talked about other concerns. Before closing the conversation, Octo warned Lyle that it could take a day or two to meet his demand. Lyle flipped the lid of his phone.

Brett finished his coffee, looked at his watch, then headed to the harbor master's office.

CHAPTER 22

New Orleans

Same day

As Lyle was driving down Bourbon Street, on his way to aunt Annette's, he contacted Patrick at the US embassy in Paris. On the fifth ring, there was an answer, "Hello, Pat here."

"It's Lyle, old buddy. I need to send you on an assignment."

"Oh, thank God, you will be saving my life. Ever since Colonel Jackson called and assigned me to work with you and Brett, I have been praying, burning candles, and hoping you would call. My COS (Chief of staff) did not initiate this move, so he has me sharpening pencils all day. Where are you sending me?"

"First, you are to call Gabriel, my precious contact in Paris. Get all the information you can learn from him about the present location of Aleksey Shamil, the Chechen. Ask him to find out if he has any leads on possible arms deals fomented by Aleksey. Once you feel you have sufficient pertinent intel, call Octo and have him get you a first class plane ticket to Moscow." Patrick mentally recorded Lyle's three requests, and said,

"By the way, your friend Gabriel was overwhelmed with joy when I presented him with the award from POTUS. He mentioned you, and I know he would give you all his blood if you needed it. Do I have a Moscow contact?"

"Colonel Jackson had the CIA assign James Rockford to be your contact. In Moscow, the COS for the CIA is not especially fond of us.

If you have any problems, don't argue, tell him to call this number." Lyle gave Pat the phone number that would prevent or resolve any future conflict.

Lyle carried on, "Take no action on your own. Get as much intel for us as you can. Sooner or later we are going to have to take the Chechen down once and for all. As you know, I thought we had killed the bastard. Good luck, and don't hesitate to call." After thanking Lyle several times, Pat ended the conversation.

Lyle knocked on his aunt's door and, as usual, was warmly greeted. As they sipped coffee, he told her he was meeting Remi at the dock shortly. Hearing that, Annette got up, walked into the kitchen and returned with a paper bag and said, "Here is a quart of jambalaya for your uncle. Make sure to tell him to bring the jar back next time he comes to town."

With a few whines of the starter, the propellers began turning on the boat old aircraft engine. Remi pushed the throttle forward, and the bow of the swamp boat lifted up into the air. The flat bottom craft moved out into the dark murky waters of the bayou with a spray of water reminiscent of a peacock tail in display behind it.

Very little was said between Lyle and Remi as the old man was working his magic between the groves of cypress trees and oaks from which Spanish moss was hanging. Almost an hour later they pulled up at Remi's hidden hummock.

At his place, the old man poured them two fingers of moonshine, raised his glass, and said, "Here's to a successful trip to the Babineaux's watering hole and back."

Lyle briefly mentioned to Remi the radiation-contaminated box he and Brett had discovered on the Russian ship. He also shared his concern regarding the missing container. After Lyle and his uncle emptied their glasses several times, the old man responded, "The boxes in question pose a serious problem, could be harmful to all of us in the region."

After a long sigh, Lyle went over the plans for the upcoming dangerous mission, "While you will be getting the Babineaux boys liquored up, I am going to check their airboats for powder, nitro, and radiation. If my equipment detects any unwanted substance, I am going to have to get Brett involved. We are going to have to eliminate this vermin, every one of them." Remi was troubled by the news concerning the boxes, he asked,

"Are you sure about the radiation? "

"I have to tell you this with the most utmost secrecy. This sale of radioactive material is not an isolated event. Not long ago, Brett and I stopped a suitcase nuke in Turkey. I believe a suitcase bomb could be on land in Mississippi, and possibly another one may already be here in New Orleans. Those are speculations; we have to find out what is going on. These substances could also be the result of spillage or leakage from medical equipment."

"Well, balls hanging from a Gator. Let's fuel up the airboat, load the crossbows, and bring a few sticks of TNT, just in case. You make us a pot of coffee and fill the thermos, son. I will take care of everything else."

Almost forty minutes later, just as they started to push off, Remi said, "Oh, shit, I forgot to feed Two Legs." Remi stepped back off the boat and soon brought back several catfish on a line. Lyle watched his uncle throw one catfish at a time to Two Legs, his pet gator. When done, his uncle fired up the swamp boat which sped out into the deeper waters of the bayou. Ninety minutes later the boat moved slowly toward the end of the old mossy dock overgrown with vines and other aquatic weeds. After tying the boat to the bottom of a cypress, Remi said, "Watch yourself when you check out those swamp boats, those people are leery of strangers and are trigger happy. I'll do my best to keep the clan happy with free rounds of white lightning. Won't take long to get them bragging about their next illegal project. Intoxicated, those jackasses love to talk. If something happens, you know the drill. You start the boat and get the hell out of here, forget about me. One request, keep your promise to feed my gator until he passes." Then, with a slight limp, the old man started walking down the path toward the run-down bar.

Chapter 23

New Orleans

Same day

Brett was in the lobby of the hotel mentally going over his agenda for the day. If things went his way, he had plans of his own for later that afternoon. Before leaving, the agent contacted Octo to get the itinerary of the Russian cargo ship which was scheduled to depart from New Orleans in the coming days, on its way back to Saint Petersburg, Russia. He picked up his Mercedes and headed straight to the harbor master's office that was adjacent to the dock. There he copied a few maps and spent some time on his iPod checking water depths the Anakriya would encounter along its route, especially as it left New Orleans. Surprised by his findings, Brett uttered a few cuss words out loud when he realized how close to several small islands the craft would be sailing at the beginning of its journey. Maybe this convenient setting, the islands, would be the sight of the dropping of the suspicious missing container. The swampy area would have to be put under surveillance. To rummage through the wet and muddy ground, Brett and Lyle would have to get the right clothes; both favored camouflage clothing which could be purchased in one of the surplus army navy stores of the city. Just as Brett was getting ready to leave the harbor master's office, one of his phones, the encrypted one, began ringing. It was Octo with more news.

"I could not get ahold of Lyle, Brett. He wanted to know about two small containers of an odd size that had been stored separately from the regular ones of standard size on the deck of the Anakriya. According to satellite photos, I can confirm his suspicion; there were two small containers on the top deck when the ship left Saint Petersburg. Presently, as you know, there is only one. Get words to Lyle fast."

"I am sure he will be excited to hear that." Brett said goodbye and left to shop for clothes. After loading the army surplus purchases into the car, he headed to the DEA office to inform Garcia that he would need to keep the equipment, the drone, and the gages, at least five more days. Wanting to test Garcia's integrity, Brett asked the supervisor a few questions.

"Mr. Garcia, my partner and I were unable to detect any signs of powder, nitro or radiation, around the cargo containers on shore. Do you know which of your men checked the containers on deck?"

"That's easy. Mr. Juarez and I personally checked between all the rows of containers on the top deck. We are extra cautious with Russian and Asian companies. We both spend time with the instruments if something looks out of the ordinary." Garcia showed signs of nervosity, with his left hand he repeatedly rearranged the hair on his forehead, moved his ashtray, and placed a pencil next to a book, and then said, "It's too bad they have already unloaded. Otherwise, I would take you with me to inspect. It requires almost half a day to check the ship before unloading can start. Nothing has ever slipped by us, I can guarantee it. Oh, I will need those instruments. Leave them there." He pointed at an empty desk. Brett politely protested,

"I told you, I will need them a few more days." To prevent further discussion, Brett handed the clerk a phone number to call if he had any questions about keeping the instruments. The number connected to Colonel Jackson. Once outside Brett asked one of the dock guards where he could find a boat and diving equipment shop in the area.

Brett made a left turn and walked alongside the historic brick building, now the home of docking personnel offices. Suddenly he heard a muffled deflating 'pfft' noise very similar to the sound of a gun being fired with a silencer. The sound was heard again, and this time dust from the wall of the old brick building spattered his jacket. Brett knew someone was shooting at him. He bent over, and while running reached under his garment to pull out his gun. While moving full speed to find cover, two more shots were fired that hit the pavement around him. Within seconds he was standing behind another building. Now protected by the masonry structure, he placed his back against the wall and slowly took a few steps forward to see around the corner of the edifice. Running away was a man wearing a shirt with a blue patch on one sleeve and the American flag emblem on the other. Brett wondered if this individual had some connection with Garcia. He could not wait to get away; this incident was unnerving.

It took Brett some time to find a sporting goods rental. When he finally located one, he rented for a week a pontoon boat, motor, and gear, which he and his partner would need later. Arrangements were made to leave the equipment in storage until needed. As Brett was finishing the last of his tasks for the day, he looked at his watch; it was time to call Lyle and Fran. Lyle thanked his partner for Octo's message. The call was brief. Next, he contacted Fran. On the third ring, a feminine voice answered. "Good afternoon."

"It's Brett. Would you like to have lunch with me?

"Yes, of course. In fact, I know of a small cafe in the park. After lunch, if you are interested, we could stroll and see the large collection of snakes there. The park also has both gators and crocs."

"I will drop by and pick you up in about thirty minutes."

"I will be ready."

After driving around in a circle, making sure no one was following, Brett turned in a narrow alley and waited. After five minutes, he pulled back out onto Bourbon street and headed across town to Fran's place, with one final stop on the way to pick up a bouquet of flowers.

Brett tapped lightly on her front door. Five foot eight inch Fran, radiant as usual, opened the door. Her gleaming and luminous eyes admired the beautiful flowers as she was inviting Brett to come in. As

Brett stepped into the room, he handed her the bouquet. Fran threw her right hand around Brett's neck and thanked him.

The couple was now hand in hand, walking across the street, on their way to a cozy cafe serving typical New Orleans food. Fran recommended the crawfish etouffee, a traditional dish that she described as a stew seasoned to perfection and full of delicious plump crawfish. Following the flavorful meal, the couple went exploring the city that Brett was discovering. Their first destination was Jackson square where late in the day jazz bands performed right in front of the Saint Louis Cathedral. The square was bustling with artists, performers, and many tourists. Feeling romantic, Brett insisted on taking a tour of the city in a horse carriage. Along the way, they could smell the wafts of delicious food escaping from the restaurants they passed. There was something magical about this ride down Chartres street when the Saint Louis cathedral came into view, and when at the same time, one could hear the sweet sound of a brass band playing in the distance. They passed historic buildings, museums, and cemeteries, they would visit later. Soon they were back in Jackson square. There they decided to enter the cathedral. They spent an hour sitting in the plaza, talking and watching people, street artists, and performers.

Unfortunately, Fran had to put an end to the fun; she was scheduled to fly in three hours. The couple returned to her apartment for one last drink. She left Brett, just long enough to take a quick shower.

Brett could hear the water running. In a daring move, he decided to join her. It took him a minute to disrobe. So far the courtship had been affectionate but not sexual, only because he was afraid to rush things and destroy the relationship. He hoped this radical initiative would spice up their romance, but he did not want this sudden decision to violate Fran's intimacy. Brett was not too canny when dealing with love affairs and women in general. He could be a bit blunt and even awkward.

Stark naked, acting like a peeping Tom, this well built and virile man slipped quietly into the bathroom where Fran's INC

International blouse, unbuckled Lee Platinum Eloise pants were hanging on the door, and her sexy black lacy thong and bra laid on the floor. Opening the shower door, he paused to admire her long firm legs. Finally, she heard him and then saw him. As if she had been expecting his company, she grabbed his hands and pulled him forward. She asked Brett to turn around and started to wash his back, then she rubbed her breast and firmed nipples against it. The welcoming reception surprised him, and the treatment that followed drove him crazy. As she slowly moved her soapy fingers on his hairy chest and firm abdomen, she could see his right hand grabbing the handhold on the walls of the shower. Brett's breathing rate began to accelerate. She let the washrag drop and faced him. His hands slid down both sides of her body, his thumbs touching the side of her breasts. With his large hands wrapped around her buttocks, he brought her tightly against him. They could no longer wait for this pleasurable moment; their urge to make love was extreme, almost painful. As they kissed, and the warm water sprayed their backs, they climaxed simultaneously.

Still dizzy from their sexual encounter, Brett pushed the shower door open to reach for a bath towel and slowly began to dry Fran off. When done, Fran grabbed another towel from the shelf and teased Brett while drying him off, all the time working her magic.

After Fran completed her playful task of drying her lover, Brett reached for his clothes. She quickly wrapped a towel around Brett and pulled him into her bedroom. With one hand she pulled the bedspread back, making sure she was keeping Brett close.

As her breast brushed Brett's torso, he picked her up and gently dropped her between the white sheets. With the precision of a surgeon, Brett began to tease his woman, running his tongue around her nipples, down her abdomen, and along her thighs. Fran was ready for her man once again.

CHAPTER 24

Bayou,

One hour later

Uncle Remi walked down the slippery path and soon was out of his nephew's sight. The agent took out two detectors and delicately laid them on the ground. Before leaving the swamp boat, Lyle took his Glock 40 from his shoulder holster, chambered a round and left the safety off. He looked around; the pier appeared to be deserted, he was alone. Carrying his instruments, he quietly walked toward the locals' swamp boats that were kept tied up about one hundred yards away. Due to the dim light of sunset, the total silence, and the presence of Spanish moss hanging from the nearby trees, the place looked eerie and even manacing. Two ospreys perched on the top of a tall tree flew off, their unexpected presence made Lyle jump. Alarmed by his arrival, several ducks swam out from the safety of the boat and worked their way into the brush and water grass.

Lyle kept looking around. He knew that all the owners of those boats were having a good time inside the tavern at the expense of Remi who was generously buying the liquor, not by the glass but by the bottle. Now kneeling down, Lyle pulled up the corner of an old tarp that had been thrown over the vessel to conceal its contents. Underneath the bleached covering, Lyle counted twelve AK 47 rifles and several metal boxes filled with clips full of ammo. Now leaning inside the boat, he found another tightly shut ammo box containing grenades. There was no sense using the powder detector. As for the radiation counter, the needle remained idle when dragged over each square inch of the boat. He pulled the tarp back over the arsenal and moved to the next craft. As Lyle worked his way from boat to boat, he found their inventory to be the same: AK 47's, empty bottles of shine and bourbon, grenades, and alligator skins of different sizes. He began to think that the detections made on the Russian ship, where the missing box had been standing, were probably from a container that had been dropped and was still floating somewhere close, waiting to be picked up.

Lyle began to worry. It was getting dark, and Remi had been gone for almost two hours. As he was approaching the bar, he could hear men shouting. Somehow in the harsh, discordant mixture of sounds, Lyle recognized the powerful voice of Patsy Cline singing Walkin' After Midnight. The intense noise must have been deafening inside the closed bar. Through a dirty window, he spotted his uncle holding a bottle by the neck, ready to serve the drunkards another round of moonshine. Lyle watched and waited. Finally, Remi gave a friendly slap on the back of one of the intoxicated men sitting next to him, got up, and left. The old man was dangerously staggering. Unsteady, he stumbled and almost fell when his nephew came to the rescue and grabbed him by his belt. Now back on his feet, Lyle led his uncle to the boat in silence, stopping once so Remi could regain his balance by leaning against a swamp tupelo tree.

As Lyle was untying the boat, he suddenly jumped back and screamed at the sight of a venomous water moccasin that was in the process of swallowing a mouse. Lyle worked his way around the pit viper and pushed the swamp boat out into the water. Rather than start the old aircraft engine right away, he used the oars to move it forward. Once they felt safe, far enough from the Babineaux clan, Remi started the old noisy engine. On idle, the propeller turned enough RPM's to push the old flat bottom boat out into the darker deep waters of the bayou.

Remi who was getting more alert in the fresh air pushed the throttle forward. The bow lifted as they sped out into an open area. With the old boat moving at half speed, they followed the shoreline where grew pines, Tupelo trees, Bald cypress, and other magnificent coniferous trees and brush. Then, without any warning, Remi turned sharply to the right and headed down Racoon inlet, a narrow water passageway that cut through several hummocks to finally reach another lake. The old man who had been quiet until then looked at Lyle and said, "I heard the alkies say they were expecting another delivery of arms in a day or so. One of the Babineaux spouted off about a load that was already there. They were waiting for the preacher to show up." The preacher was Elijah Grubbs, an ex-convict, and pimp, who was a link in the contraband chain, responsible for transportation on land. Remi leaked more news, "The drunk also said that they were to receive a weapon that could turn buildings to sand like in the story of Ado, Lot's wife, who in the Bible turned to salt when she looked back a Sodom." It looks like they are expecting more powerful weapons, maybe they were talking about the nuclear material."

Remi and Lyle were leisurely having a cup of coffee when all of a sudden they heard whack, whack, whack. Individuals were shooting at them from another boat. Immediately they dropped their cups as wood splinters flew from the sides of their craft. The throttle was pushed forward as far as it would go. The automatic fire continued behind them, and the bullets splashed water all around. The conflict was taking place in semi-obscurity, but according to the sound, the pursuing airboat was closing fast. Remi told Lyle to take over the controls, picked up his old 30-30 rifle and began to fire back. He knew it was almost useless as the craft behind them kept weaving back and forth and still gaining on them. Then all of a sudden there was a loud explosion and water sprayed in all directions. The attackers were now throwing grenades. Remi laid his rifle down, picked up his crossbow, attached two sticks of dynamite with duct tape to the long bolts. He lifted his powerful crossbow with TNT in its groove and cocked it. The weapon was now ready, he addressed

Lyle, "I want you to slow down, I am going to tell you to turn to the right suddenly. When I do, I will hit those damn rednecks from the side. I have cut the fuse close so it will blow in less than a minute. As instructed, Remi shouted, "Turn now." As the airboat slowed and turned to the right, Remi lit the fuse of the two sticks of dynamite, laid his arm against the side of the boat, aimed the crossbow, and pulled the trigger.

One could hear the drunkards' laughter. Someone was yelling, "The fucker is shooting matches at us." Three seconds later, after the point of the arrow stuck to the side of the enemy boat, the TNT blew, and pieces of men and boat flew up into the air and splashed across the water with blood dripping from the sky like rain. After his exploit, Remi was ready to go home, but first, they decided to have some coffee.

Throughout the next hour, the two men weaved among the hummocks, making sure to lose anyone following, and at last, they pulled up onto Remi's mound of land he called home.

There were animals to feed, dinner to prepare, and Lyle had to call Patrick in Paris and check in with Brett. Due to the time difference, he would contact his woman, Annie, later, much later, around midnight or one in the morning.

Lyle had been unable to talk Remi out of going along with him and Brett to the Mississippi bayou. The old man had already packed a duffle bag, extra loaded ammo, the two crossbows with additional bolts, and his potent poison for the tips. He turned to his nephew and said, "Well, son, I'm gonna catch a little sleep, would suggest you do the same soon so you can be alert tomorrow. Those Mississippi Cajuns are smarter than the brain dead Babineaux men. I sure would like to meet that convict, pastor Grubbs, and give him a good shot of my fatal mixture of venom and poisonous plant juice. We would have him sleeping with that red horned devil in minutes. Don't you and Brett worry none about me; I can carry my load. Now go on and call the little woman so you can get some rest."

"I am not sure we are going there yet. Go to sleep. I have a few calls to make."

Lyle spoke with Patrick at the Paris embassy, filling him in briefly on what had transpired in New Orleans. Patrick reported having contacted Gabriel regarding the current whereabouts of Aleksey. No information was available, the Chechen had not been located, but Gabriel was working on obtaining some intel. After saying goodbye, Lyle reached into this pack and took out a burner phone. He dialed Annie's number in Paris and waited. After several rings, he heard, "Good morning! Where are you?"

"We are in New Orleans, and probably will head to Mississippi soon. Most likely we will be here another week. I wish I could tell you more, but I can't. I am fairly sure we will have to go into Russia again, I don't know when."

"Maybe you can slip away on your way to Russia as you did before when working south of the border?" Without giving Lyle a chance to respond, Annie said, "Your mother called, she invited Jennie and me to come and visit for a week or two. Do you mind?"

"Wonderful! My mom has no one, and she loves little Jennie. The sooner you can come, the better. While in Atlanta, you could make a small detour to New Orleans and meet my aunt Annette. I could meet you there."

"I would love that. I miss you. Please take care of yourself. You have hardly any area of your body without a scar, and you better not show up wounded below the belt." They both laughed.

"I have some news. Brett met a beautiful and friendly lady on the airplane. We had dinner together at my aunt's. It looks like he has found what I have. Otherwise, nothing new. I have been in the swamp for the last two days, and Brett has been doing inspections in New Orleans and dating his new friend."

"Great news. I love you Lyle, and so does little Jennie. We hope to see you in the USA soon." Then the connection went dead.

As Lyle sat down by the campfire, the call had made him pensive and nostalgic for the happy time he had with Annie. He felt calm and a bit sad. He came out of his dreamlike state when his encrypted phone rang. It was Octo informing him that on its journey ending in New Orleans, the Russian ship had stopped off the coast of

Mexico, near Cozumel. There were two containers when the vessel left Mexico.

Lyle reminded Octo to get the ship exact departure time from New Orleans, the coordinates of the route it would be taking, and everything else he could think of. Both men said goodbye and terminated the call.

CHAPTER 25

New Orleans,

Same day

A soft breeze was blowing when Fran stepped outside of her apartment. Brett took the door from Fran, made sure it was tightly shut and locked it. The couple walked the short mile to the small outdoor cafe found nestled in the famous Jackson Park in the French Quarter.

"I am famished," Brett said. "What about you?"

"Me too." Brett was discovering all sorts of unusual sounds, sights, and culinary flavors in New Orleans. He appreciated Fran's guidance when ordering the foreign delicacies that were part of the local culture. Fran suggested the Cajun catfish and told him to go for the hot version which was pleasantly spicy. They ordered a southern salad served with a special dressing using mustard which, some claimed, the French introduced to the area.

Both lovers were finding out about each other. Brett spoke of the two different foster homes in which he grew up following the death of his parents. He had only faded souvenirs of his biological family, but he remembered the day they died in a car crash, the day his life changed drastically. On a happier note, Brett gave a detailed account of how he met Lyle on an assignment in Afganistan, ten years after he enlisted in the service. "We were soon sent to go on special ops together both in and outside the United States. In fact, that is what we are still doing today. We became very close simply because we depended on each other for survival. I like him like I would a brother."

Fran leaned over, stroke Brett's cheek softly with the back of her fingers, then standing up and leaning forward, she kissed him on the forehead from across the table.

The waiter approached with the steaming catfish and a delicious and colorful salad. An hour later as they were crossing the park, and Fran was telling Brett the difference between an alligator and a crocodile, Brett's secure phone rang. "Excuse me; it's my secure phone confidential information comes on." Brett stepped some twenty feet away from Fran and answered it by saying, "What did you find out?"

Lyle started with the brush with the Babineaux, then he mentioned the cache of automatic rifles and grenades kept on the swamp boats, but more importantly, he went over the revelations made by the inebriated rednecks in the tavern.

"The Cajuns were talking about a delivery of arms already on land and of another load coming in this week out in the gulf waters. In their euphoric state, one of the Babineaux bragged about, and I quote, "a weapon that could reduce buildings to sand.""

Lyle found strange that his partner never commented on the hair-raising intel, and never complained about not being part of the action, but he let it pass. Brett assured Lyle he had all the information they needed about the water depth and the route the ship would take right after leaving New Orleans. The agent also mentioned that Octo had called to reconfirm Lyle's findings. Before ending the conversation, Lyle told Brett he would be back at the hotel in the morning, around nine a.m. After walking back to join Fran, the couple planned their evening. Fran who was familiar with New Orleans suggested they go and spend some time listening to music. They would start at the Snug Harbor, the oldest jazz club on Frenchman street where locals and often national greats played nightly. "Brett, what do you think? Is it a good idea?"

"It sounds great. One cannot come to New Orleans and not listen to some Jazz and New Orleans blues."

They both decided to change for the evening, so they drove back to Brett's hotel and Fran's apartment. Now looking more dressy, they left the blaring cover music of Bourbon street and walked to the musical district where the locals hang. The many clubs on Frenchman street offered cheap drinks and admission, live music from jazz to blues, to reggae, and more, and plunged the visitors in a merry celebrating ambiance, a festive atmosphere for which New Orleans is known.

Later, following the trepidation of the evening, they went to a quaint small diner called Chez Louis. As the customers dined, an elder man played jazz in the Louis Armstrong style and tradition, smooth, slow, and relaxing familiar melodies. Fran and Brett laughed and talked, enjoying each other's company for almost two hours.

Hand in hand the two finished the walk in the hotel's parking lot to pick up the car. On their way back to Fran's place, Brett shared some news he had kept to himself to avoid spoiling the evening.

"I will be flying out to New York tomorrow, then on to England, and Paris. I will be gone a long three plus days without seeing you.

"I will be waiting for you to return."

Brett was not scheduled to travel to Paris or London. He simply needed to keep the upcoming mission in the bayou undercover.

After parking the Mercedes, Fran got out of the vehicle first and came around to the driver's side. As Brett got out of the car, she took his hand. "Come with me dear; I think we need to enjoy each other a little bit more while we can."

In the apartment, Fran hurridly shut the door, put her two hands on Brett's shoulders and said, "Take me to my bedroom and make love to me again. I had never had an orgasm until I met you." Brett found this unexpected declaration quite lifting since he had never been told he had the carnal qualities of a playboy or, better yet, of a Casanova.

Acting slowly to prolong the anticipation, the lovers undressed each other, one item at a time. Brett liked the foreplay to be unhurried; he was sure it added spice to the excitement and gave extra gratification to lovemaking. As they gently removed the last of each other's clothing, they slipped between the cool sheets.

Brett laid on his side up against Fran so she could feel him becoming aroused. He used his fingers to tease her, and his tongue to excite her even more. Brett's caressed Fran's slim body; she was almost quivering, they were both ready.

Just after midnight, they made love again. At six a.m. Brett got dressed, kissed Fran on the forehead and said, "I love you, Frannie. I am going to miss you, but I should be back in three days." Fran had to see him to the door; she immediately got up. Standing on the last step of the porch, they held each other for a minute.

CHAPTER 26

New Orleans,

The Bayou

After Lyle finished enjoying his scrambled eggs, fried catfish, and a cup of coffee, he called Brett on his encrypted phone, asked him to bring their swamp clothes and armory, and to meet him and uncle Remi at his aunt Annette's. Brett who was not aware of the plans posed a few questions.

"Where are we heading to, captain Lyle?"

"We are heading deep into the swamps again. As you know, I never picked up any trace of radiation on the boats I inspected while Remi was in the tavern." Lyle teased his partner and said, "There will be no charge for the snakes. Did you know that Burmese pythons are found here in the swamps, like in Florida? Have you ever eaten fried snake?" Lyle could hardly hold back laughing while waiting for Brett's reply.

"Hell no, I have not eaten snake. I cannot stand to even look at one. If it were not for protecting your ass, I would let you take Pat with you instead of me. I'm going to buy some leg protection before I meet you."

Still holding back laughing, Lyle said, "You won't need any leg protection, even the pythons prefer the sanctuary the trees provide. As Lyle hung up, his old rib injury hurt from laughing so hard.

An hour later Remi and Lyle parked behind Brett's vehicle in the alley. After a couple of knocks on the door, Annette welcomed them.

"Come on in you two. I have a hot baguette and coffee waiting."

Time was flying, soon Lyle gave the signal to leave their host, "We better get going, we have a long day ahead of us."

CHAPTER 27

New Orleans

Remis Hummock

The sun had passed directly overhead hours ago. At the table, the big meal accompanied by good wine was taking its toll on Lyle. His eyes began to close. Several times he fought this pleasant drowsiness by shaking his head slightly. It was just after two p.m. He still had a lot to do before his uncle, Brett and himself could head into the swamp. He looked at Brett, then at his uncle, and let them know they had to leave Annette. The three men stepped out into the dark alley where Remi's old truck was parked. The air which was hot and humid was more in tune for a nap than a ride in an uncomfortable old truck with poor ventilation.

The sounds from Bourbon St. caused Remi and Brett to hold back any conversation. Lyle had given them orders, Remi and Brett were to bring the pontoon boat to the dock. Then, they were to transfer from the car to the pickup, the government acquisition picked up at the airport and kept in the trunk of the Mercedes. Lyle had reminded them to be discreet while doing this transfer. The alley was usually deserted at this time of day. Lyle was responsible for the groceries they would need on the excursion, and for the gasoline. Before leaving, he said, "We should all be back in about one hour. Any questions?"

"Son, you have a good head on your shoulders. Let's get that pontoon boat; I have not driven or even been in one in years."

Two men turned left down Bourbon St., and an SUV turned the opposite direction, toward a grocery store. Forty minutes later Brett and Remi returned to the alley behind the Voodoo shop. Being careful not to arouse any suspicion, the two men placed the arms under an old tarp Remi carried in the back of his truck. Brett put the smelly crab pots on top of the tarp. Remi remembered when he had been stopped while moving arms in the bed of the pickup. The only thing that stopped the officer from looking any further was the smelly crab pots.

The old Ford truck moved out slowly from the dark alley onto Bourbon street for the third time that day.

Once at the dock, everyone was giving the last touches before the departure. Uncle Remi tied the pontoon boat to the back of the airboat. Brett nonchalantly brought the arms aboard, and Lyle lined up and secured the four jeep cans full of gasoline. Now, a bit excited to engage in another dangerous adventure, Lyle said, "We're not coming out of the swamps, men, not until we are gator food or the gators are suffering from the runs 'cause they ate one of the Babineauxs. Let's go." Now at the helm, Remi started the engine.

CHAPTER 28

Deep in the Bayou

Same day

As the sun dipped toward the west, shadows began to appear on the water. The pontoon boat was bouncing up and down behind the airboat as it pulled away from the dock. They had time to kill before the recon mission at sunset, so Remi took the long way to introduce Lyle to a different route to reach his home. Once the men reached into the deeper waters, moving along at about eight miles an hour, Remi suddenly slowed down and pulled sharply to his right toward the shore. "What are you doing?" yelled Brett who had to shout to compete with the loud noise of the old aircraft engine. "Three miles ahead, we will be in dangerous territory, that is why I want to stay close to the shore. On the west bank, assholes take shots at people like us. We are considered intruders in what they regard as their private land." Remi slowed down and spoke again, "See those buzzards?"

"Yes, so what?" Brett screamed back as he noticed the birds hovering in circles above a specific spot on land.

"Their presence means something is dead." Brett who had been raised in a city was not at all in touch with nature. Remi stopped along the shoreline; he spotted a dead deer that was missing half of the two front legs. "A gator took a few bites out of the deer, and it bled to death. This carcass will make a good meal for Two Legs, my pet gator, he will be happy to get fresh meat." Lyle took over the control of the boat while his uncle jumped out of the craft with surprising agility. With much effort, Brett and the old man pulled the deer onto the airboat. They were now heading home.

It was less than twenty minutes later when all three men heard a ping followed with the sound of a gunshot; another and another shot were heard.

Remi screamed above the sound of the engine. "I'm pulling to the right some more, keep your heads down. As I told you earlier, that area is known for shooters. In all my years living here, no one has been able to capture any of those criminals yet. "

While Remi was speaking, Brett pulled his AK-15 from his big pack, snapped it together and shoved in a mag. After putting a round in the chamber, he set the gun on three round bursts. The next shot came from the dense swamp vegetation. Brett saw the flash of the gunfire and cut loose with a three-round burst, then another, and another, to each side of the flash.

"I think I heard someone yell," Lyle said.

Remi replied with a smile, "You might have hit one of them. Don't ever set foot in that area to go after those killers. They have traps and numerous escape routes. I can almost guarantee you that you would not come out alive if you did. If not dead, you would be at least injured."

Another hour, passed before Remi tied the airboat up to a tree on the hummock he called home. "Brett, you drag the deer to my gator. Lyle, you feed the chickens. I will get us a meal started so that we can be in shape going on our night recon in a few hours." Brett was not sure about feeding Remi's alligator, "No way am I going near that killer of yours." Lyle came to the rescue, "Come on pussy, don't whine. You do not have to get close to it. I will help you."

They were now relaxing outside by the campfire when uncle Remi handed them some moonshine. After a toast to success, he announced that the steaks and salad were ready.

The dinner lasted over two hours as Remi told the two men where they were going. They would be leaving in an hour. Lyle who had never been in the area in question before was wondering how his uncle could find his way in this marshy landscape at night. There were so many reasons to get lost in the daytime; finding one's way at night seemed impossible. All the hummocks resembled each other, each new channel looked like the previous one, and there was no landmark.

"Well son, I have been traveling these waters for almost forty years. On the tip of the hummock or land, there is always a tree. On occasions, I had to create some landmarks. After missing the same turn a few times, I remember tying the Spanish moss a certain way so I could tell where I was going. It works as long as the moon shines.

I will get the two crossbows, arrows, some TNT, and my old faithful Winchester. You boys load up the arms you think you might need. I don't intend on a full out fight tonight, but if I see one or more of those no goods out on the water gator hunting, well, I am going to send them straight to where it's hot. We won't bring your pontoon boat; it will slow us down.

Don't worry we will need it tomorrow. Lyle, you mentioned you had tracking devices. If you do, bring them along, that way we can go into areas where I have never been before, and still find our way out."

As Brett was getting the armory ready, Lyle pulled out ten of the small tracking devices and the monitor. They were a bit giddy, ready to rock and roll, "We are ready old man." Remi was quick to reply, "Who are you calling an old man? I can still out shoot you with a gun or crossbow. If you had to survive out here after being civilized, you would be screaming for my help. Now you two young roosters get your ass in the boat, time to go." Uncle Remi brought in an extra jeep can of fuel after finishing topping off his boat tank. As he was pushing the throttle forward, he made one of his predictions, "The moon won't stay bright very long tonight, and there is a small chance of tule fog."

As the boat glided out into the swamp, all three men folded a large handkerchief, then tied it around their forehead, to help prevent sweat from running into their eyes, and also to keep the mosquitoes from biting that small surface of their face.

CHAPTER 29

Two hours later

Just over two hours had passed and as predicted the tule fog was beginning to rise off the murky waters of the bayou. Remi was in no rush; he wanted to keep the sound of his engine as low as possible as they worked their way deep into the green habitat. As they maneuvered deeper into the waterways, he pulled over close to shore and pointed out hanging Spanish moss that had been rearranged to form a large knot hanging just a foot above water to create a landmark. On a few occasions, while gliding along, a gator would slide into the slow-moving stream and snakes could be spotted hanging high above wrapped on branches above the men. At one particular site, where the river branched off, the men came across some of Remi's markers that indicated the right direction. The old man advised Lyle and Brett to make sure they watch for those landmarks to get back out if something should happen to him during the night.

As they puttered along, Lyle felt his phone vibrating inside his backpack which was sitting on his leg. Only four people had this number. He got up and moved as far as he could forward in the boat to get away from the noisy engine. He put his hand over his right ear and pushed the green button on his burner phone. Annie was the caller, "It's me. What is that horrible noise? I can hardly hear you."

Lyle had forgotten all about Annie calling back. She caught him at the wrong time; he was on a mission. After releasing air slowly through his nostrils, he shouted, "You hear an aircraft engine, we are on a mission."

"All I wanted to tell you is that my mother, Jennie, and I will be at your mother's in three days. Don't get hurt. I miss you." Then the line went dead.

Lyle was disappointed he could not converse with Annie who seemed so happy to announce this coming trip and who probably wanted to discuss the reunion he was not even sure he could be part of. A bit upset he had to get his composure back. Lyle tapped Brett on the shoulder and said, "Annie is on her way to the US."

"What's the matter? You look upset when you should rejoice." Then Brett smiled and punched Lyle lightly in the shoulder.

Another twenty minutes passed, before Remi pulled over next to the bank under a large cypress, and said, "You, boys, need to put a tracking device on this tree, ahead is new territory for me. If we have to get out of there fast, we better know how to retrace our steps. The Babineaux bunch are probably home in those waters."

Brett opened his pack, took out a small device, turned a little knob on it and attached it to the cypress. The same procedure was repeated several times the next hour and a half as they worked their way slowly through thick vegetation that gave way to waterways hardly wider than their airboat.

Remi, sitting on a high seat on the airboat had a better view than Lyle and Brett. All of a sudden he slowed down, looked down at Lyle and Brett, and said, "Better turn off the headsets. I can see the flames from a campfire way up ahead."

Once they reached the head of a small inlet that ran into a more substantial body of water, Remi pulled the airboat close to shore, turned it around in the direction they had just come from, and turned off the engine. Brett stepped off the boat and attached a tracking device on a tree. Back on the craft, he said, " It looks like there is firm land all the way." It was time to pack the monitoring device and the night goggles. Lyle asked Remi if he was taking his crossbow along. The old man quickly replied,

"You betcha, and the pouches of venom. I'm taking old Betsie and my 30-30 also. You boys, bring whatever firepower you think you will need."

As Lyle was taking out of his backpack the three sets of night goggles, he noticed his uncle had picked up six sticks of dynamite and a partial roll of duct tape. They had no idea what was ahead, but they knew there could be a firefight. Lyle threw a few orders at Brett, "Put the tracking monitor in your bag, two grenades, two flash-bangs, and whatever ammo you think you will need for the AR-15 and your shoulder gun." In complete darkness, Lyle quickly went over the plan with Brett and his uncle. They were ready for battle. They put their hands together and said, "Let's do it."

As they stepped on shore, Remi took the lead, with his ocular device down, and old Betsie pointing in front of him.

CHAPTER 30

Even though they had sprayed themselves with insect repellent, mosquitoes and other flying bugs swarmed around the three men as they stepped out of their boat. Sweat was dripping off their forehead around the bandanas causing them to stop often to wipe their face as they moved along the hummock's edge. Every once in a while Remi spoke into his mike and warned the agents of a limb or vine to prevent them from tripping.

It seemed like a long time before they reached the party suspected of being the retriever of the hazardous container. The trio knew of the presence of the inebriated tangos when they heard their singing and yelling. As they got even closer, they could see them dancing around the bonfire. By then, all three men flipped up their ocular on their goggles and observed the site. Lyle spoke softly into his mike. "Can anyone spot where their boats are tied up?" Remi replied, "Give me a few minutes son. I am going to sneak closer to the edge of the water. I will be back in ten."

Remi furtively moved through the lush flora, toward the murky waters to the west of the campfire. It seemed that Remi had been gone a long time when suddenly he slipped out through the bushes and tall grass. "There seems to be a small cove on the other side. I am sure the boats have been pulled close to land and camouflaged under vines so no one can spot them. Here are the plans: Brett will stay here for coverage, Remi and I will go and take a look. We must locate the boats on which they will load the hazardous container. I think they must have a special craft to pick up that bulky floating box once it's dropped off. Whatever they use, if it is guarded, we can quietly take the watchmen out with the crossbows."

Brett was the first one to react to the plans and to offer a bright idea, "I think you should place tracking devices on the crafts you think will go out to rescue that container. They have a battery life of seventy-two hours." Lyle approved the suggestion and resumed speaking.

"OK, here's the rest of the plan. Brett, if we get into trouble and the shooting starts, use the flash-bangs and grenades to buy us time to get back. If you have any doubt about us, leave. With all the tracking devices left behind, you should be able to get back to our airboat and get to safety. Once you are secure, call Colonel Jackson, give him the GPS coordinates." Lyle knew Brett was courageous and loyal, and would never leave his partner or Remi behind, but he had to try to convince him."

The scouts gave Brett a heads up and disappeared into the dense vegetation where they immediately felt lost in the darkness of the night.

Now standing close to the group of rednecks, Remi stopped and held up his hand for Lyle to stop. He whispered into his mike, "I heard someone mention the preacher. Let's move in closer and listen. After watching and listening to the group for a while, Remi and Lyle did not gather any more interesting revelations; these drunkards uttered only incoherent gibberish that sounded like Cajun. The two men continued advancing.

At last, Lyle ran across a swamp boat to which a crane and a hook had been connected to the back of it and to which a big V8 engine had been added. Another broader craft was attached to the swamp boat. Lyle attached his tracking devices on each one, then spoke into his mike. "I wonder how the preacher is going to get here?"

"I'm not sure, but most likely if he is coming in by chopper. We have what we want, let's get back to Brett and get the hell out of here."

Walking along the bank allowed them to move faster to where Brett was patiently waiting for them. Lyle spoke into his mike to let his partner know they were safe and on their way. As soon as Lyle told him about the two boats, the agent became excited and wanted to take the entire clan out while they could. Lyle easily convinced him that their priority was to determine what was going to happen to the suspicious cargo container. Now they had the proof they needed and maybe a chance at eliminating the preacher. The men would have to wait another day to witness the rescue of the container since the Russian cargo ship, the Anakriya, was scheduled to leave the New Orleans harbor the following day, at six p.m.

Relying on the few devices they had planted on the way in; they were soon back on Remi's airboat.

While Remi was starting the old aircraft engine, Brett moved toward the front of the boat to watch the red dots on the tracking monitor. An hour had passed as they weaved in and out, and around hummocks and small canals. Just as they were pulling out into the open waters, two unexpected airboats, one at one o'clock, another at eleven o'clock, appeared. Immediately gunfire was heard and resonated in the silence of the night. Spurts of water were shooting up around the men like geysers as the two boats sped toward them. Instinctively Brett grabbed his AK 15 and several mags. Lyle seized two grenades, not sure the enemy was close enough to use them.

Remi put a rope on each side of the steering wheel to immobilize it to create a sort of automatic cruising, so he could be free to reach down and pick up two arrows with dynamite taped to them. Whack, whack, whack, whack, there was a constant sound of fire coming from AK47s. Several hits had caused pieces of Remi's airboat to break off. Then they heard a harsh metallic sound; one of the bullets had hit the propeller blade. Brett concentrated and let go a three round burst. One of the men and his AK47 fell off the boat and into the water. Within seconds another man stepped forward and started firing.

Remi cut the fuse to length, and when the first boat was almost parallel with his, he lit it. The old crossbow, with the snap of a rubber band, sent the arrow close to its target. The short-fuse caused the TNT to explode near the enemies, flipping their craft over. Brett was striking the men swimming fiercely for dear life. Lyle threw one grenade, then another, as the second group zoomed by. The shock wave almost caused their airboat to flip over, the man sitting on the high seat was thrown from his perch, leaving the boat without someone to control it. As Remi resumed steering, Brett started firing his A15 again on three round burst, slaughtering the slime of humanity while the damaged craft was bouncing up and down in the choppy dark water.

With light, one could see blood around the airboats. One had lost its engine, and the other was idling. Remi yelled, "Time to head home men. The gators are on their way to finish the job."

CHAPTER 31

Same day

The pale rays of the sun were shining through the vegetation this warm and humid early morning. Remi was already at work moving and tying up his airboat closer to his hummock so Lyle would have easy access to it and ample light to conduct an inspection following the rain of gunshots endured the night before. After a thorough review, the diagnosis was good. The superficial damage would not affect the vessel's function. On land, Remi's mini zoo was coming to life with the rooster crowing, Two feet, the pet gator, devouring a piece of deer meat, and raccoons casually trotting to the water. The man of the house informed his guests, "I am getting the coffee and breakfast going."

Brett and Lyle rushed to the hand pump to splash cold water on their face and hands and raced for coffee. They ate and talked while sipping their cup of Joe until Lyle gave the signal it was time to work, "Well we have to go back to the Babineaux area, if possible wipe out as many members of the clan as we can, and solve the mystery of the dangerous container. For this expedition, we are going to need to drag the pontoon behind our boat. I want to retrieve most of what will be delivered to the Babineauxs, definitely anything radioactive. I hope we can find the signature source that Colonel Jackson wants to hand walk it to both the Chief Of Staff, NSA, and the CIA." Lyle paused.

Remi said, "Because we had this bloody confrontation yesterday, it may not be easy to eliminate most of the scumbags. By now, after losing a few partners and two boats, they know they are being threatened and may double their vigilance."

At this time, out of the blue, Lyle informed his uncle of his imminent departure for Russia. Remi was familiar with the agents sudden and sometimes erratic decisions. He should have been upset for being left in the dark, but this news did not surprise old Remi. Participating in the missions was all he wanted from his nephew to spice up his quiet life.

Lyle blew a little air through his teeth and said, "We will have to take the pontoon boat, the SCUBA gear, and the other supplies close to the camp. Since the Russian ship is leaving port at 18:00 hours, the container will be dropped about two hours later. I don't think we should go out and try to intercept while our rednecks are retrieving the radioactive box." Lyle, having uttered his last thought, Brett butted in.

"I thought about it a long time also. I do agree. When they bring the merchandise to their camp, I presume the preacher will already be there. Now we have the preacher, the radioactive material, and the rednecks in one location. It is time to eliminate most of the clan all at once." Another suggestion popped up but was immediately abandoned. Brett brought up an important reminder, "We need to plant explosive devices with timers on those two boats." Brett wanted to be the one doing the swimming to take the pontoon and the equipment closer to the camp, but Lyle objected with insistence. "That was what I was trained to do with the SEALS. I need you to work with uncle Remi to lay down a barrage of firepower, and to stop the clan members from escaping. Brett, you call Octo and make sure about the departure of the ship is still for eighteen hundred hours. We have some free time; you should call Fran. I am going to contact Patrick, and then Annie. Laughing cynically, he added, "You never know, it could be our last calls."

"While you boys are on the phone I will make sandwiches, pack my gear, and make sure we have extra fuel and water. I recommend we leave before sunset."

After three attempts, Lyle was able to get a hold of Patrick. Patrick was also part of the Vulcan mission and was presently working in Grozny, the capital of Chechnya. With the backing of the CIA, he had made contact with an informant and was hoping to have pertinent information for Lyle within the week. Next, Lyle dialed Annie. They talked for almost a half hour on his special phone. She was all excited about her coming trip to Atlanta where she was planning to spend two weeks with Lyle's mother. Her plane was leaving Paris in thirty-six hours. After declaring he loved and missed his woman, he hung up. Then Lyle walked over to see Brett who was laying out the SCUBA equipment and the arsenal.

"I tried to get ahold of Fran. I believe she has her phone off; must be in flight somewhere, so I left her a short message. Gosh, I miss her! Back on business, I have three flash-bangs, four grenades, your A15, with ten mags, explosives, and timers for the boats. Anything else you think you will need?"

Lyle studied the rest of the supplies before answering. "Good job as usual. I hope you understand; I can't let you take the swim. That water is murky, and you can't see a thing. We had people go berserk in SEAL training. The obscurity plays with your mind. I will take a compass reading, and trust it until I get there. Every once in a while, to see, you have to stop, click the light, and continue. You have no feeling of time and distance. I will be OK, old friend. I need a favor from you."

„Name it."

Looking around and making sure his uncle Remi was out of hearing distance, Lyle said, "Keep Remi as safe as possible. He hates the Babineauxs and would not hesitate to endanger himself to destroy these people. Let him work his magic with his TNT, crossbow, and Winchester, but watch him."

"I will bring him home." Then Brett took his fist and amicably hit Lyle's shoulder.

The three men rested for several hours, and just before leaving, Remi called Annette and told her if one of them did not call her by noon tomorrow, she had to make arrangements for his pets at his hummock. Intrigued and worried, she wanted an explanation which he could not give on his phone. Remi answered with caution and reassured his sister, and ended the call with, "See you in a day or two."

Now, the worst part of any op, the waiting, was just starting.

Chapter 32

Same day

Late afternoon, Lyle had tried to contact Colonel Jackson several times without success; his NSA special phone was not working. Overly cautious and in need to kill time, they checked their gear one last time before heading back toward the Babineaux's camp. During the trip, the men exchanged very few words.

Once they arrived a certain distance from the camp, they discarded the airboat that they hid with branches, vines, and Spanish moss and boarded the pontoon. The men ate their sandwiches, hydrated themselves, and sprayed on insect repellant once again. Just as the sun was setting Brett looked up into the sky and noticed an odd black cloud about half the size of football field. A bit concerned by this unusual cloud formation, he turned toward Remi and asked, "What the hell is that black mass coming our way? Are we going to be sprayed with something?"

"They are bats coming out to feed. Several miles to the northeast there are small hummocks consisting mostly of limestone with lots of bat caves. They roost in there until sunset. I took Lyle there long ago when he was eleven years old."

Once the cloud formed by the bats dissipated, the gibbous moon was bright again. Lyle pointed toward his partners and made a circle with his index finger. It was time to leave on the pontoon equipped with an electric motor which could hardly be heard. Its sound was so muffled; one could still enjoy the owls' call.

Brett, Lyle, and Remi were ready. Remaining silent, they put their fists together and somberly looked into each other's straight in the eyes for a few seconds.

Lyle's equipment was enclosed in a watertight pouch. With his foot, he pushed the sealed bag into the water, and slowly it became submerged. Once more Lyle checked a vital item, his compass. He turned on his tank valve and regulator, pulled his goggles down, and placed the mouthpiece into his mouth. Without much noise, he scuba dived into the dark murky waters of the bayou.

As Lyle disappeared, Brett said, "That man has balls. He is right. I could not have done it in that turbid water. We must show recognition, the Delta Force and SEALS; they are the best." Remi nodded. Once again the old man led the way. Even with the help of the ATN PVS7 Military goggles, the going was slow and demanding in the obscurity. It was getting close to ten p.m. when Brett spoke for the first time into his voice mike, "It's almost time, do you think he made it?"

"Quiet! I think I hear something, sounds like music." Another ten minutes passed when Remi held up his hand signaling to stop. "I am going to the right, about a hundred to two hundred feet to look for guards. You go to the left and do the same. Quiet as a fox, Remi gingerly moved without a sound, all of a sudden he detected the pleasant fragrance of cigarette smoke. This development paralyzed Remi in place. He took a deep breath and in a slow circular head motion, scrutinized the area. A few feet away, a man sitting with his back against a tree with his rifle resting across his thighs was enjoying a smoke while sipping what was probably shine. Remi delicately raised his crossbow and sighted it in. A discreet Pfffft, similar to the sound of a puff of wind, disturbed the silence when the arrow shot forward and fatally injured the guard. Remi spoke into his mike softly. "Guard down, on the way back."

Brett spoke into his mike. "Roger that, coast clear all the way to the water edge. Let's meet and then separate about fifty feet apart. We don't want some lucky bastard to get us both at once."

CHAPTER 33

Same Night
Nine-thirty five p.m.

Lyle wanted to emerge where the moon did not reflect on the water. He chose an area where the reeds were thick, and the roots of an enormous cypress gave him a place to hide. Suddenly white bubbles appeared at the surface of the stagnant water. Lyle looked around and listened to his surroundings. Once out of his wet environment, he placed his tank among the roots of the cypress, removed his wetsuit and started to get dressed in his camouflage clothes. With his shoes and goggles on, he could get organized. The agent made sure his AR-15, was loaded. Once his automatic was placed under his shoulder, and the rest of the gear was checked, he stuck a bolt in the crossbow. Now he could make contact with his partners, "Gator one onshore and ready. Are gators two and three all set to tango?"

Brett sighed with relief at the sound of Lyle's voice; he answered, "Gator two ready."

Then Lyle heard the baritone voice of his uncle, "Gator three is hot to trot. How long to a go, son?"

"The package or the preacher is not here yet. You have to be patient. Remember, Octo said the Russian ship would pass by those hummocks between eight and nine. I will be happy if they both get here before midnight. We have a lot of time so let's chow down and rest. Someone must keep his goggles on and be alert while the other rests. Out."

The time dragged and dragged until about eleven-forty p.m. when they all heard the V8 engine. Lyle had a clear view of the boat which was slowly moving toward the campsite. It was trailed by four swamp boats. Lyle informed Brett and Remi, "We have four flats and the big V8 on site loaded with cargo. I am going to need time to plant the explosives on all them. Will contact when done."

Lyle cut a couple of reeds, their straight stalk being hollow could be used to breathe underwater should someone notice his presence. Once underwater the Tangos would lose his trace.

There was screaming and yelling at the camp where the men were busy unloading the guns that had been stored inside the mysterious cargo container. Among the goods, Lyle spotted a large black case he was familiar with. This dangerous item which contained nuclear material was in the wrong hands.

After a while, the frenzy slowed down, but the noise did not subside. About thirty individuals were standing and drinking their shine around the fire that had been revived. They were probably celebrating the successful arrival of the merchandise. Lyle took advantage of the slowing of the activities to crawl and plant the explosives and timers on the five boats. He was watching the scumbags chugging the shine like water. Lyle had finished his work when he heard the sound of a mighty loud boat engine approaching. It was a speedboat that moored just a few feet away from the agent.

Lyle counted six men aboard, the pilot, five heavily armed men, and one individual, the preacher, who was noticeable due to his size. Lyle was now retreating, moving away from these well-armed guards who were now splitting up. Based on their demeanor, Lyle thought they were military trained. One of the five guards was carrying a heavy box. The morbidly obese gentleman, the preacher, was carrying a case probably full of cash. The guards remained close to the preacher as they joined the party.

"Gator one. The preacher has arrived. He has five trained guards. The explosives are in place. I need time to plant an explosive on the boat that just came in."

Feeling secure in his hiding spot Lyle took the time to adjust his gear. Now ready to leave, he picked up the crossbow, cocked it, and placed on a bolt. With his night goggles down, he moved like a snake and watched his surroundings like an eagle. He had spotted two guards talking. When they separated to continue patrolling the area, he raised the crossbow and aimed at the one closest to him. The guard targeted slumped to the ground with the feathers of the arrow sticking out of his mouth.

Lyle knew the next guard would be harder to take down. He was equipped with night-goggles. After a while, he would be questioning the absence of his partner on whom, as trained, he was keeping an eye. Lyle spoke into his mike, "One guard to go, be ready." Remi and Brett were on full alert, all psyched up, ready to put their arsenal to work.

Lyle was as close as he could get to the second guard. Just as he pulled the release on the crossbow, the guard turned his head slightly to the side. The Arrow hit the night goggles before piercing the side of his face. Instinctively, the guard pulled the trigger on his weapon which was set on automatic. As the man slumped to the ground dying, the gun kept firing until empty.

After a short pause, the shooting was considered an accident rather than an attack; the party continued. Brett and Remi had changed their position. Now closer to the site, the carnage could start. An arrow with TNT hit near the campfire, immediately exploding. A few men were thrown outward; others were blown with such force that body parts were flying in all directions. Brett threw a grenade as far as he could on the opposite side of that nightmarish scene. A few survivors were running for cover. The battlefield was scattered with limbs and blood. The sound of the injured was atrocious. Their distress, pain, and fear were palpable. This attack was causing complete pandemonium. Unfortunately, not all the members of the clan were dead. The few who survived started to retaliate with fury, they were shooting their AK47s anywhere and everywhere for they had no idea where their enemy was. Fired weapons never disclosed their location since none had been used.

CHAPTER 34

Next day

Two minutes past mid-night

By chance, not due to martial expertise, one clansman randomly shot Lyle who felt a hit, so violent on his armor, that he was knocked to his knees. His ribs that had been cracked in a previous mission were interfering with his breathing. The pain was intolerable. Crawling along the ground, gasping for air, he, at last, hunkered against a big oak tree for comfort. The battle was not over. While catching his breath, Brett threw a grenade that was followed by a TNT blast targeting the outer perimeter of the camp. Although incapacitated, Lyle found the strength to pull a flash-bang from his belt, even though he was not sure how far he could throw it. Lyle spoke into his mike, "Flash-bang, cover-up." Within seconds the whole sky lit up, again, there was loud screaming and chaos among the few survivors. With each flash-roll, victims rolled on the ground with their hands over their ears. Within seconds, Lyle heard on his mike. "Flash-bang, cover-up."

The second flash-bang had created more havoc to all but three men. The three remaining guards who, right after the first explosion had put in special military earplugs. They had gone low to the ground while pulling the corpulent preacher toward the water edge. Brett had seen the scene, so he opened up with a three-round blast hitting the closest guard in the chest, the man stumbled backward, then continued to move toward the water edge. Brett then spoke into his mike. "The guards have special armor, aim for their heads."

Lyle had also opened up, using three round blasts taking down tango after tango. Then he pulled his last grenade and threw it with anger toward the preacher who fell to the ground, bleeding profusely from an injury to his arm. The guards helped him up. The site was quiet until Lyle heard "Grab the money and let's go." Someone else still standing took hold of the uninjured arm of the preacher and pulled him into the shallow water. The exchange of fire continued.

All of a sudden Brett felt the impact at the level of his left shoulder, just above the body armor. It did not hurt much at first, but he knew the pain would come. He said nothing. Remi had no more TNT to shoot off, so he used his old 30-30 Winchester.

Minutes later they heard the loud roar of a boat engine start. They all smiled; in under ten minutes, the sky would light up. To Lyle's surprise, several wounded rednecks also made it to the water's edge. Once onboard they pulled out into the bayou, not knowing that within minutes they would be blown to pieces. As the boats pulled away, Lyle saw an opportunity to work his way toward where Remi and Brett were. Several Rednecks had deserted from the battle scene and were hiding in the reeds were now trying to escape into the bayou.

Brett, though wounded, spoke into his mike. "My last flash-bang, cover-up."

The desolated site was quiet. Only the campfire was still throwing some light. Lyle said, "I'm going after the suitcase and that other case. Cover me." Then with his gun pointed forward, Lyle worked his way to what used to be a lively camp. Stepping over body parts and bodies, he saw no immediate danger. With great effort, the agent grabbed the black suitcase and the bag the preacher had been carrying earlier. He was back to safety in less than twenty-five seconds. Lyle gave the case to Brett, not knowing his partner was wounded, and said, "Get this to the boat, let's go!

The old man and his two invalid partners left and worked their way to the water's edge. Lyle's arm was resting over Remi's shoulder.

His breathing was labored, and the pain was severe. Brett carried the heavy case using only one side of his body. The old man installed the patients inside the boat and took over the control of the craft. The sound of the engine was like a bowl of fresh air, a rebirth. Remi felt relieved thinking about the cruel and harmful people he and his partners had killed. He did not expect any more fighting on the dark water of the river that was leading to his hummock.

CHAPTER 35

Next day

Twelve forty-two a.m.

The trio was now aboard Remi's boat. Reaching it had been difficult. Lyle had noticed that his partner was carrying the heavy suitcase with his left hand; something was wrong, he was right-handed. On the way back, Lyle had turned around twice to help his old friend who was falling behind. Finally, Brett admitted having been wounded. Lyle said, "Where were you hit?"

"Top right shoulder. It's nothing, let's go."

"No way, let me put a pressure bandage on first."

The bullet had damaged only flesh, no tendons or ligaments, only a steady oozing of blood. For support and to stop the light bleeding, Lyle put on a tight pressure bandage.

Remi jokingly stated, "The old man is in still in good shape, he can help you. Which one will accept my assistance?"

Lyle, the macho man, replied, "Brett has an injured shoulder. You take the small case, and I will carry the nuke." Remi knew the agents were hurting, he offered his shoulder to Lyle who was hurting. Drained of all physical resources, his nephew accepted the help.

With night goggles down, looking like aliens from outer space, the three men, worked their way back to the pontoon boat. Once the cases were on board, Remi untied the boat and pushed it out into the darkness.

The men each chugged down a bottle of mineral water, sipped lukewarm coffee, and ate a sandwich in silence. Almost a half hour had passed before they transferred to the airboat. Uncle Remi said, "Lyle help me pull the pontoon and hide it in the weeds, we will pick it up later. Right now, we need to get back into familiar waters before daylight. I am damn sure the Babineaux clan, what's left of it, will come looking for us with fierce rage."

The gleaming light of the stars began to fade as the old airboat pulled up alongside Remi's hummock. After tying up the craft, Lyle hid the nuke and the other case, and Remi prepared some coffee. Lyle cleaned Brett's wound, used butterfly bandages to stop the bleeding, covered it with a sterile dressing, and bandaged it.

Remi came back from the chicken house with a dozen eggs. In the kitchen, he dropped freshly ground coffee into boiling water, and mumbled, "One hell of a night, man! Breakfast will be ready in ten minutes."

CHAPTER 36

Bayou

Same day

The rays of the sun were trying to push their way through the tule fog. Remi poured himself some coffee. After taking a few sips, he left the house to feed his chickens and throw a slab of deer meat to his alligator. When he returned to start breakfast, both men were sound asleep with their head leaning forward. He awakened them and ordered them to go to bed. Remi took his Winchester, laid it on his lap, and sat next to the old Cypress tree, near the water, to discreetly stand guard.

The Babineaux had no idea who was responsible for the attack the night before. Remi was vigilant; he knew how unpredictable and erratic the Babinauxs were. Enraged by the defeat their clan had endured, the survivors of the battle were probably cruising the slow-moving streams, lakes, rivers, and canals, in search of suspicious, unwelcome prowlers. The loss of men and merchandise had been humiliating to the rednecks and was a threat to their livelihood. It represented a defeat that was unforgivable. Working for the Chechen had been a blessing, especially following the loss of Renard's business. It had provided some income and most of all, state of the art arms they could not have acquired otherwise. Losing this source of work meant losing their livelihood. The people of the area, for the majority, depended on odd jobs that did not demand order or control, and indeed were not abiding by the law. Poverty was rampant.

On the water, the men were concentrating their hunt among individuals living in the hamlet, or close by. Some were envious of the Babineaux clan's sophisticated guns and also of the easy money the scumbags were dishing out freely at the tavern.

Three hours later Lyle woke up. With moans and groans with each step and each breath taken, he worked his way to the kitchen and poured himself a cup of coffee. He sat down with his uncle who was concerned with his nephew's suffering. Remi addressed the problem, "You've been banged up pretty hard, son. I need to take a look at your chest and see how bruised you are. Since you can't do much, you could stand guard.

As you know the Babineauxs must be on high alert, with retaliation on their mind. As a precaution, we need to keep an eye on any visitors. I am going to get some herbs that will help you heal faster, and for sure breathe easier. I hope Brett's wound does not get infected. I will get some herbs to prevent that too, and when I get back, we should eat a bite before we open the hospital." Remi was laughing as he limped to the front door. He left and walked to another hummock he called his pharmacy. There, many medicinal herbs and plants grew: the groundsel bush, the goat weed, the coral bean, the sorrel, and many more. Remi was fascinated by the Indians' high knowledge of natural curatives. He had in his possession a book, History book of Louisiana written by Antoine-Simon Le Page-du Pratz who had lived with the Natchez from 1720-1728. This old publication was a rich source of Indian plant medicine.

Remi retuned with several plastic bags containing leaves, seed, flowers, and something that looked like mud that Lyle did not recognize. The old man grabbed his mortar and pestle and with a rapid and forceful twist of the wrist started to crush several ingredients. The leaves and seeds were now mushy and had released an unpleasant acrid smell. When the brownish mixture took a smoother consistency, Remi grabbed several layers of a flannel rectangle, measuring twelve by eighteen inches. With a wooden spoon, he smeared the mixture onto the cloth and obtained a perfect poultice. Brett was getting up;

he immediately poured himself coffee. "Where are you going to place that horrible smelling stuff? Not on me, I hope?"

Remi, sharp-witted as usual, responded. "It's an underarm deodorant for people who don't shower. If needed, it can be applied to all parts of the body. Are you ready?"

Brett and Lyle stepped backward when Remi said, "It's for Lyle's sore ribs. A for you, Brett, we have to sew up that wound of yours. We can go to town and have the Voodoo witch do it, or Lyle or I can sew it up here. Who do you think will hurt you the least?"

Lyle was almost choking trying not to laugh. Remi kept a straight face, then Brett said, "Give me the shine, and let's get me sewed up."

Lyle stood up and said, "I will get what we need." As part of the pre-op, Lyle returned and handed Brett a small jar of moonshine to drink on an empty stomach. While waiting for the alcohol turned anesthesia to relax the patient, Remi applied the poultice to his nephew's thorax and held it in place by wrapping a towel around his torso that was held with several safety pins.

Lyle opened the suture kit, washed his hands, and put on latex gloves. He filled a syringe with lidocaine and observed Brett's mouth twisting into a grimace as he was injecting the burning local anesthetic. The wound was clean. Due to its depth, it required sutures. It took half an hour to finish the job with the application of a non-stick bandage.

During the procedure, Remi had been busy in the kitchen preparing an omelet, grits, and fried potatoes. He encouraged his guests to taste the raccoon stew. There was some hesitation, but once tried, Lyle and Brett were surprised at how tasty the dish was. Remi jokingly said, "Next time I will prepare an opossum tureen you will love." They ended the meal with coffee and made themselves comfortable. The three men discussed the events of the night and went over the pluses and minuses of their strategy. During the talks, productive criticism and suggestions were offered by all.

Remi proposed they take a short walk to the end of his hummock. Lyle was very cautious with each movement, somehow this time, getting up from his chair seemed less difficult, even his breathing appeared less painful.

He turned to Remi and shared his improvement. Remi ordered the repeat of the treatment at bedtime. Although far from being healed, Lyle was amazed by the drastic improvement. He thanked his uncle. "Feels good doctor. My breathing is more comfortable and does not hurt so much to inhale."

CHAPTER 37

Same day

At this time of day, the sun had just passed it's highest point in the sky, and the bayou became less active and less noisy. The birds were no longer present except for some herons, hawks, and ducks.

When the men finished eating, they prepared the airboat. Lyle had isolated to call Colonel Jackson to inform him the mission was completed and its objective, rescuing the suitcase, had been met. Unfortunately, the colonel was not answering his phone. Brett who found himself idle decided to call Fran who was flying back from Boston.

Annie and Jennie were scheduled to arrive in Atlanta sometime early this morning. On the hummock, Lyle was improving fast, so happy of the progress that he was talking to himself, "I am finally recovering and enjoying my time off." He no longer saw the need to leave for Russia, not until Patrick received more intel about the Chechen, mainly his location.

Lyle picked up the encrypted phone and reached the colonel on the seventh ring. "Sorry, I was in a meeting. Give me your ID code please."

Lyle gave his code, then said, "We have a suitcase for you. We need a pickup."

"Is either one of you hurt?" As always, Colonel Jackson cared about his men first. Lyle gave a ten-minute debrief but avoided any bad news concerning injuries. He informed the colonel that he and Brett would be in New Orleans within the hour. The colonel advised the agents to stay put until secure guarded transportation was ordered to pick up the nuke. Lyle remained on hold for several minutes.

"I will be sending one AH-64 Apache gunship from Huston for support, and Major Redford will be arriving on an MD 500N to take possession of the suitcase nuke. Are you close enough to the pickup site to activate your cell with the beacon."

"Negative. But we are leaving for New Orleans. It will take us about forty minutes; there, we will activate our tracking device so the choppers can track us. The meeting place will be on a deserted bank of the river, SW of New Orleans, where there will be plenty of room for the choppers to land."

"Roger that. Activate at forty minutes. Your country and I, thank you once again. Once the nuke is picked up, you boys take a week or more off. Earlier today, I got a call from Patrick; I will call you back and pass on the intel in later."

"Roger that." Lyle terminated the call. "Come on guys let's finish loading up and head for Orleans." Brett was curious about the cash the preacher had brought at the delivery site, right before the beginning of the battle. It is Remi who out of curiosity brought up the subject.

"What about the brief-case with the money?" Remi asked. Lyle answered jokingly, "What brief-case? The poor of New Orleans needs it far more than the gun builders and politicians of DC. We will use the money with sound judgment and fairness."

Ten minutes later, one could hear the loud whine of the old four-cylinder aircraft engine as the airboat worked their way through the brackish water of the swamp, on their way to New Orleans.

Forty-five minutes later the MD 500N held back as the Apache came in swept the area, and flew over the top of Remi's airboat.

As they moved along, Lyle could see Brett smiling; he seemed happy. Lyle was delighted for his old friend who had saved his life so many times. "You look happy Brett. I guess leaving the bayou makes you smile. Getting away from snakes, gators, bats, armadillos and more is a relief." This area takes time getting used to it.

"Not that, Fran will be arriving in the Big Easy tonight about ten p.m. and God Lyle, I miss her."

"I understand the feeling. You don't have any idea how pleased I am that you have found someone who seems to appreciate you. You will be staying here. As for me, I will be leaving to Atlanta as you already knew. I will miss you on this long ride. Would you mind if I take the Mercedes and you keep the SUV for a while?"

"Not at all. Fran loves walking; she couldn't care less about the car."

They passed the dock area, soon Remi began to slow down the swamp boat. They could hear the high pitch sound of the rotors slapping the air. Remi tied his boat along the shore. The Apache came in and swept the area twice more before the MD 500N landed. First, a man all decked out in black body armor got out of the chopper, and took a position. Then, in uniform, Major Redford got out and, approached Lyle and Brett. When close enough to hear over the sound of the chopper, Major Redford looked at Lyle and then gave him the prearranged code and a handshake. Lyle handed the major the nuke, and said, "Handle the egg carefully major, and a safe trip home."

"Thank you, captain. You men saved a lot of lives. We are heading to the Louis Armstrong Airport to meet up with a plane coming in from Washington DC; I understand Colonel Jackson will be on board. Let him have this egg." No one saluted as the major turned around and headed back to his chopper.

"Well men, let's head to Annettes before we start going our separate way."

CHAPTER 38

Same day

After the delivery of the suitcase, the men felt relief. They moored the boat and rode to Annette's in Remi's truck. Lyle knocked on the alleyway door; there was no response. His aunt was expecting their visit. Lyle said, "Just a minute, she might have a customer, I am going around through the front."

Minutes later, Lyle opened the door for his two partners. After the rapid ritual of the kisses on the cheek, Annette told her visitors to sit down while she got an aperitif and mixed nuts for them. This time the drinks were one of the famous cocktails served in New Orleans. This one was named after a New Orleans neighborhood, Bywater. The mixture combined aged rum, green Chartreuse, and Averna on shaved ice. To the amusement of Brett, the conversation conducted in English was occasionally intersected with a few Cajun French phrases. Two hours later, the party came to an end, and the three men left Annette.

Remi had to replenish his pantry in the city and head back to the hummock. He still had the shore of recovering the pontoon which had been left hidden under weeds on the way back from the massacre of the Babineaux clan. Lyle offered to help him bring it to the rental place. Remi said, "I will get it tomorrow and bring it back here to New Orleans. I can float it over to the shop where you rented it and get a cab to return to my boat."

Brett immediately offered his help, "Give me a call. Tomorrow I will still be in the area."

Since everything left to do was under control, Lyle could think about his departure for Atlanta. "I plan on taking the Mercedes and head for my mom's in Atlanta early tomorrow morning, maybe even this evening. It takes six and a half hours to drive there, at least."

"If I were you, I would not drive anywhere until I shower. With that heat, the mixture I put on your ribs will soon smell like cat piss mixed to skunk spray. It's the nature of the concoction; it deteriorates with time" Remi squeezed his nose as the others laughed.

Lyle could have spent his last night at Annette's, but he chose to join Brett who had reserved a room for himself in one of the hotels near Fran's apartment. It was after six p.m. the two friends walked into the hotel lobby."

Lyle dropped his cases in the room; he did not want to leave them in the car. New Orleans had a high rate of property crimes.

Lyle who was still very tired due to his round-the-clock pain, said, "I think I better leave in the morning. By the time I clean up and take care of the gear it's going to be late, and I am hurting. I respect Remi's unconventional healing methods, his treatments twice a day helped me. How about you? Are you better?"

„Sore also."

Brett looked at his watch. "Beer at the bar in an hour. I am going to lie down for half an hour, while you take your shower."

Lyle tried the bed which was comfortable. He got undressed and showered, not wanting to smell like cat piss and skunk spray. Remi's poultice was carefully wrapped several times in a newspaper that had been dropped on the nightstand, courtesy of the hotel. Once Lyle was under the hot water, he exposed his sore body to the spray, hoping the heat would hasten the healing and decrease the constant aching felt in the entire thorax. The dried the mush left on his skin by the poultice was dissolving and disappearing down the drain. Drying off and putting on his clothes was still difficult and awkward, but with extra effort and ample time, he made it and walked into the bar with Brett. For safety and privacy, they picked a table where the dim light created a relaxing ambiance.

Contrary to the hotels and restaurants on Bourbon Street, the background music in the lounge was soft and inviting. In this atmosphere, Brett and Lyle were unwinding. Two days ago, the big battle had been a test of nerve, and no matter how mentally tough the agents thought they were, their mind was still affected by the tremendous emotional strain.

After the waitress brought two mugs of beer, the two men went over the operation which they had already done briefly at Remi's. They knew they would be de-briefed eventually, and they wanted to report identical details. The operation talk ended, and the beers began to kick in. The men told a few jokes and discussed what they would do with their time off. Lyle finished his beer, sat it down on the small round black table and said, "I'm so tired and sore, I will leave early tomorrow. I think I am going to retire and try to find some comfort in my big queen size bed. What about you?"

Brett looked at his watch and said, "It's late, so I am going to stay right here, and in twenty-five minutes, at eleven, I will head for the airport. Fran is supposed to be in at 11:40 p.m., give or take. God, I will be glad to see her."

The two men said goodnight and Lyle headed back to the room.

CHAPTER 39

Next day

It was four a.m. when Lyle left the hotel room without a sound. At this time of day, the restaurant was closed, so he relied on the coffee machine in the empty reception hall. Later, he would stop on the road for breakfast. It was a long drive to Atlanta, some 480 miles; it would take him six to seven hours. Of the two main itineraries, he picked the northern one which was longer by thirty miles but had less traffic and no construction work. He knew interstate 59 N was desolate and did not go through any major city. Not like the other interstate which crossed Mobile, Biloxi, and Montgomery, cities that offered interesting sites to tourists. But Lyle was not touring; he was in a hurry to reach his destination.

In Hattiesburg, a medium size town, he stopped in a cafe, The Java Werks, where he ordered a copious meal, a combination American and continental breakfast, eggs, croissants pancakes, the works.

He was now back on the road. I-59 meant a boring ride. He stopped two more times before seeing this large road sign that read, Welcome. We are glad Georgia's on your mind. The message was adorned with the picture of a peach, of course.

To make his entry, Lyle had left his bag in the car; he needed both his arms to hug his mother. He walked up to the front door and knocked firmly. Monique opened the door. She reacted with excessive enthusiasm as if Lyle's visit was a total surprise. Monique was expecting him; he had called her twice while on the road. She wrapped her arms around him, squeezing Lyle's sore ribs with too much ardor. Monique stepped back when he gently grabbed her arms and said, "Not so hard." She was upset to discover Lyle had been injured once more, "You got wounded again. Oh my God! Please retire, find something else to do."

"I just slightly cracked a few ribs, very painful, but harmless. They will heal in no time." He changed the subject abruptly, "At exactly what time are Annie, her mother, and Jennie landing?"

"At five-thirty p.m. Come on in, don't stay standing in the doorway." They sat at the table and Monique served a light late lunch. Having Lyle's company provided ample pleasure to Monique. They always had a lot to discuss, and Lyle liked to help his mother with her house; she would always find little jobs and minor repairs for him to fix.

It was time to get ready to pick up the guests at the airport. While on the road, Monique raised the subject of marriage, a topic that irritated Lyle. He was in favor of marriage, but at this time he could not see it taking place, especially not the way his mother conceived things, the church ceremony, the reception, the honeymoon. They had tried that already, mostly to please their families, and he did not wish to repeat it with the unnecessary hoopla. He and Annie wanted a simple stop at the courthouse in the company of very few guests, followed by a well-planned gourmet meal served with champagne in a reputable restaurant.

Lyle drove Monique to the large Atlanta airport. Inside the terminal, they verified the arrival time of Air France flight 256 on the monitor. Thirty minutes later the three women came through the door. Annie, carrying two small suitcases was leading the way with Jennie following closely. Marguerite, Annie's mother, was not far behind. Jennie saw Lyle, she thought she recognized him, but was not sure. Hesitant, the little girl stopped in her tracks. When she saw her mother rushing in his direction, she immediately run to him and jumped up into his arms.

At the house, Monique knew the women were tired and would not expect an elaborate meal, so she had prepared something simple, a large green salad and shrimp skewers, and for dessert, a scrumptious peach cobbler. The next day, she would take all of them to a restaurant known for its excellent and authentic southern food.

At the table, the conversation revolved mostly around the things the guests would be seeing in the coming days. Lyle helped Marguerite carry her suitcase to the spare bedroom where she and Jennie would sleep in the twin beds. The little girl was impressed with the colorful matching patchwork quilts on the beds. Giggling, Monique said, "Without wedding vows, I guess we will put Annie in Lyle's room, and Lyle on the sofa." Annie laughed, Monique was pulling no punches to push the marriage scene again.

There would be no shower love scene in the hallway bathroom. Lyle entered his old room, the same room where he grew up. He was wrapped in his soft terry robe wrapped around his firm muscular body. After he locked the bedroom door, he turned toward the woman he loved. She was sitting up in bed with her beautiful long dark brown hair pulled to one side. He had desired her silently every day he was separated from her, "I missed you."

As Lyle walked toward the bed, Annie said, "I heard you moan with pain when I hugged you. Please, open that robe; I want to see how bad you were hurt again."

"It was nothing. I just banged up a rib or two."

Lyle had allowed the robe to drop below his stomach exposing the black and blue thoracic cage. Annie grimaced and put her hand over her mouth for a moment; then she took a deep breath. "You have been hurt. Turn around." He put his robe back on, but Annie insisted. She gasped for air with her mouth wide open as she could not believe how black and blue and swollen, Lyle's back was. All the bruises were turning yellowish on their edge. Slowly she pulled the sheet back as she stared at Lyle. "Get in here dear before I feel too sorry for you and find you too fragile to make love with you."

Lying on their sides as first, Lyle looked into the eyes of the woman he loved. With his finger, he played with the lobe of her ear and leaned over to kiss her lips lightly. Then their lips came together, then Lyle ran the tip of his tongue down and around her neck. As

Annie moaned, he began to bring her closer. She was excited and could not wait to feel him. Laughing, she said, "I think you are injured below the belt; there is a lot of swelling down there. It's going to take a couple of special lips to reduce it." She straddled her man with caution, scared to hurt him. Reaching down, she guided the tip of his swollen phallus inside her swollen and moist vulva and vagina. Lyle tried to participate, but the broken ribs on both his back and chest caused him to pull back down into the softness of the bed. Annie kissed her man on the lips softly. Lyle being incapacitated, she was in charge of the physical agility needed for the lovemaking. Soon the two lovers moaned in unison. Lyle was squealing with pleasure. Exhausted, Annie fell flat on her back following the massive orgasm.

Ten minutes later they both rolled on their sides and looked at each other. Lyle spoke, "I love you Annie Poo." They wrapped their arms around each other and began to caress one another. Annie's right leg went slowly up over Lyle's upper thigh, then she grasped the firm phallus which was still hard, and guided it with tenderness and love inside her once more. The lovemaking this time was not rushed, and once completed, the two slept the night away, never really knowing when they separated.

CHAPTER 40

Same day

Loui Armstrong Airport in New Orleans was bustling; people were coming and going, and all the travelers seemed to be in a hurry. Brett parked in the short-term lot, made sure everything was secure in the SUV and headed inside with a small bouquet of flowers in his hand. Nothing outlandish, and there were no silly balloons. Many times, Brett had watched Lyle be selective in picking just the right bouquet for his Annie. To welcome Fran, Brett was wearing khaki sports pants and a tight black polo shirt which enhanced his muscular physique.

Waiting for his girlfriend to come through the exit door, somewhat nervous, he moved from foot to foot. Fewer passengers were now passing him on their way to the baggage claim. It was way after twelve a.m., the flight had landed at 11:45 a.m. Emotional, Brett had forgotten he was meeting a flight attendant and not a passenger. Finally, the uniforms closed the parade of travelers. As Fran stepped through the door, she spotted Brett and was somewhat startled. "Brett, what a nice surprise to see you here! Thank you for coming." She waved at her two colleagues, "Gloria, Mary, come and meet my friend." The other two attendants walked toward the couple. Brett shook hand with the two women who were mentally and visually undressing him. They all shared a few mundane remarks and separated. By then the hall leading to the exit was deserted. Brett held Fran in his arms for a few seconds and handed his bouquet that was well received. Hand in hand, they walked off in a different direction. Fran was admiring the delicate bouquet and commented on the originality of its composition. Looking at him straight in the eyes, she said,

"Those flowers are beautiful; they were selected with good taste." Brett felt satisfaction in hearing the flattery. "We should have lunch, do you have time? I can't wait to relax. It was a long flight from Paris this time. I don't usually accept replacing anyone, but it was an emergency that popped up at the last minute. I did it, but I prefer my short commute, it is less demanding. If you don't mind, I would like to change before going out. Out of the blue, she stopped, leaned forward, wrapped her arms around Brett, and kissed him so sensually that instantly, he became aroused.

It was getting late, at the apartment, she changed into comfortable slacks and tee shirt, and they left.

CHAPTER 41

Atlanta Georgia

Same day

Monique was beaming with happiness. Her son was home with the woman he loved. It was the first time they were under her roof, and their company provided immense pleasure to Lyle's mother who was terribly family oriented. Monique was always ready to celebrate family events, big and small. She gave importance to all the steps in one's life, birth, promotions, weddings, birthdays. The day Lyle married Annie in Paris was the best day of Monique's life. Unfortunately, due to the assassin who interrupted the church ceremony, the couple's marriage never ended with what Monique considered sacred, a marriage license. Being from the old school, cohabitation without being married was not acceptable. She tried to reason. Maybe the couple was right; their love would not be more sincere and stronger with that document.

She smiled when she joined the company in her small and beautifully laid out backyard. Surrounded with tall pink hollyhocks, her guests were still in their robes, sipping a fresh pot of coffee Lyle had just prepared. Monique sat down and addressed Lyle, "Where are you taking our guests today, son?"

"I am taking everybody to the Atlanta Botanical garden. There are several exhibits offered right now. The one I know all of you will enjoy is the orchid display that will be open until the end of the month. At 2:00 there will be a carnival for the little ones with clowns, magicians, sing along, storytelling and acrobats to entertain children. I know Jennie would love this. If not too tired, we can stay for the concert on the grass. On the way back I would like to introduce Annie and Marguerite to the best barbecued ribs in Georgia. I am taking you to a restaurant called The Southern Gentleman, an institution in Atlanta." Annie was quick to come up with a silly remark, "I know where there are some black and blue ribs, right here at home.", Monique went along, "Oh yes, but those cannot be consumed." Monique added, "Lyle is like his father. He would not find strange to sacrifice himself for his country; I don't approve. My son is not an offering to any country. For now, let's enjoy our time together."

The Botanical Garden was magnificent with its lush exotic plants, fountains, sculptures, and the walk across a 600-foot suspension bridge.

It was late afternoon when the family of five sat down to enjoy southern food. Annie and Marguerite shared items they had never had before, besides the excellent and tender ribs, they sampled fried green tomatoes and collard greens. Full, they shared some pecan pie served with bourbon sauce. By ten p.m. that night, everyone was in bed and asleep, except Annie and Lyle who were talking about the future and the excursion they had gone on earlier.

The following morning, after breakfast on the patio, Monique brought out a second pot of coffee. Lyle had planned activities for the day, "If everyone is up to it, I thought we should go to the Centennial Olympic Park. It serves as Atlanta's legacy from the 1996 Olympic Games. Marguerite remembered well the 1996 athletic competitions, and especially the bomb that had exploded during the games. "We'll have lunch, then take Jennie Anne to the Kiddie Six Flags park. How does that sound?" Monique had another idea in mind for the afternoon, she said,

"Let's take both cars. While Annie, you, and Jennie are visiting Kiddie Six Flags, I will take Marguerite to downtown Atlanta to do some shopping. We will have lunch in the city.

Annie warned Lyle that Jennie had ridden only merry-go-rounds, nothing fast moving or dangerous. He would have to ride with her. Lyle reassured her, "We will ride the little train and go on the carousel. All the rides are designed for children and their parents, nothing dangerous. For lunch, we will go to Goodie Burger, winner of the 2012 Battle of the Burgers." Now addressing his mother Lyle offered to bring back dinner. "You will be tired, let me bring the dinner home."

Later that night Annette called her sister to invite the five of them for a visit to New Orleans. Sleeping arrangements were already in place; she had room for everybody. Going to New Orleans was very tempting, Annie and Marguerite could not miss that opportunity even though they were aware that the trip was a long one by car, some 900 kilometers, almost the length of France! They decided that they could leave the next day and take the tedious road to go because of the fluidity of the traffic and the absence of constructions. Coming back, they would take the southern route and make a few stops in cities along the way and play tourist in Biloxi, Mobile, and Montgomery.

The following morning with Lyle and Annie in the front, Marguerite, Monique, and little Jennie in the back, the Mercedes headed for New Orleans. But before hitting the road, Lyle called Brett and announced his coming visit at Annette's. His partner and Fran would join them the next day.

Chapter 42

New Orleans

Next day

During the drive back, time seemed to slow down for Lyle, and a calming peace settled over him. The conversation never stopped once the four adults, and Jennie was in the car. Before driving on into the city proper, Lyle filled the Mercedes with fuel, while everyone took a brief walk. Once they were into New Orleans at the beginning of Bourbon St. Lyle stopped to purchase a good bottle of wine for his Aunt, and the three woman almost talked themselves into an early grave about which flowers to buy. It was Annie who settled the problem when she told her mother to purchase the baguettes, Monique to get the flowers and she would choose an excellent aperitif.

Marguerite was overwhelmed at Bourbon St. as Lyle drove the length of it slowly. Then he turned and parked in the alleyway behind the Voodoo shop. Lyle told the ladies that they should go to the front of the store to enter. Annette saw her sister, almost cried but held her composure. Lyle introduced the others, and Annette was beaming. Once seated, Annette poured the aperitif that Annie had brought, and then the French conversation picked up in both speed and loudness. As they ate Jambalaya and Gumbo for dinner, it was washed down with bottles of wine; the talk was reaching a high peak. Lyle was tired from the drive and told Annie they needed to walk to the hotel, which was only a few blocks down the street. After saying goodbye, Annette had carried little Jennie sound asleep up to the bed placed in Marguerite's room.

Lyle took a deep breath of air on the street, placed his hand in Annie's, and pulled her close to him. "I love you, my dear. I hope my relatives did not overwhelm you."

"You are kidding; I love them. What a great time I am having, and my mother also."

As they approached the hotel, they spotted Brett and Fran walking toward them. A person would have thought it had been at least a year since the two men had seen each other, they wrapped their arms around each other, slapped each other on the back, then stepped back, "Fran this is the love of my life Anne-Marie, we call her Annie." The two ladies touched hands and spoke in French. Then Brett said, "Lyle and Annie, Fran and I have been enjoying ourselves. We walk almost everywhere, and I see and feel things that I have not seen before Lyle."

Annie smiled, looked right at Fran and Brett, and said, "That will happen when two people find each other and become like one. Would you like to go have a nightcap with Lyle and I here at the hotel?"

"I would love it; what do you think hon?" Fran was always involving Brett.

"Anything, if I am with you."

The next two hours were spent talking as the two woman got to know each other. Lyle, at last, broke the somewhat of an interview. "Annette is taking the ladies around town tomorrow, Brett I think you should go with Remi and me back to the site." Lyle was careful not to disclose anything.

"That will be fine. Fran has an early flight to DC, and she should be back about four p.m. Is that right hon?"

"Give or take a few minutes. Why don't we all go out to dinner tomorrow at that fish place where we first went to dinner Brett."

Brett was looking at Lyle, waiting for an answer. Lyle looked at Annie, then said, "Do you think the two mothers would agree on that dear?"

"I will drag them. Brett, you make arrangements for seven."

"Annie you are a beautiful, and warm person. No wonder Brett spoke so highly of you."

"Thank you." Lyle was overjoyed when he met you. He and Brett are like brothers, who have been to hell and back. After the couples entered Annettes house they talked for several hours. At last Lyle looked at Brett and his Uncle and said, "I need you two to go down town with me. We won't be to long."

Uncle Remi was ready to go anywhere. He was not accustomed to so much talking, or noise as he often said.

CHAPTER 43

New Orleans

Next day

Atlanta to New Orleans on I-59 is a long way, some 480 miles of desolate road. Jennie fell asleep right after leaving Atlanta. To kill time Annie started reading aloud surprising information about the beginnings of New Orleans. At one time Louisiana had the third largest Native American population in the eastern United States, the Tchimachas. Like in other parts of the country, the European encounter decimated the population by introducing diseases. Annie was discovering bits and pieces of facts that amazed her audience and helped cope with the ride. After a while, Monique took over the reading of the resources. She picked a section dealing with the arrival of the French-speaking Acadians, refugees who resettled in Louisiana after being expelled from their home, in Eastern Canada, by the bullish English. Those Acadians are the descendants of the Cajuns.

In Riverside, Alabama, one-hundred and ten miles from Atlanta, the travelers stopped for breakfast. The break was welcome and allowed everybody to stretch their legs and relax in the small but hospitable cafe. Lyle warned his passengers that the next stop would be 260 miles away, in Hattiesburg. He filled the Mercedes with fuel while everyone took a short walk.

Once they reached New Orleans, Annie asked to stop where she could buy some flowers for their host. They went to Winn-Dixie, a large grocery store. There, Lyle took time to select two bottles of wine, and Annie found a bouquet of fresh daisies, pink roses, and baby breath combination, a sophisticated flowers arrangement sold with a vase that was decorated with a gold colored ribbon. Monique wanted to bring something too. She bought a bottle of Martini red vermouth, a before dinner aperitif.

As a preview for things to come, Lyle took the travelers the length of Bourbon Street. Annie and Marguerite could not believe their eyes. Who would have thought that someday they would visit New Orleans?

Lyle turned and parked in the alleyway, behind the Voodoo shop and told the ladies to go to the front of the store to enter. Annette was all dressed up to meet her guests and had visited a hair salon. All made up; she looked ten years younger. The two sisters hugged. Lyle introduced his woman, her mother, and little Jennie. Annette was beaming. Once inside the house, she sat with them and poured the aperitif that Annie had brought. The conversation picked up in both speed and loudness. Marguerite and Annie appreciated Annette speaking French Cajun even though it was a bit odd and demanded concentration. Having studied and taught French in school, Monique spoke the language with total fluency. Hearing Annette's was a little strange, and on several occasions, she had to paraphrase to be understood. When speaking Cajun, her speech was slow and had a sing-song cadence that was pleasant and amusing. Annie enjoyed the language and asked Annette to teach her a few expressions to take home.

To introduce her guests to New Orleans cuisine, Annette had spent the previous day preparing Jambalaya and Gumbo for dinner. Both dishes were washed down with red wine; the ambiance was warm and free of tension. Three hours later, tired from the drive, Lyle decided to walk to the hotel he had reserved for himself and Annie. Annette's walls, he thought, were too thin. The women stayed up a little longer to pick up the dishes and clean up the kitchen with their host. Marguerite and Jennie would sleep in Annette's spare room which had been decorated with the little girl in mind. Annie left an hour later and walked to the hotel which was located five minutes away. Lyle was sleeping when she arrived at their lodging.

The following morning Lyle called Brett, gave him the name of his hotel, and invited him for a cup of coffee. In the restaurant, Lyle and Brett hugged as if they had not seen each other for a year. They wrapped their arms around each other, slapped each other on the back, then, finally stepped back. Then came the introductions, "Fran, this is the love of my life, Anne-Marie, we call her Annie." The two ladies shook hands. The next hour was spent talking, and the two women got to know each other. Lyle was already planning a side job with Remi, and some sightseeing for the ladies.

"Annette is taking guests around town this afternoon, do you think this would interest you, Fran?

"That would be fine except that I have to work today, and I will not be back before seven p.m."

Brett who had not seen Annie in a while was genuinely happy to talk to her. He was excited recounting his first encounter with Fran who was laughing listening to him.

Before separating, Brett and Lyle made plans to meet in two hours and drive to the dock where they would meet Remi.

Being together in New Orleans, the two friends decided a get-together had to be organized. This time they would invite and treat Annette to a feast at the Commander's Palace, a beautiful, elegant, and expensive restaurant that has been a New Orleans landmark since 1893. The cash found in the preacher's pouch would cover the bill.

CHAPTER 44

New Orleans

Same day,

Claiming to have some urgent affair to take care of south of the city, Lyle asked Remi to come long. With Brett already in the passenger seat and the old man in the back seat of the Mercedes, Lyle drove in the direction of a boat dealer who had sold him an airboat that his uncle deserved to own.

They had driven toward the bay for almost thirty minutes when Remi demanded an explanation; he said, "Why are we going to the bay, I thought you said we were going to your aunt's."

"Yes, we are, but first I have to pick up something in the Plaquemines parish. Won't take long." Brett was smiling; he knew what was going on. As Lyle pulled into the boatyard, Remi, enraptured by the boats on display at the Bayou Boat Shop, shouted, "Look at all those boats, son. I guess you are going to rent one to take me home because it is going to take a while to fix mine."

"You are going to take yourself home. I am not going back in your swamp for a while. I have a little surprise on layaway for you." Suddenly Remi looked worried, he did not understand Lyle's half hidden message. After the salesman came out, said hello, and shook their hands, he led the trio to the boat that Lyle had chosen and for which he had paid a deposit. Remi, still unsure this new boat was going to be his, gasped for air, put his right hand on his chest, then said, "It's made of aluminum, long, narrow and sleek— with a carbon-fiber propeller. Lyle, I can't, I can't take this."

"You paid for it with the work you have done." Ralph, the dealer, asked Remi to take the new boat for a spin while Lyle took care of the paperwork in the office.

Brett and Remi were on the boat. Remi took a few minutes to admire the craft and become familiar with the instrument panel. He turned the key and raved the engine up. As he sped from the dock, he soon turned left creating a wake, passed where Lyle and the salesman were standing, then pulled out into the bay. While the two men were testing the airboat, Lyle paid the balance with cash he was carrying in his backpack. When Remi came back, he was shaking his head, still not realizing this beautiful new boat was his. After all the ownership documents were completed and signed, the salesman handed a folder to the new owner.

"I don't know what to say, son. There is no Babineaux on land or in hell who could catch this baby; that engine roars like a tiger. With that canopy, I will no longer get sunburned. Thank you."

"You take your boat to the dock. We will meet you at Annette's. I called her, and she has coffee and two sorts of beignets ready for us. You will get to meet Annie, her mother, and my little girl."

Remi started up the engine, waved his dirty old hat, and pushed the throttle forward; his boat moved out into the bay with a large wake behind it. Remi still had to tie his old craft behind the new one, get his truck, and meet Lyle's family before returning to his hummock in his spanking new airboat.

He had never been so proud and so happy as he worked his way toward the dock.

CHAPTER 45

New Orleans

Following day

The next morning, at the hotel, the two lovers were enjoying each other. The lovemaking was exquisite. Annie wanted to feel her man, touch him, hold him. She seldom got a chance to do that; he was in the habit of vanishing without leaving any trace. She never knew when he might return or not return. He was going to be embarking on a black ops mission again, and soon. Annie could always detect the tension in Lyle, just before he would leave.

Once Brett and Lyle left, Annie walked to Annette's to join Jennie who was being pampered by her great aunt. Annie caught the two of them preparing bread pudding. The little girl had been wrapped in a dish towel to protect her clothes. To gain a foot in height, she was standing on a small platform. Annette was showing her how to measure the ingredients; she would demonstrate and return each one to its container. Jennie would repeat the procedure, and dig into the flour with the measuring cup. Annie was watching how applied, absorbed, and precise the little girl was, and how Annette was not short of words of approval.

Lyle had called Remi early that morning. He wanted the three of them to return to the site of the recent battle that had ended with the rescue of the radioactive material. Lyle and Brett were at the dock waiting to hear the sound of Remi's old airboat. Each man had brought his case, and an extra one containing dry ice. They had no idea what they would encounter so Remi, the proud owner of a brand new vessel, took no chance with his new boat. He pulled alongside the dock and left the engine running waiting for Lyle and Brett to come aboard. Remi pushed the throttle forward and said, "Since we are going back to the killing grounds, we will need to take some water and sandwiches from my place."

Back at the hummock, Brett fed the chickens, prepared the crossbow, the TNT, the duct tape, and loaded the jeep cans of gas. Remi gave a few more orders, " Make sure you have your guns loaded and ready. Just because I got the pontoon boat out without incident, does not mean we're not going to be facing a firefight. Lyle, maybe you should attach the silent running engine. I will get the water and the rest of the goodies." Remi was the man in charge when engaged on the water of the bayou. A wise man, he always was direct and precise when giving orders, using short phrases clearly stated in an authoritative tone of voice.

Nothing more was said as the three men prepared to go back into Babineaux country, a dangerous territory where one slip up could make anyone gator food. Remi untied his boat, started the engine and once more the trio moved out across the murky water. An hour later, Remi said, "Turn on your tracking device, son. If it still works, that will save us some time."

"It's been over three days. We're just about at the limit of the batteries. Let's see." Brett opened the tracking device box, flipped a switch. "Nothing yet." Then ten minutes later he spoke louder than normal. "I got a red dot Remi; you're right on course."

An hour later the boat pulled into the small cove where they had hidden the airboat once before. Now on foot, they moved through the woods with Remi in the lead. Even with the two-dimensional image resulting from the green hue of the night vision goggles, walking through the dense brush and trees was difficult. Although they felt safe, they chose to keep separated a short distance as they worked their way toward the campsite where the carnage had taken place. Speaking into his mouthpiece, Remi asked Brett, "What are you looking for?"

"Wallets with names, guns, any IDs." Lyle addressed his partner "Brett, you know the procedure, you take the water line, I will move over to the west where some of the scumbags disappeared the other night. Uncle Remi, you will have to stand guard with your 30-30, and take out anyone out who shows up."

Lyle and Brett turned over stones, kicked the dirt, looked in the water along the bank, and even dug in the ashes. Forty-five minutes later, they reunited with Remi. Lyle was the first to speak. "I found a wallet, one military seal knife, and I could have picked up a few teeth from different areas. What did you stumble on, Brett?"

"Pretty much the same. I got a partially burned belt with a seal knife still attached to it. The way the guards responded to the attack, I am sure they were former military. I found an ID and some money in a blackened leather wallet. I guess the colonel wants to track down who those traitors are." Then Brett held up a couple of fingers, two different hands, and a foot. "We have to get these on ice, somebody might be able to get prints, and for sure DNA."

"Great going. The colonel wants the men responsible for selling this radioactive material to be stopped, and this evidence will help track the nuke back to its source. All we are waiting for now is a word from Patrick, then my friend, we are going on a paid vacation to Chechnya."

On the return trip down one of the canals in the bayou, the trio came under heavy fire from land, and sparks flew from the hull, the engine, and the propeller. Brett, within seconds, raised his AR15 and opened up with return fire which was followed by distant screams. The roaring sound of the engine of the attack boats became louder as they got closer. More gunfire hit the stream, spraying the men continually. Lyle took control of the craft so Remi could start attaching the TNT to his crossbow.

As they turned the corner from the narrow channel into a more significant canal, two flat bottoms boats came straight toward them. There were two men with AK 47"s firing on full automatic in the front of each craft.

At one time, a piece of their propeller broke off, and their boat was taking hit after hit. Lyle jerked sideways as a bullet skimmed along his body armor. Then like a ghost, Remi raised up with his crossbow and fired. As the arrow moved along its trajectory toward the oncoming enemy boats, it left a slight trail of whitish smoke from the fuse attached to the dynamite. Then, within seconds, there was a loud explosion, which overturned the Babineaux boat in front of them and caused the other one to turn sideways.

As the other boat leaned to turn, both Lyle and Brett fired at it, round after round. They saw the pilot fall over the side. The craft started spinning in a circle as no one was guiding it. The two remaining men attempted to get ahold of the steering handle, but never did, Lyle and Brett tore them apart with bullets. Remi cut the speed of the engine as the aircraft engine was smoking, it had taken a hit, and someone needed to bail water from the holes made by the enemy bullets. As Brett and Lyle were scooping the water out, Remi was looking for survivors. Two men were spotted briskly swimming away; he cut them down with his 30-30. Finally, the silence of the bayou was back, Remi turned his boat around and headed for his hummock.

Once back on land the three men examined Remi's old craft. The old man shook his head; his dependable boat had significantly been damaged. He walked over to his little shed adjacent to the house and brought out a bucket with a brush in it. While Remi was using his homemade tar to patch the holes, Lyle picked up his backpacks and walked out behind the trees where the preacher's cash rescued following the night of fighting had been hidden. Once in the airboat, Lyle kept an eye on his pack. Remi wiped his hands, sat down the rag and said, "Well, that should keep my old boat from sinking until I get you boys to the city and back, I think it's on its way out. One could detect a little mournfulness in the face and voice of the old man.

The three men sat quietly in the boat as Remi steered them toward the city. As they moved along slowly, they were afraid the old aircraft engine would catch fire or blow up. The prop was out of balance, whining and slapping the air, the rickety old boat was falling apart. The coughing and gagging of the engine did not give any confidence to the men about making it. Usually, it took Remi about forty-five minutes to an hour to get to the dock. This trip took an hour and a half. Remi's old faithful boat pulled up to shore, it gave a loud bang and quit running.

Once at the dock, Lyle entered the address of the FBI in his GPS. He took all the evidence gathered at the battle site to the New Orleans field office of the FBI. While Lyle was taking care of important business, Brett and Remi went across the street to have a beer. "I won't be long; I expect some questions if I go in looking like I do." Lyle pulled off his body armor, shook off some dust from his trousers, then tucked in his shirt. He walked into the FBI office with the case containing the severed body parts preserved on dry ice and a pack full of potential evidence. Immediately the uniformed guard posted at the entrance put his hand on his gun and approached Lyle.

"This might look funny sir, but to explain my presence, I am going to give you my ID and give you a phone number to call. Once your agent in charge calls that number, I am sure you will relax. The guard took the number to the clerk at the desk. Lyle gave him the same directions, "Call the number at the white house, please. What I am bringing is of national security."

The agent got up and took the phone number to another agent higher up the pecking order. Five minutes later two agents came back and took the case and the pack. There were no hands on guns now, it was yes sir, no sir, can I get you anything? Lyle smiled, then said, "I am sure the man on the phone told you to fly this to Washington ASAP. Thank you for serving your country." Lyle walked out with a big grin on his face and crossed the street to join uncle Remi and Brett.

Chapter 46

New Orleans

Same day

Brett and uncle Remi were watching for Lyle to come out of the brick building. Lyle joined his partners, ordered a beer and shared his encounter with the guards, how each man had to shine the others shoes to get one of God's assistants to get one to collect the physical evidence.

After a few laughs, Remi said, "It is still early, why don't you boys take a ride back to the hummock. Today I am going to retire my old boat as soon as I get home. We will come back to the city with the new one, but first, we'll take a detour to go gator hunting. You won't get sunburned with the handy canopy, and you will have another chance to feed my gator pet, Two Feet."

Brett categorically answered, "I am not going near that pet of yours."

To settle things, Lyle asked the old man to go back to his home alone. "If you decide to come back, we will be at Annette's. Remember you will get a chance to meet Annie, her mother, and Jennie."

"You forgot Fran, Lyle; she will be in later. I will pick her around seven."

They drove back to the dock with Remi. The old airboat, although on its final voyage, surprised Remi, it started arrogantly without any problem. Talking about his craft, he mumbled, "That boat is a dependable friend I can count on." He waved his dirty, faded hat, pushed the throttle forward, and soon disappeared out into the bay. Minutes later, they were back in the car and on the way to Annette's. During the short drive, somewhat puzzled, Brett asked Lyle what the proper way to approach the purchase of an engagement ring, "Do I pick out the ring, or do I go with the lady and let her choose what she wants?"

Lyle felt like laughing but did not. He had never bought a ring for a fiancee before. He had given Annie the money. She had sped to a jewelry store to get her ring. On cloud nine and excited, she had been pulled over by a gendarme for speeding. After shaking his head from side to side for a few seconds, he said, "Let me ask Annie when we get there. Lyle knew his partner was in love with Fran, but he never expected this development so soon. He had not realized Brett was so serious about the relationship. "I see things are moving, I know she is a beautiful lady, kind to you, and she thinks the world of you, which is essential, but I am surprised and at the same time happy for you." Lyle kept his left hand on the steering wheel and reached over with his right hand to shake the hand of the man he considered a brother. "I wish you a happy life with Fran." Brett appreciated Lyle's approval; he knew he was wise and sincere.

"You think you will try tying the knot again after almost being assassinated in Paris during the first attempt?"

"Yes, someday we will."

"We are here. Take the Mercedes to go pick up your bride."

Chapter 47

New Orleans

Late afternoon

After being out in the hot, humid air all day which encompassed most of Louisiana that day, the three men were relieved to open the door at the Voodoo shop and step into the air-conditioned house. After several aperitifs consumed, the conversation became louder and louder as each bottle of wine was consumed. Remi never said anything about his new boat as he Lyle paid for it from either the money taken from the night before, or one of his and Brett's other black op assignments. But he was the happiest he had ever been in a long time. Marguerite was enjoying her self; she had been stuck in a small town ever since her husband retired, and hardly ever visited anyone. Monique was happy and overwhelmed with joy to visit her sister and have her son, the woman he loved and a potential granddaughter visiting. And now she had a real friend in Marg as Lyle called his future mother in law.

It was Fran who announced she had to go first. She had to be at the Delta desk at four a.m., as her flight left at five a.m. Brett and Fran hugged and said goodbye and went. Jennie Anne had fallen asleep several hours ago, and Lyle had carried her upstairs to her bed. Uncle Remi said he needed to be going as he had to come back to the Big Easy again the next day. "You're not going to try and go back to that hummock of yours in the dark, are you?" Annette said with concern.

Remi looked at Annette and felt like saying something stupid back, but said, "I hooked up some lights on it. Won't be any problem. I will see you early in the morning." What Remi wanted to do was transport what things he wanted to keep off the old boat, tow it out a ways and sink it. He had loved his old airboat, and it had served him and others well.

While Annie and Lyle walked down Bourbon Street toward their hotel, Lyle turned to Annie and said, "I have a critical question."

"Oh my god Lyle, you want to know where we are going to settle down at." Then Annie beamed and waited.

"I wish it was that simple. Brett has a problem. He wants to get an engagement ring for Fran. Does he buy it, or hold the money out like I did, and Fran goes to buy it." Annie did not hesitate; she started laughing immediately.

"It's nice when a man will ask for a woman's hand and give her a ring. I know our situation was different. How about we both go with Brett tomorrow while Fran is gone. I know her well enough to know she would not want something godly. She loved the one you should have picked out." Then she laughed about the ring again.

"Ouch, you got me, but I had no choice. Besides the ring you picked was perfect. Your plan sounds good. I will stay home though. You take Brett alone like he is buying for you. He will feel more comfortable."

"I am happy for Brett. Fran and I talked a lot——she is a kind, considerate and a pleasant person. They will make a perfect pair. I never thought anyone as beautiful as she would love the outdoors and would want to walk so much. Yes, yes I am for their marriage."

After Lyle and Annie had showered, Annie was all smiles. Just the thought of marriage had changed her composure. She kissed Lyle softly on the lips, then ran her fingers along his firm chest, down to his stomach and would make a circle around the inside of his thighs. Then she leaned down and ran her tongue around Lyle's nipples; she could feel his engorged instrument against her. Then Lyle pushed Annie on her back, kissed her neck, and softly sucked on her nipples until they became hard. He slowly brought the tip of his tongue down across her belly and ran his tongue around her bush, making sure to touch her lips between her thighs, As Annie began to moan, Lyle new it was time to become one, or he was going to explode.

After they made love, they, fell into a deep sleep with their arms wrapped around each other.

Chapter 48

New Orleans

The next morning

There was soft music playing in the apartment where Brett and Fran were childish in the shower. Both were covered with soap bubbles from a gel she was squeezing on his shoulders. The foamy suds were running down the back of their bodies. The slimy sensation from the soap was deliciously slippery when their bodies connected, giving both lovers a bit of a thrill. It was very early in the morning, and Fran was getting ready for work. In the warm spray, Brett teased Fran, kissing her neck, ears, and anywhere on her bare skin. With a keen eye, he was staring at her attractive and well-proportioned figure, and making compliments on her looks; she enjoyed his flattering remarks.

Making sure his fingers performed magic on the different parts of her body; soon, she could no longer wait. She turned around and pushed herself against his firm erection. Motionless now, they let the warm water run over their skin. They were sexually aroused. The two became so excited, that, for an instant, they became unconscious in unison, unaware of their surroundings. After they caught their breath, Fran started giggling as she was returning to being rational, and finally decided to get ready for work. As they walked toward the bedroom, the towels fell to the floor, their lips met, their breath accelerated, they were hot again. Without a single word, they ended up between the white sheets.

Fran laid on top of Brett's body smiling, worn out, at peace. Running late, she put on her uniform but took time to drink a cup of coffee and eat the waffles Brett had prepared for her while she was getting ready. She appreciated all the simple little things he did for her without asking, serving her a glass of chilled orange juice, folding a napkin by her plate, warming the maple syrup. All those ordinary details made life pleasant. She would always thank him for all the attention no one else had ever given to her, except for her mother. He had picked up these thoughtful habits while living close to Lyle. Lyle had been raised by a warm and dedicated mother who had transmitted to her son some civilized manners as she called the little favors.

After dropping Fran off at the airport, Brett returned and laid down on the sofa to watch the news. The apartment was quiet; he fell asleep. When Brett woke up, almost four hours had gone by. He prepared a fresh pot of coffee and called Lyle to find out if he had any jobs for him. Lyle informed his partner that Annie would be stopping by his hotel in a few minutes to take him to look at engagement rings. Lyle also suggested having the preacher pay for the diamond. Lyle was laughing as he offered the deal. "I leave it up to you, please have no scruples, it is our money. Personally, I would not hesitate, we deserve it. And remember, with this mode of payment, the size and the quality of the stone are no object." Brett needed time to think about it.

Less than ten minutes later, Annie knocked on the door. Once in the living room, Brett offered her some fresh coffee, and they discussed the engagement. She suggested celebrating the event. "One must always mark the happy occasions." Brett grabbed his jacket and they left. At the hotel reception, the concierge wrote down the name and the approximative address of two reputable jewelry stores located not too far away.

At the first jewelry store, both Annie and Brett became overwhelmed by the choice of rings to chose from. There were yards and yards of cases full of beautiful rings. It was Annie who helped limit the selection by asking to see the solitaires. She had a preference for this kind of setting which isolated the diamond and allowed it to be emphasized. They selected two rings and asked to see another type of mounting, something with gems surrounded with smaller diamonds. They started with the halo engagement rings. The jeweler explained the term "halo," which he said referred to a gemstone completely encircled by smaller accent diamonds. Annie was now trying rings to give Brett a better idea of the true results once on one's finger. She was gesturing her hand under the light to give more brilliance to the stone. Brett kept coming back to Waverly, a halo style band mounted on 18K white gold with a stone of half a carat. She left him alone for a few minutes as she did not want to influence him with this critical decision. The choice having been made, Annie admired the jewel with Brett. "I would be on cloud nine if a gentleman gave me this ring. Fran will love it."

The engagement ring was strategically placed in a box lined and covered with burgundy velvet. The jeweler deposited the gift in an elegant tiny little bag decorated in black and gold and closed with a gold string.

Brett felt relieved, he thanked Annie for her help, and she assured him she had enjoyed being there. Happy with his purchase, he invited her for lunch on Bourbon street. He said, "You advised me to celebrate happy events, let's start now. I am taking you to Cafe du Monde, a nice little bistro." There, while enjoying their meal, they talked about Fran, life, and marriage. Before leaving, Annie stressed that any woman loved it when a man presented her with an engagement ring, especially one as beautiful as the one he had selected.

After lunch, they separated, and Annie returned to her hotel where Lyle had been busy doing paperwork and making phone calls. He was happy the shopping had been successful.

Chapter 49

New Orleans

Next day, late

The full Strawberry moon, also known as hot moon and Oak moon, was glowing bright that evening, and the humidity was relatively low for New Orleans. A couple walked hand in hand toward the Galatoire restaurant, where they had eaten on their first date and had returned many times. As they entered the building, Brett and Fran were met by the maitre d' who took them to a small table in the back of the room where it was less crowded and more intimate. Brett quietly noticed that some of the men seated across from their big mamas were staring at Fran; she was wearing a Calvin Klein ensemble with spaghetti straps supporting a cleverly designed lace bodice. Her skirt was calf-length and slit on one side. Brett was proud of her; she could be sexy without trying. He was the happiest he had ever been in his life. After a few minutes discussing their food order, the waiter walked away. Fran and Brett talked and laughed as they sipped a glass of Zinfandel and shared an appetizer, fried eggplant on a stick, while awaiting their food.

As usual at Galatoire the dinner was delicious, crawfish served with creamed spinach sprinkled with buttered pecans. And for dessert, both ordered caramel cup custard. They took their time enjoying their meal. Brett told Fran that Lyle and himself would be leaving on another mission for at least a week, maybe longer. Fran's face saddened, her hand slowly reached across the small table and grabbed his hand as to retain him from going. "Think about me when you are gone, don't get hurt. To reassure him, she added, "I understand the importance of your work."

Half an hour later, as signaled by Brett, the waiter brought two champagne flutes and poured the wine from a bottle that had been sitting in a bucket of ice. "Will there be anything else?" the waiter asked. There was a smiling "no" from Brett, the waiter turned his back and walked away, also with a smile on his face; he could tell love when he saw it. Brett reached into his pocket and brought out a small burgundy velvet box. He opened the box slowly, all the time looking into Fran's beautiful green eyes, and said, "Fran, I love you. Will you marry me?"

There was a pause due to surprise, and maybe shock. Fran knew that someday he would propose, but she had no idea this development would take place so soon. Glistening tears formed on her cheeks as she said, "Yes, yes, yes. I love you, Brett." Then Fran put her left hand on top of Brett's left hand. He slipped the engagement ring on slowly, but nervously on Fran's finger. Size six ring, Annie's size, was correct for Fran.

"Brett, it's beautiful."

Fran admired her ring while moving her hand so the diamond would shine in the light. She got up, walked around the table, sat down on Brett's lap and kissed him, for what seemed like forever. Once she came up for air, she placed her two hands, one on each side of Brett's cheeks, looked into his eyes, and said, "I love you. Let's go walking as soon as we finish our champagne."

The couple kissed briefly on and off as they walked down Bourbon Street. After an hour, Fran led Brett back to her apartment.

At bedtime, after so much excitement, Fran became silly, "Brett, would you take the future Mrs.Francine Thompson to our bed please."

Brett picked up Fran in one swift movement, carried her to the bedroom, and as he laid her between the white sheets, his lips were on hers.

CHAPTER 50

New Orleans to Cancun

Fran and Brett were still wrapped arm and arm around each other when the alarm clock rang the following morning. After shutting off the clock alarm, Fran, still naked, made sure the water was spraying warm in the shower, while Brett made coffee. Thirty minutes later while walking to Brett's car, the last night of the Strawberry moon was still prevalent in the night sky, even though clouds were moving in over New Orleans. Arriving at the Louis Armstrong airport a few minutes before three, Brett took Fran's hand and walked with her to the Delta desk. They gave each other a long hug and sensuous kiss. Fran said, "I love you, Mr. Brett. Come back to me soon, uninjured." There were tears of joy, and some sadness as they separated from the long sensuous hug.

"I love you also Frannie. I have so much to live for now. I will call when I can, if possible as I know your schedule. Please don't try to call; we will have our phones turned off, because if a phone should go off and give our presence away; we might get injured or killed." As Brett was driving back to the Hotel, Lyle and Annie were hugging, each other tightly in bed. They had just made love, and both knew it might be the last time; no one ever knew during a black operation.

Lyle got out of bed, and while he put on his clothes, he was running the op's information through his head. Annie had made coffee and helped her man pack what few clothes he would take in a pack. She looked at the two particular cases sitting on the bed but never asked what was in them; Annie knew it was part of the job, a job she hoped would soon be over. When everything was ready, Lyle said, "If you decide to stay or go home early, have my mom drive you back to Atlanta in the Mercedes, if you want. One of us will pick the car up. I will call as soon as I can."

"I think we will stay two more days, your mother misses her sister, I can tell." Then Lyle's phone rang.

"What's happening?" Lyle said.

"I'm ready. Which car are we taking to the airport?"

"Your SUV. I will be at your door in a minute."

Lyle kissed Annie goodbye one last time, met Brett and within the hour were at the airport. After turning the car in, they headed for the Spirit Airways counter, as their flight left for Cancun at 08:40 a.m. to Ft. Lauderdale, leaving there at 11:16 a.m. for Cancun and arriving in Cancun at 1331 p.m.

During the flight, Brett caught severely needed sleep, while Lyle's head was swimming with ideas, permutations, and possible scenarios that Brett and himself would be faced with. About halfway through the flight he was finally able to snooze. Before landing, Lyle said, "I keep forgetting to ask you about a cut or scratch near your right ear late afternoon the day you went to the port authority. Do you remember what happened?"

"Sorry, I should have told you. My mind has been elsewhere boss. Won't happen again. Just before I left the office, Garcia made a phone call. After I left his office and just down the street, someone took a shot at me. When I hugged the brick corner for cover, he fired off two more shots causing a piece of the brick to cut me. The shooter took off running down between the cargo containers, and I was unable to fire back."

"I figured the guy was dirty. We will need to visit Mr. Garcia when we get back. With a little persuasion, I am sure we can get some information. Maybe he should have a heart attack, or at least we feed the fish with him."

"Sounds perfect for me. Are we going to stay near the airport again at the Courtyard Marriott?"

"Already booked, open-ended date. Two SUV's are on hold also. I contacted Octo yesterday. I still need to call our CIA contact in Cancun or Merida as soon as we get settled. We need to get into action as soon as we land. The agent should have the special extra gear I requested."

The two men had coffee, and shortly afterward the announcement for landing came.

The aircraft turned out over the blue waters of the Carib, then began losing altitude as it lined up for its approach to land. Within minutes it bounced three times before it's landing wheels settled down and rolled smoothly along the tarmac in Cancun. The two men passed through customs without a second look using their diplomatic passports. They picked up two SUV's, one blue, and one black and headed for the Marriott.

After the two men settled in their room with two beds, Lyle placed a call to the CIA office in Merida. Within minutes John Alston was on the line and said he would bring their package to their room that night. "What information do you have about a possible cargo container being dropped off a Russian ship in the waters off Cancun? Lyle said."

"I have been up to Cancun and with help found out all I could get. We are confident that MS-13 picked up the container and distributed the goods."

"What can you tell me briefly about that group?"

"MS-13 is an international criminal gang that originated in Los Angeles, California, in the 1980s. The group later spread to many parts of the continental United States. We have confirmed over the past year that they are now working with a Drug Cartel called 'The Templars.' Are you aware of them?"

"A lot more than you can imagine. Do you know where they might have unloaded the goods?"

"The police found what they think was the container outside of the city of Ignacio Zaragoza. Take highway 180 from Cancun, turn right on 180D to the town. There was nothing left in the cargo container if you can believe the Police force. Rumors are that the goods are headed north to be given to Coyote's and others to move the goods into the Los Angeles area. Give me a phone number so I can keep in contact and provide what assistance we can."

Lyle gave him a phone number of one of his burner phones, and also one of Brett's. Then he gave John their room number. After a few more questions they closed the conversation. "Time for some chow and beers my old friend. Our goodies are on the way here from Merida. It looks like we are heading inland and up toward the border. We are going up against MS-13 and some of the Templar Cartel again. I hope we have not bought off more then we can chew."

Brett thought for a moment and responded. "Do you think there was another suitcase nuke in with the armory?"

"I hope not. I will ask the local Police Chief if he has a radiation monitor we can borrow. All I have with me is a dosimeter." The time passed slowly at first until the first two beers kicked in. Two hours plus later a man from Merida came into the Marriott and soon approached them where they were still drinking and just finishing eating."

"Are you Mr. Lyle Mercer sir?"

"Yes I am, may I help you?"

"I'm John Alston, your contact, and I have a box of supplies from Washington in my vehicle outside for you sir. Do you want me to bring the box to your room?"

Lyle introduced Brett, then told John thanks, but he and Brett would go with him and get the goods. Outside away from other ears, the three men talked for almost thirty minutes about the Templars and MS-13. After John had left, and later in the room, they made sure they had tracking devices, two sniper rifles, rapid-fire guns, and the bricks of Semtex, flash-bangs, and timers Lyle requested. After finishing the inventory, they split the supplies up as planned and would take them to their vehicles in the morning. Then Lyle and Brett checked their night vision oculars, earbuds, and other voice contact devices. As Brett looked into the bottom of the box, he saw two new armor vests and a note. Brett read the brief handwritten letter out loud. "Major Mercer and Sargent Major Thompson; if you could, please bring the body armor home with no scratches, cuts or bullet holes. Good Luck and God Bless. Colonel Jackson."

"I think the Colonel is overworked and there is too much on his mind. Twice now he has referred to me as Major. I know he worked for my father, a Major when he was a Captain. Have you noted any changes in his character Brett?"

"None. But Colonel Jackson referred to me as a Sargent Major. We need to meet with him if we get back. "Satisfied at last the men showered and hit the sack.

CHAPTER 51

Cancun To Ignacio Zaragoza

Brett and Lyle decided not to contact the Cancun Police Chief to borrow a radiation detector. During the black operation, "The Yucatan Connection," they had discovered how crooked the police department of the city was. After breakfast, they took the road in their two vehicles. It was six a.m., and they were going to Ignacio Zaragosa. As instructed, an hour later they turned right on the 180D and were in Ignacio Zaragoza, a village in the State of Quinta Roo, not to be confused with the town of Ignacio Zaragoza in the state of Chihuahua, close to the border with the United States, some 3000 km away.

Brett's command of Spanish was much better than Lyle's; he would be the one inquiring in the cafes and bars about a large box or a small cargo container that had been discarded somewhere in the area. Two hours later Lyle met up with Brett. "No one was aware of this box. Somehow I am sure they know something but are afraid to speak. Let's get off the main drag and see if we can find young kids who may know where that thing is. We can always resort to bribes. A one hundred dollar bill should help some."

Both men made sure their shoulder holster guns where chambered with noise reducer screwed on, and with the safety off. They were in drug cartel country where protecting the illegal business occasionally led to stabbing or shooting innocent people. An hour later, while walking down to the end of the Avenida de la Reina, just outside of town, they spotted the container on its side, among tall dry weed.

Behind it was an old run down house where chickens, goats, and two dogs were running loose, one of them had tits hanging to the ground. Within seconds both dogs ran back behind the shabby building.

Brett told Lyle to watch as he calmly walked up to the poorly kept building. As he moved forward, an old man with gray hair and dark wrinkled skin walked out on the porch with a cigarette in his mouth. With a smile, Brett slowly approached the man. All Lyle could see from a distance was the individual shaking his head "No." An instant later, a young teenager came from around the side of the house and stood close to the old man as to protect him. Suspicious, the boy asked Brett what the purpose of his visit was. Probably out of fear, no one seemed to be willing to answer Brett's questions concerning the cargo container that had been dumped on the property. As speculated, when Brett offered two one hundred dollar bills to the older gentleman, more came out of the kid's mouth. Lyle who was waiting on the side of the road could hear most of the conversation over his earbuds. His limited Spanish did allow him to pick up a few words, la linea, California, el Norte, all keywords meaning border, California, north. Lyle saw Brett handing a third bill, and heard him thanking his witnesses for their help. The agent turned around and headed back to where Lyle was waiting.

As Lyle and Brett were walking back to the container, Brett relayed what the young boy and his grandpa had no idea who had discarded the box but the teenager who had watched the activity remembered clearly that the next day he saw a white van stop where the box laid, soon followed by a second identical van. He observed four men unloading the contents of the big box and putting the goods into the vans. The strange activity terrified the boy, he kept quiet and out of sight. Two men, well armed with assault weapons were patrolling. The kid counted six men in all, and said that the shortest man with the longest hair was called Escobar. He heard one of the men yelling that the Templars needed to get the load to the MS-13 gang in Heroica Nogales since the tunnel was ready."

Lyle remained in deep thoughts for several minutes, before he answered. "Let me get my dosimeter; not the best to measure radiation, but it's better than nothing, and let's figure the fastest way to catch up with that bunch. Did the kid or the old man say when they left?"

"They have about a twenty-four-hour head start on us."

Brett returned to his SUV and consulted his iPod to get an idea of the distance they would have to cover to reach the destination of the goods. He said, "Those two places the smugglers mentioned, Nogales and the tunnel, are about 3,700 klicks or 44 hours driving time from here. No way we can catch up with them by road in time." Before leaving the site, Lyle entered the box that had been left wide open and tested it for the presence of radiation.

"My dosimeter indicates there is either a suitcase nuke in that load or radioactive by-products to make a dirty bomb. Let's head for the airport fast. We'll turn the cars in and charter a plane to Nogales, Mexico. We should be able to land just ahead of them. So close to the border with the US, it will be easier to question people, and we should be able to get some support getting our hands on the smugglers once they reach Nogales. I don't know if you realize, Nogales, Mexico is abutted to the north to Nogales, Arizona.

Chapter 52

Cancun To Ignacio Zaragoza

The two men sped back to the Cancun airport. An hour and a half later a Cessna 310 was cruising over 200 miles per hour, with the two agents aboard. The pilot was flying toward the Arizona border to an old town called Nogales, on the Mexico side of the border. Over the sound of the twin engines, Lyle who was sitting in the back seat was trying to make a phone call to Colonel Jackson. Using code words, he informed the colonel of possible radioactive products or bomb arriving via two vans in the Mexican town of Nogales. Two gangs were involved in collecting, securing, and distributing the contents of the container that had been picked up forty-eight hours ago in the city of Ignacio Zaragoza, two days away by car. One of the two gangs involved in the delivering the goods is MS-13. Using more code words when necessary, Lyle asked the Colonel to gather information available about the location of a drug smuggling drug tunnel opening in the US from either Nogales or somewhere close. Colonel Jackson informed Lyle he would get the information for him within the hour. Lyle laid back against his seat and turned on his iPad to connect with the government satellite. As the time passed, he read all he could find about the MS-13 gang, a famous international gang notorious for its violence, and renowned for its trafficking of drugs, weapons, and humans between Mexico and the US. He learned that their presence had extended to countries like Australia, France, South Korea, Egypt, and others.

Later, he linked up with Octo, and using code words again, asked the clerk to gather available information from the DEA and border patrol about both the Templars and MS-13 and any information they had on drug smuggling recent arrests.

The Border Patrol agents were suspicious the dope and arms coming from Heroica Nogales were channeled through tunnels, but no organization had ever been able to locate this sophisticated mode of entry. What Lyle wanted to do was to get tracking devices and Semtex placed on both the arms loads and whatever was causing the radiation spike. When sure the loads were deep inside the tunnel, he would blow them up by using a phone call connected to a device placed in the Semtex. The two partners wanted to kill as many gang members as possible and to render the arms, explosives and suitcase nuke harmless. But first, they had to find the vans with the goods.

The pilot looked over at Brett sitting in the front seat and showed one finger. They would be landing in under an hour. Brett spoke into his headset and asked the pilot if there were SUVs available for rent in Nogales. The pilot got on the radio and contacted Nogales airport. The cars were available could not be reserved; they were rented on a first come, first serve basis. Next, Lyle asked the pilot if he could drop down low and follow the highway 150 leading into Nogales from about three hundred miles out. After some discussion, the pilot agreed.

Meanwhile, Lyle had taken out two pairs of military binoculars from their packs on the back seat. He gave one to Brett, and they watched the highway as the plane flew as slow as it safely could, about a thousand feet above the roadway 150. Brett, excitably yelled, "Two vans and two SUVs straight ahead."

Lyle told the pilot to pull to his right so he could get a better view of the Vans and SUVs. Once he was sure the vehicles represented the expected convoy on its way to Nogales, he asked the pilot to pull back up to flight altitude, and land as soon as possible. Immediately, Lyle got on his government phone and ordered Octo to make contact with the car rental agency at the Nogales airport, and asked him to bribe the agency to make arrangements to rent two dark-colored SUVs.

There was no hesitation when the pilot asked in Spanish for landing instruction in Nogales. The wheels no more than touched the tarmac when the pilot taxied as close as he could to the vehicle rental office. Lyle paid the pilot his fee, added two hundred dollars for the individual services and another two-hundred dollars to have him forget he ever saw him. As they were walking inside the white rental building, the plane pulled toward the fuel depot, and would soon be on its way back to Cancun.

Within forty-five minutes, Brett and Lyle found themselves at the wheel of an older, slightly banged up black SUV, and a shiny dark blue newer model. Time was of the essence; they needed to get south of the city to pick up the tail of the vans and the rest of the caravan.

CHAPTER 53

Heroica Nogales

The sun was past the zenith, and the temperature was high. Lyle and Brett drove out of the city in a southern direction. The two vehicles pulled through the bushes about ten miles south of the town and parked. Now they would wait for the two vans to go by. They did not know when the smugglers would leave the highway or where they would end their long journey.

In Nogales, a city of more than 212,000 souls, it was known that in general the local police were corrupted and that sometimes were paid bonuses by the cartel for protecting criminals. Even though shootings and stabbings happened, life continued, and the residents were not barricaded in their homes as some would like us to believe. On the weekends, the main street would attract American visitors who enjoyed bargains and most of all the colorful trinkets so readily available in Mexico. At night, and mostly on weekends, the Gringos still took over la Avenida Primera where they took advantage of the cheap beer while gambling at the Camino Caliente or at the Palace Bingo where they could gorge at the 24hour buffet. Underage young men continued to invade the Casino Palermo where striptease was part of the night show and where the drinks were available to all.

When the four vehicles drove by, Brett and Lyle followed behind them as close as they could without being spotted. The traffic was light, but they always managed to keep several cars between their SUVs and the convoy. Before long, the motorcade turned right on a dirt road, just outside of the Nogales city limits. Lyle called on his com unit and told Brett to break off and turn around to avoid being spotted, but most of all he wanted him to climb to the top of the water tower they had just passed in order to watch the next move of the smugglers.

Five minutes later Brett was on top of his mirador. He contacted Lyle, "There is thick dust indicating several cars following each other or a huge truck made a sharp turn about two miles up the dirt road. I can hardly see the outline of the building which could be a ranch. I am sure this is where they stopped. The air is free of dust once you pass the structure and there is only one isolated truck on the dirt road.

"Also, those guys have had a long drive; they need to rest and celebrate before taking the goods over to the US at night."

"I agree. We need to find a way to get close so we can place our tracking devices amongst those weapons and that case. If we succeed in planting the Semtex, then blow it when both men and goods are inside the tunnel, we will have accomplished our mission. We need to find out how close the border is. I don't think they would try smuggling anything in daylight; remember, they fear our drones."

They both decided to drive and see if they could find a trail that they could ride on to bring them closer to the ranch house. Driving as slowly as they could, not to raise dust, they came across what looked like a goat path bordering a ravine. The men put their vehicles in four-wheel drive and worked their way along the narrow path, never reaching more than a few miles an hour. They worked their way, getting closer and closer to their destination. Soon the goat path took them down into the canyon itself. The rolling boulders soon stopped their forward movement. "At least our vehicles will be hidden Brett said."

"Roger that. Let's turn them around just in case we have to get out of Dodge fast." After turning the SUV's around, they started laying out the supplies they would need to take on the trek to invade the ranch. As they talked and organized their gear, they drank lots of water and ate protein bars. They were not sure when they would be able to hydrate or eat again.

While waiting for sunset, Lyle and Brett realized their good fortune. The deep canyon ended less than a quarter mile from the building. The tall sagebrush and dry weeds blanketing the entire area, plus the few scattered dwarf pines and huge boulders would offer the men some safety as they worked their way to end up inside the building.

CHAPTER 54

South of US border

The Hacienda

Well hidden behind brush at the top of a small hill, Brett and Lyle continued to watch the men carrying the weapons into the house under the vigilant eye of the patrolling guards. They counted fourteen individuals involved for this lucrative entrepreneurship. There was no doubt, the entrance of the tunnel was located inside the house. Lyle had radioed Colonel Jackson who told him that anyone surviving the explosion would be captured on the US side. In the meantime, the authorities were busy locating the general area of their arrival. The colonel informed Lyle that the Border Patrol agency had the most sophisticated radiological monitoring device available, it was expected to pick up signals from the suitcase nuke.

At the ranch, most of the weapons had been transferred to the tunnel. Several guards were asked to watch closely the door through which the merchandise had been delivered. "Stalker one to stalker two. Are you protected enough for a shootout?"

"Roger that. And from my spot, I can exit with cover back to our vehicles."

"It's funny; I don't see the tangos taking the rest of the goods into the house. I am going to get closer to the second van and see if I can find out what is holding them back from finishing the job. I want to be damn sure that the nuke is being channeled when we blow the tunnel. Right now, the leader, the man with the black hat who was shouting orders earlier seems to be getting ready to leave in one of the SUVs with his driver and two individuals. They will escape the explosion. I must warn the colonel." At this time, two men with long black beards and matching long hair stepped forward. They handed the leader a brown sack that probably contained money.

"Roger that. I suppose the colonel is all set to send a drone to follow them."

Lyle and Brett were ready to act. They had flash-bangs, grenades, extra mags, and the devices ready to set off the charges. Lyle was now looking straight into the well-lit hallway of the main building, and in his night ocular, he could see a guard handing armors down to a man standing with only his upper torso out of an opening in the floor. After the armors, the black box was lowered into the tunnel. The two vans were now empty, and the merchandise was ready to be shipped. Only a few guards were left behind to watch the place.

Lyle took a mental note of the time, eleven-forty-two p.m. He called Colonel Jackson to let him know the firework would start in thirty minutes or less.

Brett and Lyle were now ready to take out the tangos guarding the farm. As predicted, the men felt free to unwind now that the leader was no longer present. They took off their shirts and dropped their rifles so they could have a little fun playing soccer. Brett counted six guards kicking the ball. Killing those guys proved to be unchallenging. They were given no time to hide; as a result, they never retaliated. In a few seconds, six bodies were scattered on the gravel of the inner courtyard. Following this short interlude, Lyle made a fatal phone call that triggered a spectacular explosion, shook the land and sent a cloud of dust flying into the sky. Brett made two more phone calls from his burner phones to set off more explosions that caused the main building to vibrate. There was dust rising from not only the small hill but also from the front of the house.

All of a sudden Lyle's phone rang, he pushed the lid open, "Colonel Jackson here, we found their exit point in the States, there is no one coming out. I am sure the tunnel collapsed, and everything is buried. Our meters are picking up the radioactive signal. Great job men! Be careful. It is time to head home. We will take care of things here on the US side."

"Rodger that." Then Lyle contacted Brett to share the colonel's message. All he heard back was, "Stalker two. Rodger that."

"OK Brett, let's do some inventory." In the courtyard, blood was running from necks, torsos, and legs. The shooters were so good; no coup de grace was needed to be administered, the guards were lifeless.

The agents were intrigued by the tunnel; they decided to enter the dusty hallway where its opening was. Just by looking at the floor, it was not possible to detect where it was. The tiles on the floor had been laid back in place with perfection. Lyle kept hitting the floor to find a change in resonance. He gave up. As Lyle was inspecting the house, looking for evidence of further trafficking, Brett chose to check the vehicles that were still in the front yard.

All of a sudden there was a moan as Brett took two rounds in the front of his bulletproof vest. Lyle's body rotated at the speed of lightning, he sighted the man's head in the scope and fired. The shooter's head disappeared, completely shredded to tiny pieces. Following this lethal attack, the man's body remained standing, perfectly erect for a few seconds, and to the two witnesses' disbelief, it even took a step. This ghostly apparition shook the two agents who watched in awe with their hand covering their mouth. They looked at each other, and Brett reacted, "It reminds me of the chicken's reflex where the bird can run away with its head freshly chopped off."

Following this incident, Brett and Lyle realized they had neglected to take some precautions merely because they had not anticipated such a significant number of workers on the ranch. After disrupting the soccer match and killing the six players, they were sure they were alone. But the fighting was not over. Lyle turned around and saw the SUV leaving with one man at the wheel. They fired at him in unison; the vehicle soon stopped. The driver was now headless. The agents realized that maybe other guards were still present on the premises. They would investigate. At this time, Brett made another phone call, the small device in the Semtex received the signal, and the SUV with the dead man inside became pieces of junk covered in blood. Brett said, "One van left. If there are a few men still inside the building, maybe we should back off, let them get in the vehicle, and take them down. What do you think?"

"Great idea. I took two hits on the colonel's new vest. We have to take points off for that." All of a sudden Lyle heard Brett yell. Lyle looked east, a tango had come behind Brett and had raked him across the back with a three-round burst. Fortunately, his partner was wearing the latest bulletproof armor that could stop an AK47 round. "Lyle sighted in the tango and emptied a three round burst of his own into him; one in the chest, one in the neck and one that decapitated him. It was not over. The two men heard the cranking of a starter, the van's headlights came on, and it began to move forward. They both switched their guns to automatic and emptied their clips into the sides of the vehicle. Brett again pushed a small button that caused the immediate destruction of the van.

Lyle called Brett and told him they had to get out of Dodge fast; he could see bright lights through the dust on the horizon, the police were coming in mass.

As Lyle and Brett were retreating toward their SUVs, Lyle's phone rang. "Colonel Jackson here, mission completed. There is a drone high in the sky tracking the SUV. The Department of Defense has been assigned to clean up the US side. Concrete will be poured in inside the tunnel, so thick that no one will ever be able to dig anything out."

"We are heading back to New Orleans and will be waiting to hear from Patrick. He knows where the next loads of arms will be coming from and how they will be getting to the Black Sea, and maybe to the Mediterranean Sea. We will call when we head out."

"Major, your country thanks you once more."

CHAPTER 55

Mexico To New Orleans

Next day

As Lyle was speaking with the colonel, Brett was catching up with him, sliding and running down the embankment of the cliff-like edge to reach the flat and sandy bottom of the canyon. In doing so, Brett who was involuntarily speeding down was unable to slow his descent by grabbing branches or plants; they were nonexistent on the dry steep-sided walls of the deep gorge. On his mad race down, he tore his pants an seriously injured his leg. When Brett finally stopped his fall, landing on his butt on what had been the bed of a stream. There, feeling squeezed in by the vertical walls of the canyon, he took a few minutes to wipe and cover his bleeding wound with the small dressings he was carrying in a mini-first aid kit. He contacted Lyle to let him know he was on his way to their SUV but did not mention his accident. Once the two men were together again, they hastily loaded the SUVs and drove slowly along the goat path, all the time making sure they kept their speed to a crawl to prevent creating any dust that could give away their position. They pulled up on the road, stopped, turned off their engines, and listened attentively to make sure the Mexican Police were not coming their way. Once on the blacktop, they went straight through to the Nogales International Airport. Before turning in their rented vehicles, they changed their clothes and washed their face and hands the best they could in the first airport bathroom they found. Some of their dirty clothes that had turned earth color were discarded in a garbage can. Now more presentable, they headed to the car rental agency. Once in the terminal, they shipped their cases with their guns to New Orleans via air freight. Afterward, they bought tickets for the first flight to Mexico City. Over a beer, enchiladas, and tacos, they waited for their next flight to Houston.

On their flight from Mexico to Texas, both men were in and out of sleep, still tired when the plane landed at the George Bush Intercontinental Airport. The short hop to New Orleans, their last leg, would leave no time for a nap.

It was seven p.m. when their Delta flight landed in New Orleans. Going through customs, they were looked over several times when they showed their passports. But when they laid their cases bearing the United States seal on the counter, they were waved through without question. From the airport, each man made a personal phone call. Lyle contacted Annie at her hotel, and they talked quite a while. She advised Lyle that her mother, his mother, Jennie, and she were getting ready to drive back to Atlanta, and were thinking about leaving the next day. With some sarcasm and lassitude in her voice, she asked him, "What about you, what are your plans? Am I going to see you for more than twenty-four hours this time?"

"Hey, cheer up, I will meet you in a few minutes. Brett and I have to finish a short assignment tomorrow, here in New Orleans, and then, eventually, we will have to fly to Russia." Lyle knew this was not quite true; his real destination was going to be Chechnya. "Tonight, let's do something, just the two of us. I am taking you on a carriage ride through New Orleans. At night, it is magical. There are people everywhere. The music, the bright lights, the colors, the sounds; you will love it. But first, I have to shower." Annie was concerned about Lyle's next mission which he had kept to himself. She was well aware that he was not free to divulge details that could compromise the outcome of his project, but he could reassure her by not leaving her completely in the dark. Being a frank, straightforward person, she did not appreciate the lack of transparency. Lyle knew he had to appease her and to do that he gave her unimportant details about his next assignment.

"We intend to finish a job we thought we had completed before. The man who hired the assassin who almost killed us at our wedding is still alive and involved in other operations. We are going after him."

"Yes, I agree, catch that bastard." Annie was still upset knowing that he would be gone in a short time." Before ending the conversation, she just said, "OK, I will see you later."

Brett had contacted Fran who told him she was arriving at MSY, Louis Armstrong airport, at ten forty-five p.m. Since he was already there, he decided to stay at the airport and meet her upon arrival. Lyle and Brett discussed the plans for the next day before going their separate way.

"Tomorrow, after the women leave to Atlanta, you and I are going to visit Mr. Garcia, the man you said was responsible for shooting at you. He is a traitor; he will be treated like one. We will induce a heart attack."

"I hope you let me insert the needle this time, Lyle. That crooked bastard almost had me killed."

Lyle took the cases and placed them on a cart so he could wheel them out to the SUV. He hugged Brett and told him to meet him about nine the next morning at his hotel. Having nothing to do but wait for Fran, Brett decided to catch a nap.

It was late when Lyle gave his secret knock on the door of the hotel room. He was a bit apprehensive about the reception he would get after the quarrel over the phone. He no more sat the cases down on the floor when Annie threw her arms around Lyle and held him tightly as if she was not going to let him go. He was relieved to see that she loved him no matter the awkward and not always pleasant situations he had dragged her in. Then her plump lips met his dry, chapped, and even cracked lips, and silently they kissed and hugged for several minutes. She firmly grabbed Lyle's hand and told him, "I am ready for this carriage ride you offered over the phone. I imagine you are tired, but you must realize this is my last night in New Orleans." They left immediately.

It was the last carriage ride of the day. They boarded the large mule-drawn open coach on the Decatur Street side of Jackson Square. It was Painted bright red and almost luxurious with its polished well-padded leather seats. Being the only guests on the smooth ride, they misbehaved like two young lovers, exchanging little pecks, allowing traveling hands to caress bare skin, biting earlobes, whispering naughty things, etc. while the driver was entertaining and enlightening his guests with true-life scary stories and amusing anecdotes about the French Quarter. Following the excursion, the couple decided to stop at the Sugar Cane bar to get a drink and listen to zydeco music by a group called The Bayou Stompers. Annie was discovering this lively music which could lift anyone's spirit. The group was singing in Cajun French, but she could not understand much, "Can't understand a word but I love it, it is so stirring, a one-legged man would want to dance! I don't see how people can stay still with this energizing music. Since we are here, we are going to have a Sazerac cocktail. I read that New Orleans is where the first cocktail, the Sazerac, was created. In the beginning, this drink used to be made with brandy, and later rye whiskey was substituted for cognac." By the time they returned to the hotel, it was almost one in the morning! Lyle decided to take a shower before bed. His hair and neck were still dusty. He was tired, Annie offered to wash his back. As the warm water ran down Lyle's body, it started to revive him. He tried to turn around several times to face Annie, but she would not let him. As the soapy water and bubbles ran down his tight firm body, she would gently tease him in the sensitive spots to arouse him. Lyle took her hands in his and intertwined their fingers. He turned her around and lifted her. Annie could feel the heat of his breath on her neck and the firmness of his arousal. It was time to surrender; she guided him inside her.

Later Lyle shaved, then he joined Annie between the white sheets. This time the lovemaking was slow, and the little bit of heaven lasted way into the early morning.

Fran had never seen Brett in his working garb before, let alone with dust on him. Having only one clean polo shirt when he changed his clothes in Nogales, he had kept his dirty pants on. Since he had fallen in the canyon, he was not only dusty; he had crusted dry mud at knee level. She was so glad to see her fiancé that she wrapped her arms around him at the arrival gate as her two friends stared and probably wondered about Brett's appearance. Fran took him by the hand, and they walked out to her vehicle. Now alone in her car, Brett kissed her again and again with passion and love. She was so thankful that he had returned.

Brett showered, shampooed his hair, shaved his three-day stubble beard, and changed clothes. They decided to celebrate his return by having a glass of wine on the terrace at one of their favorite bistros. So happy to be together, they talked for a good hour and watched the pedestrians going by. She wanted to serve a meal to her man at her place. They stopped at Meals To Go and picked a three-course dinner. At Madeleine's, a gourmet pastry shop, Fran chose the dessert, two servings of Mexican flan. They had a good evening eating and watching TV. Both were tired. Brett lifted Fran and carried her to the bedroom. She let him remove her clothes and giggled like a little girl. As they kissed, Fran unbuttoned Brett's shirt, one button at a time, and unbuckled his pants belt. Brett removed the rest of his clothes as Fran was too slow. He turned off the lamp next to the bed, and slowly slid in against Fran now lying on her side. His fingers gently touched her in the sensuous and exciting parts of her body while his lips teased her ears, neck, and lips. Soon Fran had reached a point she could not wait any longer. She pushed Brett on his back, straddled him, and guided him into her.

After making love, they took a short breather. Brett slowly brought the woman he loved to a peak once again, then as he looked into her eyes he lowered himself down slowly, and they repeated their coupling. Sleep soon followed, each one on his half of the queen size bed.

CHAPTER 56

New Orleans

Awake and rested, Brett pulled his arm slowly from behind Fran's shoulder, now free, he looked at the clock on the nightstand. It was six a.m. He got out of bed quietly, so as not to wake Fran, and went to make a pot of coffee. Like Lyle, Brett liked the smell of coffee in the morning. This unique fragrance evoked several things to him, friendship, togetherness, and life. With a cup of steaming coffee in hand, he stared out the window of Fran's living room. A few dark cumulus nimbus clouds were hovering over the city, and the sun was already up. Brett was thinking about the job his partner and him had planned to do this morning at the docks. It was so calm, and he felt so serene in this apartment with his Fran just a few feet away, he became reluctant when thinking about eliminating Garcia; he was ready to reconsider.

Deep in thoughts, he did not hear Fran come up behind him. She had sat her cup of coffee down on the table and was now slowly sliding her hands underneath Brett's robe. Her fingers began working slowly up his hard firm chest. She kissed Brett's neck, and she let her fingers walk there way down his rock hard abdominal muscles and get lost in the vicinity of his manhood. Completely absorbed, Brett was still debating in his mind the best course of action to take concerning Garcia's fate. He was not responding to the attention he was receiving, all the cuddling and fondling did not bring the response Fran was hoping to trigger. To reach her goal, she was now teasing him by lightly brushing the inside of his thighs. Finally,

Brett became aroused. He congratulated her on her perseverance, dedication, and her skill. They both started giggling. As his lips found hers, she leaned against Brett's now firm manhood. His body began to quiver as she led him to the couch.

Brett put his left hand behind Fran's head, and with the right one, he gently laid her down on the couch. With her legs wrapped around Brett's waist, Fran pulled him inside her. The rhythm was slow at first and kept the beat with the heavy breathing. Shortly after that, there was moaning, a sound of release coming from the lovers.

Lyle was still asleep when Annie got up and made coffee. She could tell her man was awake even though he pretended the contrary; his face had a happy look, and a satisfied smile on it. Annie sat a cup of coffee on the nightstand on Lyle's side of the bed. She kissed her man on the forehead then walked back to her side of the bed, sat her coffee down, removed her robe, and slid between the sheets. Lyle kissed his woman's on the ears, cheeks, and on the nose and lips. Leisurely lying there together was very relaxing. Rarely did Annie enjoyed this simple pleasure with Lyle. They stayed there immobile and quiet for a while until both needed a refill in their cups.

The closeness brought about petting and necking. The couple wrapped their arms around each other and shared some hot passionate kisses that led to lovemaking. The moans of pleasure soon followed.

CHAPTER 57

New Orleans

It was just after eight a.m. when two friends sat together in the lounge of a hotel for breakfast. The rays of the sun glowed through the blades of the Venetian blinds facing East, creating parallel golden lines on the wall behind their table. As part of one of the walls of this popular hotel was a waterfall continually running down a giant slab of marble to land in a pond filled with fish. On a plaque to the right of the fountain was a list identifying the fish visible in the freshwater, small and colorful danios, common guppies, and a single tiger placo hiding in the gravel at the bottom of the aquarium could be easily recognized.

As they drank their freshly roasted coffee, Lyle broke the silence, "I was thinking about Fran, not only is she pretty, but she has her head on her shoulders, and for her sake, I do intend to bring you home safe." Brett was beaming. He had a tendency to appreciate flatteries directed at Fran, and also to brag about his fiancee, "She is very practical, has more wisdom than most. I am lucky. We're both lucky. I did not think there was another woman on this earth like your Annie; there is one more."

Lyle was also practical; he returned to reality by bringing up what had been arranged the day before. "Let's kill that bastard, Garcia. After that, we will have to discuss our trip to Russia. While we are over there, we should have opportunities to wipe that scum of the earth, the Chechen. This mission better be without calamities. Remember we have to come home safe as we have weddings to attend. Have you discussed with Fran our plans to marry in a double ceremony in New Orleans?" Their conversation had jumped from assassination to a trip, and now to wedding bells.

"Yes I approached her with that possibility, she is all in favor. "Brett held his fist out toward Lyle, who also made a fist and connected with Brett's.

"I mentioned to Annie our intention to combine the two celebrations last night, she approved, and in fact, she found this idea quite original. I am sure this is going to please her mother and especially mine when Annie brings that up while driving back to Atlanta."

Lyle had no more than finished talking when Fran walked in. They invited her for a cup of coffee, but she declined the offer. They left the pleasant dining room, Lyle got in the SUV, Fran and Brett hugged for a second before he got in the car. As the partners started to pull away from the curb, Fran, with a grin on her face, looked at Brett, showed her left hand with the ring on it, and then blew a kiss to Brett. As they started to turn at the corner, they slowed down, and both waved one last time and honked the horn lightly twice. A short distance later they made another left turn toward the docks. Fran walked back to her place to change clothes and head for the airport at 11:30 a.m.

As they were driving through town, Lyle had to maneuver the SUV through the crowded streets of New Orleans. When they were just two blocks from inspector Garcia's office, he pulled off the main drag and parked behind some old rusted cargo containers. The two men remained silent while they changed their clothes. They switched to tight black polo shirts, slipped into close-fitting black pants, and changed their footwear to tennis shoes.

Lyle reached under the driver's side of the front seat and brought out a metallic blue box, about the size of a small book. He opened it up and removed a vial full of a clear liquid. He picked up two syringes, inserted each needle into the fluid, and sucked it into the syringes until they were full. With their plastic caps in place, he put both syringes into a small tube similar to a cigar holding tube which he placed inside a pocket held secure with a velcro holding strap on his military belt.

Brett had strapped on his gun holster under his left shoulder with his Glock 40 and silencer screwed on. Both men made sure a round was in the chamber, the silencers were screwed on tight, and the safety was off. The bulletproof vests, earbuds, and mikes were packed in a backpack. With their dark baseball-like caps on and dark glasses over their eyes, they walked into the office of the DEA and dock inspector. As usual, there was no office staff present. Both agents walked into the back room, Garcia's office, and Brett locked the office door and stood guard.

Garcia was behind his desk. He sucked air into his lungs, pushed his chest out the best he could over his fat belly. To Brett and Lyle's surprise, he recognized Brett and said, "About time you brought back my equipment. Did you leave it in the front office?"

"Yes, it is there," Brett said. "I would like to thank you for letting us use it."

Then Lyle stepped toward Garcia and stuck his hand out like he was going to shake hands with him. When Garcia was within range, Lyle brought his right arm back as fast as a rattlesnake going to strike. His fist moved forward with brutal force and hit the obese man in the windpipe. The blow was so mighty, the inspector flew off his chair and landed on the floor, gasping for air. Still conscious, with an extended arm and his hand curved, he was sweeping the floor, trying to gather his front teeth, incisors and canines, that had been jerked out of his mouth under the savagely violent stroke. Brett was watching the scene, shaking his head, feeling a little perturbed. Lyle pulled the velcro strap loose, opened the container and took out a full syringe that he shoved into Garcia's protruding carotid artery. Within seconds, a moaning Garcia grabbed his left chest with both hands. He died within a minute from a heart attack. Brett felt like kicking the man before leaving the room, but instead, he walked into the front office and said, "One down. Let's go see if we can find a file with a picture for the gunslinger who shot at me."

Twenty minutes later, with no success finding the file and picture of the assailant, the agents furtively left the office. On their way back to the SUV, without intentionally looking for him, Brett spotted the man who had shot at him. He was entering a bar just outside the main gate. He was wearing the same vest with the identical insignia, a detail Brett had mentally recorded the day of the attack. Lyle immediately grabbed the second syringe that was filled with succinylcholine, that muscle relaxant that, in excessive quantity, can rapidly mimic a heart attack. According to Lyle, it is a murder weapon of choice for its easy administration and rapid action. Best of all, it is almost impossible to detect it by forensic labs. This time Lyle handed the Sux, as it is sometimes called, to Brett.

It was plain daylight. Inside the lounge, one could see two patrons perched on high stools who were drinking at the counters. Outside, the two agents took a second to concoct a scenario for their intervention which was going to take place in the presence of witnesses. "I will approach your friend from the front with a glass of beer in my hand. I will stumble and spill the content of my mug on him. I hope he will start yelling, maybe grab me, and swing his fist. Being a good Samaritan entering the bar, you will pull him away from me. At that instant, you will shove the needle into his thigh. Don't linger inside the bar, keep walking right on out the front door. As for me, I will offer my excuses repeatedly, but will also make a fuss regarding my attacker's aggressive attitude toward me. He will start stumbling around, his respiration will become depressed, and soon it will cease. I will leave. After the incident, let's split up and meet back at the car."

Lyle stuck to his plot. He entered the bar and walked to the counter to order a beer, the stalked man had just purchased his drink from the bartender and was going to a table. Lyle caught up with him, and without being seen, pretended to accidentally bump the targeted victim who was now drenched with Lyle's beer. An argument followed, Lyle whispered a few expletives to agitate his opponent. The insulting language incited the fellow to swing at Lyle. At this time Brett showed up and as a good citizen, calmly separated the two patrons. As planned, the Sux was injected successfully. Lyle and Brett left going their separate way.

The respiration of the victim started to become depressed, his muscles began twitching, and soon the man became inert on the floor. By then the bartender was on the phone, calling for an ambulance. Back at the SUV, Brett said, "That's the last threat anyone will receive from the scummy bastard."

As Brett drove, Lyle called Octo and gave him a list of items he wanted him to have sent to the embassy in Tbilisi, Georgia, a county of 69,700 square kilometers with a population of just over 3.7 million. This nation is located at the crossroads of Western Asia and Eastern Europe, bounded to the west by the Black Sea, to the north by Russia, and to the south by Turkey and Armenia. He also asked him to get two tickets, first class of course, for him and Brett to leave that same day for Tbilisi via Istanbul.

Octo called back an hour later and told them he had a flight reserved to leave just before three, arriving in Tbilisi at 5:30 p.m. the next day. Lyle said they would take it, and asked Octo to reserve them a hotel for two nights in Tbilisi as that would give them time to get the arms at the embassy. Before closing the phone call, Octo said he would send a text with the follow-up information, and wished them good hunting. It took Lyle and Brett less than forty minutes to pack. Once at the airport they turned in the SUV and still had an hour to have a beer before heading to JFK, then to Brussels and Tbilisi. These two men could sleep at the drop of a dime and would do so on each leg of the trip.

CHAPTER 58

Tbilisi, Georgia

The aircraft carrying Lyle and Brett was approaching the capital of Georgia, it was flying low over the orange and tan roof tiles of the city of Tbilisi. A few minutes later one could hear the dull sound of the wheels being lowered from the body of the plane which began to flare out as it approached on its final leg at TBS airport. It had taken the two agents over twenty hours to travel from New Orleans to their destination. Having slept during flight time, the two men felt rested. As usual, the passengers rushed to line up in the aisle, eager to escape the confinement of the aircraft. Lyle and Brett left the first-class cabin with two sensitive cases each and headed for the baggage claim section to pick up their backpacks. There, they sat down on a bench to look for the name of their hotel, watch the passengers go by, and discuss how they would travel from Georgia to Chechnya.

They went over the pros and cons of renting two SUV's or just one to drive over the border of Chechnya which was about one hundred thirty miles away. The primary purpose for their journey was to take down Aleksey Iman Shamil, once and for all. This dangerous man meant trouble as tens of thousands of lives; possibly millions depended on Lyle and Brett for stopping the flow of suitcase nukes. Lyle leaned back against the backrest of the rod iron bench, rubbed his head as he watched the suitcase carousel go round and round. Pensive, he said, "Let's rent two units, pick up the armory which will not be in before tomorrow, rest and have fun exploring the area one more day." They collected their backpacks. Lyle added,

"We'll use two vehicles. I believe there is a little more risk splitting up, but if one of us gets caught, the other will still be able to finish the mission." Lyle took the lead and said, "Let's get the cars, get to our hotel, clean up, and then chow down. I smell like garlic bread; a shower is highly recommended. I wonder if Annie is home or in flight to Paris right now, this time difference is confusing, I don't know what day of the week it is."

Brett had punched in the numbers to call Fran and when she answered her voice and breathing denoted surprise. "Oh, am I glad to hear from you, Brett. I did not expect any news that soon. The thought of being with you again has kept me going through a hectic flight today. Tonight I am glad to be home."

"Slow down. You sound nervous. What happened?"

"Nothing important. People get to me, everyone is in a hurry, very demanding, on the verge of being rude. How are you? Where are you now? How soon will you be back?"

"We just landed in Russia." Brett had no choice, he lied. The agents knew they had to be cautious about their location. "Our plans are preliminary, but we hope to return in ten days or so. What we do changes from day to day." Brett was extra stingy with information he shared about the operation. Fifteen minutes later, he was still talking and pacing.

Lyle had let the phone ring ten times with no answer. After he looked at his watch, he figured she was not home yet. Lyle sat down and typed out a long text message. He asked her to make sure she mention his name to Jennie. Then he looked at Brett who by now was still on the phone sitting on a bench where he had gathered the cases and the backpacks at his feet. Lyle sat down next to him and whispered into his ear. "I will be at the car rental just outside the gate. I am taking my cases and backpack."

Lyle was completing the paperwork for two four-wheel drive SUVs with GPS when Brett came up behind him. "Fran is fine Cap. Oh, I mean Major."

Handing Brett his keys, he said, "You get the dark blue one. Let's head for the Iota Hotel Tbilisi. It's well located, close to the Embassy and airport. Can't wait to get to the hotel, I need to clean and feed. What about you?"

"Same. I stink so bad the mosquitos won't land on me. Did you make contact with Annie?"

"I know she is already airborne; I sent a text." After walking around the vehicle, looking for tracking devices and signs of bomb, Lyle opened the front passenger door and placed the sensitive cases on the passenger seat next to a gun he could reach in a hurry. He set his backpack in the back of the car and walked over to see his partner who had just finished inspecting underneath his SUV. After reviewing the directions to the hotel, Brett programmed his GPS and headed out. Lyle slipped in behind the wheel and followed his partner.

Over an hour had passed before the two men sat in the hotel restaurant for dinner. Without ordering it, the waiter brought them a small plate covered with all sorts of appetizers. Next, he brought beans and salad called meze, a small Turkish pizza called pide, and kofta — a stew of ground beef and lamb meatballs, a specialty of Turkey served only at a few restaurants here in Tbilisi. As Lyle ate his Turkish specialties, he thought about Istanbul, the warm red roofs of the buildings leading down to the blue waters of the Golden Horn river. He was dreaming about how pleasant it would be to meander through the markets with Annie, and sample many of the delicacies that Turkey has to offer. As Lyle's mind began to drift, Brett popped the cap off a beer, bringing Lyle back to the present. While consuming several bottles of beer, the two men to sample another dish, menemen, a combination of tomatoes, green peppers, spices and olive oil to which Turkish feta cheese is added. After the waiter left, they discussed their plans for the following day. They had thought about taking some time to wander in Tbilisi, a town full of charms. Their dinner and conversation lasted over two hours. Brett stood up, stretched, and said, "Let's go walk to let our stomach settle before we hit the sack. We can go over a few of the operation fine points while we walk."

"Good idea, we need exercise after being cooped up in those planes. Back in the hotel, am going to go through the cases and clean the guns, want me to do your tools also, boss?"

As the two men started walking down the cobblestone road, Lyle said, "Naw, I will do them early in the morning, I need to clear my mind tonight with meditation. I still have some thinking and planning to do. There will be no room for mistakes when we go after The Chechen."

After a four mile walk, they returned to their room where they relaxed with a beer.

Chapter 59

Tbilisi Georgia

Thick black clouds and a heavy wind had moved over the town of Tbilisi during the night, leaving the air crisp and bright when the rising sun started filtering through the purple clouds over the Eastern mountains the following morning. The sky slowly turned a pinkish glow with light strokes of lavender here and there. Two men holding coffee mugs stood in their boxer shorts on the cold stones of their patio watching the spectacular sunrise. The cool temperature, the stillness of the air, and the silence were refreshing and encouraged idleness. No words were exchanged for a while.

Now ready to face the day, Lyle and Brett needed food to be able to achieve anything. They walked to the restaurant wondering what would be served for breakfast in this part of the world. They realized their nice hotel was occupied mostly by visitors from neighboring countries, and also from Eastern and western Europe. The usual Danish, croissants, waffles, sausages, and eggs, were all available in this establishment that catered to different tastes. Lyle and Brett decided to go native. Their waiter advised them well, and the result was more flavorful than they had expected. Lyle ordered an omelet with fried sulguni cheese and Georgian bread. The bread, their waiter explained, is spread with butter and roasted in the oven at high temperature until golden brown and pleasantly crisp. A simple treat that surpassed what Lyle imagined. Brett went for chirbuli; a delicious egg dish served with a peculiar sauce made of tomatoes and walnuts. He was pleased with his selection.

Now full, they pushed back their chairs and enjoyed a last cup of coffee that they spiked with a local liquor called chacha, a strong Georgian brandy sometimes called vine vodka, made from grape residue left after making wine. They left the hotel an walked to their vehicles. Lyle had decided he would go to the embassy to pick up the rest of their weapons. While there, he would get a few maps and speak with the local spook to see what intel he could get about the region. Maybe the CIA would be aware of a road leading to an unguarded section in the border with Chechnya. With a load of arms in the vehicles, they could not afford to be stopped. Brett was to stay behind and go for a walk in the city to meet individuals who, if possible, might know a safe way to get across the border without being detected. Giggling, Lyle said, "Get friendly with someone who looks like a goat herder. They usually know where all the passes are in the mountain. I will contact you later. You know the drill, if something looks and feels good, go with it, my friend. Beer is on me tonight."

An hour had passed when Lyle discovered the embassy located on Georgian-American Friendship Avenue, a big white building in the shape of boxes with numerous narrow and high windows. From a distance, it looked like a prison without electrified fences. Getting closer, and facing another direction, it lost its dismal looks thanks to its immaculate lawns. At the embassy gate, Lyle presented his military ID to the guard who examined it carefully and returned it along with a visitor pass that was to be posted on the left corner of the windshield. After he directed Lyle in the right direction, the young guard gave him a salute. The agent met another Marine who took him to the office of the COS.

The COS remembered Lyle from a previous visit. The man informed the visitor that his packages would not arrive at the airport before six p.m., and would not be available for pick up, here at the embassy, until morning. Lyle was upset. He was about to tell the COS to call the White House which would have been arrogant and of no use. Instead, he took a deep breath and thanked the COS who said, "You may come early tomorrow, seven a.m." After Lyle obtained the maps he wanted, he headed for the front door.

As he was walking across the yard of the Embassy, he dialed Brett and told him about the delayed delivery of the weapons. Brett was in town looking for a shady individual who might have suggestions about the border. Lyle knew this method was not too promising; it was absurd. They would have to research on their own, and they would do that today. In the morning they would check out of the hotel, pick up their arms at the embassy, and head into Chechnya.

During the drive back into the city, Lyle made contact with Patrick who was already in Chechnya. Pat said he had a general location where the fishing trawler would be bringing the arms into, the county of Dagestan and about thirty to forty klicks from a city named Makhachkala. After answering a few questions from Lyle, Pat said he would leave a map inside an envelope at the hotel reception. Lyle told Pat he would be arriving the day after tomorrow around eleven p.m. "I'll be picking up the weapons first thing in the morning, and Brett and I will be heading your way shortly afterward. We will meet at the Grozny City Hotel, where you are staying." Pat immediately said, "I will reserve you a room with two beds. Can you give me the name I should register you under?" Lyle pulled out his passport with the name he used to go through customs in Georgia.

Pat's voice faded for a moment, then he said, "The hotel is a 4.5 stars establishment located in the center of town." Pat paused and resumed, "Grozny is beautiful, new buildings everywhere, parks, promenades, and more. Following the bombing and the complete destruction of Grozny during the war, Russia spent a fortune to rebuild the city entirely. Right now I am on my way on E119 to an area near Sulak Cynak. I may not be back when you get there. You are going to be traveling on a road that is very rutted, especially coming over the mountain. You will need a four-wheel drive."

Lyle shared a few more details with Pat and headed for his SUV. On his way into the city, he contacted Brett again. They met at the city outdoor market just after ten a.m. By chance, they came across two older gentlemen when they sat on one of the few benches that were found along a pedestrian path bordered on both sides by plane trees. In the shade of these majestic trees, the older locals stroke a conversation with Brett and Lyle using a combination of words and gestures. After a while, Lyle took out some paper and pen and was able to convey that he was looking for an exit to Chechnya where the traffic was light or absent. Adding naive illustrations to the conversation, Lyle and Brett ended up with two possible roads that would take them in Chechnya without going through a guarded checkpoint. Satisfied with the information, they treated both gentlemen to a couple of shots of chacha, the local brandy.

The remainder of the day, they spent their time looking for the roads the old men had mentioned. They found both of them and both were not maintained and were more like broad trails nature was reclaiming, but they were passable and led into the foothills and across the border.

Once satisfied that they had the right route, they spent some time in the capital where they visited the immense library, admired the Akhmat Kadyrov mosque and many other interesting structures. Georgia is attracting tourism and is developing this industry with five-star hotels, gourmet restaurants, and art galleries. The country is also opening ski resorts, trails, and many more outdoor recreation facilities.

Two hours later they returned to their hotel as they needed to clean up before going to dinner. Now in the restaurant, Lyle and Brett sipped a glass of Tbilisuri semi-dry wine made from Cabernet and Rkatsiteli grapes. They were not surprised to find out that good wine was produced in Georgia, a very small country which manages to be the 22nd wine producer in the world. The waiter placed plates of meats, cheese, and seasoned slices of tomatoes on the table and brought a straw basket full of warm Turkish bread. It took the two men over an hour to eat their light dinner before taking a short stroll on their quiet street. They needed rest to face the next day. They were not sure what awaited them in the mountains, and even more puzzling, what was going to happen in Chechnya where security was not guaranteed.

CHAPTER 60

Tbilisi to Grozny

It was a sweltering sunny day, and the air conditioners had been on almost the entire time they traveled, passing through forests of beech, birch, oak and pine trees. The rutted road with numerous tracks left by the passage of vehicles suggested that other individuals had taken this difficult route to travel from and to Chechnya. So far the agents had not come across any suspicious encounter and, in fact, had felt safe in this traffic free mountainous region. The grueling drive did not allow any speed, there were potholes and ruts most of the way, but the situation improved when they finally reached a paved road. Lyle who was in the lead vehicle looked at his watch. "Two p.m.," he said out loud to himself. The agents were tired of driving; they needed to take a break, urinate, eat, and rest. Lyle slowed down when he spotted a small stream flowing between yew and birch trees. He pulled his vehicle into the shade and made sure he parked so he could leave in any direction. As he was getting out of his vehicle, Brett pulled up and backed in beside Lyle's car.

The total silence of this place was almost eerie. After looking around, with his gun within reach. Without any delay, they chose a tree trunk to empty their bladders.

Once finished relieving themselves, Lyle laid an army blanket on the grass, and like a nice little couple on an outing in the countryside, they displayed their picnic. Brett had brought two bottles of water, salami, cheese, and the unusually shaped bread that was round and looked like a thick pancake. He reached into another bag and laid out apples, oranges, and some delicious treats he had purchased at a bakery earlier that morning. Both agents had a sweet tooth, so Brett had bought some gozinakis, treats made of nuts and honey, and plum fruit rolls. It was far from a Sunday picnic as automatic weapons, loaded with a bullet in the chamber, safety off, rested against their legs. Kidnaps for ransom were unusual but still happening along the border. Although the trip, so far, had been without incidents, they had been warned that traveling solo in deserted places could be dangerous. After a toast to a successful mission, the men gorged themselves on the generous supply of goodies that Brett had brought along.

Before getting on the road again, they consulted their maps. The next leg of their journey would take them to an area the old men had described, in so many words, as being troublesome. To face any danger, they would keep their automatic weapons on the passenger seat of their cars the rest of the way. Now ready to leave, Brett would lead the way.

"It's my turn to take the lead for a while," Brett said. "Maybe you should drop back farther than I did following you. If someone stops me, I can let you know over the com unit, that way you can be prepared to come from behind with your AR15."

Lyle paused before saying anything. "Great idea, I 'll do that."

The two men picked up their stuff and made sure their guns were chambered. Before leaving, they walked over and picked and ate some blackberries. And after they relieved themselves once more, they filled their gas tanks from jeep cans and washed their hands and face in the creek. Brett got into his SUV, stuck his left arm out the window with his thumb up. "Locked and loaded," Lyle said into his mouthpiece.

"Roger that," Brett replied while moving forward. Lyle followed about three hundred feet behind his friend as he drove about thirty-five mph down the narrow road which was better but far from being smooth.

Another two hours had passed when Lyle heard a voice speaking in his headset. "I smell an ambush. Five individuals are coming out from behind a clump of trees, and there are branches blocking the road. I am slowing down. You better stop and work your way behind the trees as we planned. I am putting my mouthpiece, leaving it on, and hiding it under my shirt, so you know what develops. I am completely stopped now due to that barrage, I see them walking in my direction, and they are not smiling. Oh my, I see arms, AK-47s. I will stall as long as I can inside my car. I may need you."

Brett felt like a stagecoach traveler in the seventeenth century who was about to be robbed by bandits when the roads were not secure. He remained in his vehicle as two men with AK-47s approached on the left side of his SUV. Another man with an automatic weapon was now standing on the right side, with another one not far behind. Brett began to sweat as the men kept their guns pointed at his head. All of a sudden they stopped about eight feet from his car window. An individual, about five foot ten, dark skin, black hair, and unsightly brown teeth, shouted something. Brett did not grasp what seemed Arabic or Turkmen words. After repeating himself on a firm tone of voice, the desperado pointed his gun at Brett's head. Then he dropped the tip of the AK toward the ground. Brett knew what he wanted, so as he opened the door, he pulled the car keys from the ignition and quickly slid them under the seat. Once out of the vehicle, they signaled Brett to put his hands on top of his head and sit on the ground. Almost five minutes had passed now. Although tense, Brett knew his partner was not far.

While one man kept his AK pointing at Brett, another one opened the rear door of the SUV. He raised his voice and started giving loud orders so fast; it sounded like gibberish. On the ground, with his hands above his head, Brett watched. He was thinking how pleasantly surprised the robbers would be the minute they discovered the gold mine, the unexpected Ali Baba's treasure, the cases full of modern weapons. The other two men who were guarding the road began walking toward the vehicle. All of a sudden Brett could hear, "Allahu Akbar (God is great), Allahu Akbar, Allahu Akbar." They had found the sniper rifles, automatic rifles, and the rest of the armory Brett had been traveling with. This unexpected stroke of luck incited the men to express their joy through what looked like a circular dance. Then, to continue the celebration, they shot their AK into the air and yelled Allahu Akbar over and over.

The sound of another gunshot came from the trees, about a hundred feet away. Brett noticed his captors were now turning their attention to the clumps of trees the attack was coming from. The man guarding Brett was Lyle's first victim. The blow caused blood and brain matter to shoot from his head, one of his eyes was dangling at the end of some slimy tissue, and jelly-like fluid was dripping from the eye socket. Being in the proximity of the injured man, Brett was sprayed with blood and brain tissue all over his face and chest. When the man hit the ground, Brett opened the rear passenger seat door and slid across the back seat of his SUV. He pulled his SIG Sauer P226 from his holster. One of the attackers pointed his weapon toward the trees but never had a chance to even aim at the enemy due to a fatal injury. He dropped his AK and reflexly grabbed his neck that was bleeding profusely. The rapid loss of blood killed him; he was dead before he hit the ground. Armed, Brett was now ready to engage in fighting. Someone was now running was toward the trees as two of the men crouched on the ground at the front of Brett's SUV. There was another loud gunshot; the fellow running had been decapitated, his blood formed a fine spray in the air as he fell forward in the grass.

Brett could see the legs of the two men in the front of his car. He walked slowly to the rear of the SUV, his automatic was loaded and ready. Brett pulled the mouthpiece from under his shirt and spoke into it. "Thanks, my friend. Can you get the attention of the idiots hiding in front of my car? I need to get behind them from the driver's side."

"Copy that. Give me a few seconds."

All of a sudden Brett heard the two men yelling in the front of his SUV. He kneeled, looked under his car, he could see their legs almost up to their knees. He fired two quick shots, one into each man's leg, they screamed and started crawling away from the vehicle. Just as Brett rolled to the ground, he fired into the head of the first man. Then he aimed at the second one, at the same time Lyle did; the two gunshots pulverized the victim's head which was no longer attached to his neck.

"Stay close to the SUV; I am going to remain behind the trees and will come out about a hundred yards away. I want to make sure no one is hiding."

"Roger that. Usually, the big chicken shit man in charge always stays away from the action. I guess he is in no hurry to meet the seventy-two virgins."

"You don't see the brass at the front fighting our useless wars either. Oh, by the way, how come not seventy-three or four virgins, Brett?"

"Maybe it is the number of wives the prophet Mohammed had. Good hunting."

Just over ten minutes had passed when Brett heard a gunshot down the road, then another. A couple of thieves had stayed out of harm ways. Five minutes later Lyle appeared walking up the road. "I am sure they were planning to pull something," Lyle said, panting a little for air.

"You out of shape, boss? You are panting."

"I had to drag the two fat bastards into the brush to hide them. Some wild animals are going to have a feast; those guys are big. We better get the others off the road. Since I am out of shape, you take the big ones." Both men laughed as they were dragging the headless corpses away from the road.

Twenty minutes later, with Lyle in the lead, the two-vehicles continued their ride toward Grozny. Before pulling onto highway E50, they filled their vehicles with gas, ate the rest of the salami and cheese, drank lots of water, then hid their guns the best they could under the seats and spare tires, and headed toward the city.

Just before eight p.m. that night a man named Carl Henderson (Brett) stayed with the vehicles while another man named Jack Wilson (Lyle) checked in at the Grozny City Hotel. As usual, Lyle or Jack left the date to depart open. They had no idea when they would get back to Grozny once on the Chechen's trail. No one spoke a word until they had their gear and other supplies safe in the room. With their guns cleaned, everything checked, Lyle finally asked. "Who is going to hit the shower first?"

After a rock, scissors, and paper challenge, Brett said, "See you in ten, I need to soak."

While Brett was taking a shower, Lyle called room service and ordered dinner and beer. As Lyle drying off, the meal arrived, and soon one could hear the clicking of glass. Both men emptied their bottle half way before coming for air. As they ate, they talked and enjoyed the warm and tasty food. Then there was a codified knock on the bedroom door, a loud tap, three light, two hard, and three light. Both Lyle and Brett knew it was Patrick, their partner. Lyle hurried to open the locked door to welcome the visitor with a hug.

Pat gave Brett a long hug, and Lyle handed him a beer. The three men gave a toast to a successful mission. Lyle wanted to order a third dinner, but Pat had eaten earlier. More beer was brought in. It took Pat filled Lyle and Brett in on what had transpired since his arrival in Chechnya.

CHAPTER 61

Grozny to Dagestan

Deep in thought, and preparing their plan to attack the terrorists, the three agents had forgotten the time. They had conversed back and forth for several hours and gone over details of their eventful journey that could have ended dramatically. There were maps and papers with notes laid out on the top of two beds, a coffee table, and a nightstand. Without realizing it, they had worked and talked past midnight. It was now almost one a.m. Lyle looked at his watch and said, "It will be one shortly; if no one has anything to add, let's hit the sack and meet downstairs for breakfast at six a.m."

"Sounds good to me." Addressing both Brett and Lyle, Pat said, "What did you decide about my taking my SUV tomorrow?"

Lyle was watching Brett, waiting for him to reply. He shrugged his shoulders, which meant he did not care either way. "I say bring it; we will spread the explosives between the three vehicles, place your car at a third possible escape route, just in case. You have full insurance coverage, don't you?"

"Roger that. I have insurance. In the morning we will have to discuss how we proceed to our destination because if all three vehicles travel together, a caravan of SUVs on the road is going to look suspicious.

"Settled. See you downstairs at six." Pat left for his room that was one flight up, on the third floor. Brett and Lyle hit the sack following a hectic day spent in an unpredictable and risky part of the world. Within minutes, they were sound asleep.

Four hours later Lyle slipped out of bed, washed his hands and face with cold water, and brushed his teeth before making coffee in their room. Tired from a lack of sleep, Lyle went for a cold shower, cold water always helped him wake up; it stimulated his brain. Brett got up and poured a cup of fragrant coffee and sipped it with his eye closed. Leaving the bathroom, Lyle appeared in the bedroom wrapped in a fluffy terry robe and wearing matching slippers, all five-star hotel gratuities. Brett was giggling when he noticed and then pointed at the girlish slippers on Lyle's feet.

Lyle had just talked to Annie who was back in Paris. "Her mother is going to stay a couple of days before she catches a train home. She said the flight back was very smooth, and Jennie slept the entire trip back, some six hours. She had a phone call from Fran who is fine too. Before we go downstairs to eat breakfast, call home if you want, but watch the time difference, you may startle her in the middle of the night. I think Grozni is seven hours ahead of Atlanta. With Annie it is simple, Grozni is only one hour ahead of Paris. When we head out this afternoon, it might be several days before you will get another chance to speak with Fran."

Brett swallowed a mouthful of coffee, then said, "Go ahead, get us a secure table if you want Cap, sorry, Major. I won't be too long on the phone. She should still be up or ready to retire. Just hearing that woman's voice perks me up. God, I miss her."

Lyle put on his shoulder holster, chambered a round in his SIG Sauer P226, placed the safety on, then screwed on the sound compressor. He placed it in his quick draw holster. Lyle gave Brett a thumbs up, grabbed his light jacket to cover his weapon, and headed downstairs.

When he walked into the spacious dining room, it was empty. Lyle noticed the elegant decor of the space. On the walls, one could see tapestries representing rural life in Chechnya and richly framed contemporary paintings by local artists. Found here and there were well-composed bouquets of fresh flowers in magnificent vases. As Lyle moved across the room, he suddenly spotted Pat sitting at a table for four in a corner where two rock walls joined; not far away from an exit. As Lyle approached the table, a waiter was close behind with a pot of coffee and three cups. The dim light was perfect for this time of day. In this quiet atmosphere, it allowed to relax and enjoy the company.

Once Lyle was sitting, the waiter smiled and poured his coffee, and refilled Pat's before leaving as the men were not ready to order yet. As soon as the man was out of hearing range, Lyle spoke, and his voice tone typically flat, devoid of inflection, said, "As I mentioned last night, we have to get Brett in a sniper position so he can cover both of us while we plant the tracking devices and explosives on the trucks in case they get away. I need to put the explosives on the boat while you plant tracking devices on the rest of the vehicles. We will go in before midnight using our NVG's. Remember, everything will give off a ghostly green image. Probably been a while since you have worn one Pat?"

"Almost three years now. The weather report predicts a cloudy sky, with a quarter moon. There will be no moonlight near the Caspian Sea, as it's foggy down there at night. Lyle, if I should get in trouble, move on without me, you understand. Stopping those suitcase nukes is priority one."

"The mission takes priority, but Brett and I leave no one behind. If we have to, we blow ourselves up; no one gets captured." As Lyle waved at Brett, who was coming in with a big happy grin on his face.

"Howdy men. I could eat a horse. Have you guys ordered yet?"

"We were waiting for you," Pat said.

When the waiter returned, the three men gave their orders, causing the waiter to look in disbelief at the amount of food the trio ordered. Almost twenty minutes had passed before their food arrived. They stuck with what they were familiar with, the basics, bacon and eggs. Several side dishes were added, fried potatoes, toasts, cheese, and Danish. While eating, their conversation stayed away from the mission. Pat talked about his life in Paris when he worked at the embassy. "I was so glad to leave the place, but now I realize how lucky, how fortunate, how blessed, how privileged I have been for having spent a year of my life there. I will return someday. Pat became pensive, almost sad while thinking about this magical city.

Once they finished breakfast, they ordered another pot of coffee, and Pat laid out the directions to take to both leave the city and then head down toward the Dagestan and the Caspian Sea on R306 and later on E119. The distance to their final destination was between one hundred and seventy-five to two hundred miles. Pat looked around before handing Lyle and Brett a folded city map and map of the country. "I have marked the route in yellow to get you out of the city, and the direction to where the boat lies anchored north of Makhachkala in Dagestan; just in case we get separated. At the end of the road, when you cross the bridge, you will find a dirt road to your right. It is not very wide, and you could miss it.This road will take you out to a ridge overlooking the sea."

Pat looked at the check the waiter had left, took a roll of money out of his pocket, counted out a number of bills and laid them on top of the table, then he said, "If you two follow me, I will stop at a gas station so we can fill the vehicles and the extra cans. There is a little grocery store next door to it. I suggest you buy food there, bottled water, and fruit for a week as I am not sure what is ahead of us."

"I will get the beer," Brett said grinning and with a slight laugh.

Almost twenty minutes had passed when Pat spoke into his mouth mike. "Ahead is the Akhmad Kadyrov Mosque. One of the largest and people call it the Heart of Chechnya. It was built in the Ottoman architecture and opened in 2008. We have to turn right up ahead. Be alert as we are going through what was a war zone of 1999 and 2000 between during the Second Chechen war, between Chechen and Russia.

As the three cars pass through just a small section of the area, they could see the devastation that had not yet been completely rebuilt like the center of the city had been. "No one wins except those who make the weapons," Lyle said, dryly.

They were now on the road, on the most demanding and dangerous part of the mission. We turn onto the R306 in a couple of blocks." Pat said as they were leaving the city of Grozny behind.

"It will be several hours before we stop for gas again, in Levinkent. We can have a cold beer there and eat. It will take us several hours to get into Dagestan. After that, we will turn north on the E119 and soon cross over a small river. I am not sure of the name, but you will see an old rock hut on the right before you drive onto the bridge. Remember, I repeat, once across the bridge immediately turn onto what looks like a dirt road with tracks in the dirt from a lot of vehicles driving out to the Caspian sea."

It was close to six p.m. when the men pulled into a small gas station with several older run down buildings on both sides. After filling their vehicles with fuel and eating lunch, they headed north. Just over an hour later, they were crossing the bridge, and as directed, they pulled off on the dirt road. Pat got out of his SUV and told the men to put an automatic weapon and grenades on their passenger seats up front as from now on they were in an insecure territory.

CHAPTER 62

Caspian Sea

Several miles north of Makhachkala

Slowly, two vehicles were following a third one on the dirt road that appeared to come to an end. Pat who was in the lead never slowed down, he kept driving, and so did Brett and Lyle. At this time, Pat spoke into his mouthpiece, "We have about half a mile to go, no use to panic, the road is full of potholes and ruts. Just stay in my SUV tracks." The trio, having reached their destination, could not wait to stretch in the fresh salty air. Pat parked his vehicle facing the opposite way. There was ample room for the other SUVs to do the same. There was no conversation as the three men, almost like robots, laid out the gear they would take to the ridge overlooking the sea. Each man knew what he had to do, and what weapons he would need. Lyle and Brett were ready to go. They waited for their friend who was more familiar with the area and was going to lead them. As the three agents crested the small ridge in front of them, they could see the waters of the Caspian Sea.

Pat had researched this body of water, the largest lake or full-fledged sea on earth. It is bordered by five different countries and has 44% of all lake water in the world. Its salinity is about a third of most seawater. Many islands are scattered in the Caspian Sea, and most are uninhabited. The sea region has a rich biodiversity, 850 animal species, among them 115 species of fish and 500 species of plant.

Carrying a heavy load, the three men appreciated the cool mist coming off the water. From their elevation, they could see fog beginning to form along the shore. All of a sudden, Pat gave a signal to stop walking. An automatic response was to drop flat on the grass. Lyle released a strap on the side of his pack and pulled out his military binoculars. From their mirador, the men could observe any activity taking place below. Lyle studied the people, the boat, and the trucks parked on a dirt road which wound along the seashore. He spoke softly into his mike. "The name of the boat is the 'Salambek.' Must be named after someone's family. I count five trucks, two Toyota 4Wheel Drive and thirty-one tangos. Pat, how many did you spot when you were here before?"

"Counting the men on the trawler, forty-one, there could be more in the hold of the boat. That dirt road works it's way along the shore and ends at the foot of a cliff overlooking the sea. Let me use your field glasses a minute, that will save me from opening my pack."

Pat studied the boat and trucks for several minutes before he spoke. "See the three trucks in the front?" Pat paused and waited for his two friends to answer. "They are loaded. The canvas is tied down; the others are not. Some of the transfer of goods has been done. I suspect they will be leaving out of here late tonight, soon as they load the other trucks. Maybe in a few hours. I think we better move it if we are going to stop them."

Both Lyle and Brett acknowledged Pat's evaluation of the situation, then Lyle spoke. "We still have a lot of daylight even though the fog is getting dense. We are going to have to get closer and wait. I think we should work our way down to that gorge and stay behind this white boulder."

Before handing the glasses back to Lyle, Pat studied the ground cover, and said, "Let's back up slowly and then work our way to to the right, there is a depression there that will provide some cover on our way to that boulder. Follow me. I was in that same spot not too long ago."

Fifteen minutes later, the three men pulled their packs off and laid their loads on the cold ground; they needed to catch their breath.

"That's the spot. Brett, this is where you are going to provide cover for us. Your call sign will be the eagle. Here, take my field glasses and survey the area the best you can while we have light. Pat, you and I will take ten tracking devices with us. We will leave the rest with Brett in case one of us gets hurt. Pat, you put tracking devices, one on the two pickups and the first three loaded trucks behind them, and you attach a Semtex along with the tracking devices. I will place trackers on the other vehicles and the boat, just in case, it should get away. We can't fail with explosive and tracking devices on the boat and vehicles. We will wait until it's darker and use our night goggles. Your call sign will be 'Mongoose,' mine will be 'weasel.' Use two clicks for yes and one click for no when we are unable to speak. No one takes any chances, understand?"

After Brett and Pat shook their heads OK, Lyle continued to go over the action plan. Brett lowered the pods on the Russian SVD Dragunov sniper rifle. He took out four ten round magazines with 7.62 Nato rounds, checked them, and then took a bullet from a box in his pack and chambered it. Then Brett shoved the magazine with some force into the gun, to make sure it locked. He laid out five more magazines filled with 7.62 Nato rounds and placed them in the holders on his belt. He looked through the scope, checked the wind, made adjustments, and set the safety. "I'm cocked and locked, Lyle. It's almost time boss." Brett was anxious to get the job done and head back to safer territory.

Pat and Lyle checked their gear, placed flash-bangs and grenades on their belts, made sure their holster gun was chambered, and then chambered their automatic weapons. Each man carried a military first aid kit, water, and protein bars. Lyle took out each one of his spare magazines, checked the rounds, and then placed them back in their slots on his ceramic armor vest.

Darkness was filtering in, and the fog was hovering over the water, both allowing very little moonlight to show through. "Time to move out Pat." The three men bumped their fists together, and two of them slid out into the darkness of the night.

Thirty minutes later Lyle and Brett heard, "Mongoose in place."Two clicks from both men followed the transmission. Then a few minutes later Lyle said, "Weasel in place, and going for a swim." Again two clicks followed to let Lyle know that both his men understood he was on his way to plant the explosives on the hull of the boat. Lyle speaking into his mouthpiece said, "I am going for a short swim, give me twenty minutes max, if you can. Lyle lowered himself off the rocks into the cold waters of the Caspian Sea. He swam on the other side of what had been a boardwalk for only a short distance to study the possibilities. Lyle swam back under the boardwalk moving arms and legs carefully not to make a splash. He was now against the side of the boat, and the engine area was to his left. After swimming to the back of the vessel, he took out a block of Semtex, set the timer and stuck it against the hull of the craft. Everything was OK and ready. Lyle swam to the center of the craft, placed another block of explosive, and set the timer again. As an added precaution, a tracking device was also added. The agent spoke softly into his mike. "Job complete, I am on my way back."

He heard the two clicks from both men as he swam under the boards, back to shore. Almost ten minutes had passed before Brett and Pat heard Lyle speak again. "Charges have been planted. Mongoose clear to go. Pat's turn."

"Mongoose copies. I will work my way into the three trucks first. Out."

As before, two single clicks followed. Brett watched intently using his night scope as Pat crawled along the ground and through the couch grass. So far, the few men actively working on the beach had remained in one spot. Out of forty-one men Pat had reported present, only a handful had been observed after the darkness fell on the area.

All of a sudden Brett saw two men walking toward the trucks where Pat was to place his explosives. "Two tangos to your right, coming around the engine." As Pat was rolling and lying still under the six-wheeler, Brett sighted in the first man who was holding a rifle. He observed this individual walking, stopping a moment to listen and look for enemy presence. After a few long minutes, he walked away, probably feeling reassured. Then two sea gulls flew in and landed where the man had thrown something on the ground. This man was well prepared to face any imminent danger. He was keeping his finger on the trigger, ready to fire. No longer anticipating risk, the two men stopped walking. One put his foot on the running board and lit up a cigarette and offered it to his partner. After lighting one for himself, the two men started walking away, moving toward the next truck.

"Area clear Mongoose." Brett and Lyle heard two clicks on their headset. Pat placed devices on the rear of the truck and below the cab of the vehicle. After looking out in all directions, he started crawling on his belly toward the next unit.

Brett soon picked up Pat on his infrared unit and said, "Area clear to go." Pat clicked his mike twice once again.

Lyle had watched the tangos tie down the straps on the fifth unit in line, just over thirty feet in front of him, and now the men were finishing loading another truck. "Weasel to eagle. Is it clear to next unit?"

It was almost forty seconds before Brett answered, "Area clear, it's a go. Mongoose is set to proceed to the first truck in line. I will have him hold while I'm your eyes. Do you copy mongoose?"

"Roger that. Truck units two and three are ready to blow."

Lyle was crawling in the dust of the road with his wet clothing, turning the dust to mud. Just as he pulled his legs under the rear of a truck, he heard eagle speak. "Four men coming your way from the boat. The two in the middle are carrying a case of some kind. Could be one of the nukes."

They were too close for Lyle to speak, so he clicked his mike twice."

The men were speaking a Russia Chechnya Dagestan dialect. Lyle was able to make out some of the words since he spoke Russian. He did not like the few words he understood; they had mentioned suitcase nukes. One man took the case and headed toward the front of the convoy. The other three men then headed back toward the craft. "Lyle you have one man in the front seat. Two men just got in the front of the next truck. I think they are getting ready to leave."

Lyle clicked his mike once and then crawled slowly out from under the truck. Just as he dropped into cover behind the tall grass, eight men carrying boxes approached the rear of the vehicle. All Lyle could do was watch. After they had loaded the truck with there goods, the men left and headed back toward the boat; he called Eagle. "Status on mongoose?"

"All trucks are ready to blow; he is still unable to approach the pickups. Be advised that four men are getting in the back of the loaded trucks. Suggest you pull back."

"Mongoose here. I have an opening to plant an explosive and tracking devices on the second pickup. Give me cover if you can."

Brett hit his mike twice, and slowly swung the muzzle of his sniper rifle back toward mongoose. I have you covered, go, go."

Pat had finished planting the explosives and was strapping on the last tracking device when he saw a pair of legs approaching from each side of the pickup. He heard the doors open, and two men got in. Then two more men climbed into the back seat. Pat crawled slowly to the back of the unit, and he could see men already sitting in the big six wheeler behind. He had no way to get out. He spoke softly into his mike and said, "Devices planted, don't worry about me. Blow the units when you are ready."

There were two clicks from both Brett and Lyle. "Standby mongoose, we will get you out of there. Weasel out." Then there was silence.

CHAPTER 63

Just after midnight

Five minutes had passed, and they were still plunged in complete silence. Pat had checked the front, rear, and sides of the 4 X 4, there was no way he could get out yet without being spotted. Then his lower jaw dropped, there he was, the man with a limp. The Chechen, Aleksey Iman Shamil, was getting into the passenger side of the first SUV. "I just saw Aleksey get into the lead unit. Forget about me, and blow the units." Pat was breathing hard, and his voice gave away his excitement and concern.

"Mongoose, I need another minute or two. I am climbing up the ridge so I can get a better shooting position. Be ready, and when I say go, roll out toward the sea and get protection behind anything you find, the fireworks will start then." Lyle heard two clicks from both Pat and Brett. Lyle found the outcropping of rocks he wanted to use for protection and laid down with his AR-15 pointing toward the tangos. "Back to you Mongoose, I am going to blow the boat, and that will surprise those guys, they will stare at the conflagration in dismay before throwing themselves to the ground or running from the inferno. You will roll fast out and down toward the water. Eagle will take down as many men as possible to give you a chance to work your way around and back. We will blow the other units two minutes after the first. We should be able to catch up with the lead vehicles later. You copy?"

Brett clicked his mike twice, then lined up on one of the tangos with his sights. Pat wrapped his arm around his AR-15 strap and pulled himself to the very edge of the truck. "One, two, three, go, go." Lyle pushed the button, and one loud and massive explosion followed. The fire on the boat was intense, and due to the smoke, the visibility was poor. Pieces, of the craft, small and large, were thrown into the air. More flames erupted as more detonations were heard, all due to the blowing of ammunition. The noise, the airshow, and the energy created were impressive seen from the ridge.

Pfft, was all that anyone could hear as someone fell flat on his face on the waterfront with half of his head missing due to the bullet that Brett had fired. Two more men fell as Lyle opened up from his location. The remaining hands on the shore and the ones on the road began to panic, and chaos took over. The big diesel engines of the six-wheelers fired up, and the two 4 X 4 pickups started to move forward as fast as the road allowed them to go. Lyle triggered the explosives on the last truck to explode. The sky lit up like the 4th of July as box after box of ammo blew, legs and arms began to drop from the sky like rain. Of the vehicles, there was nothing left but pieces of the chassis.

All of a sudden the tarps on the back of the remaining six-wheelers were pulled up; big 50 caliber machine guns opened up firing hundreds of rounds a minute up toward both Brett and Lyle's position. The rocks that provided cover were turning to sand as the rounds tore up the hillside. Pat had crawled back up to the edge of the road and aimed at the gunner in the back of the second 4 X 4 just as it was pulling away. Lyle hugged the ground as he pushed a button and truck four exploded, more body parts and blood rained down from the sky. Meanwhile, the two 4 x 4s were out of sight around the bend in the road with only one truck close behind that now pounding their position with their big 50s, Brett and Lyle were thankful for having the ridge for protection. They continued to hit with rounds as they were rushing to catch up with the lead units.

Just as the third truck was starting to pick up speed, Lyle pushed button three on his activation device. As before, explosions went off as the red rain along with parts of bodies, covered the landscape. All of a sudden part of a head rolled next to Pat, causing him to jerk and feeling nauseous. He looked both ways, the coast was clear, so he ran across the road and started working his way back up the embankment toward the ridge. "Mongoose retreating to cover." Two single clicks followed his words.

As Lyle started to climb, all of a sudden a bullet round from a Ak47 hit his body armor in the back. He stumbled forward, gasping for air. "Tango on Weasel's ass old buddy, need help."

"Roger that." He just dropped behind a boulder, powerless for a short instant. "Keep on climbing." Then Lyle heard the big Dragunov speak. He knew that was the end of that problem; Brett almost never missed. As Pat climbed the hill, grabbing onto the grass and rocks to keep his balance, he took one hit, then another into the body ceramic armor on his back. Fortunately, the rounds were coming at an angle and glanced off, his body facing differently, the bullets might have penetrated enough to cause serious damage. Then he was hit on the shoulder with a round. Pat never felt the pain when first shot, the adrenaline was high, but he knew he would feel it soon. "Mongoose hit, leave me and catch up with those trucks."

"Brett, I'm dropping back down on the road and going to work my way over to Mongoose. Cover us the best you can."

Brett clicked his mike twice. As Lyle passed the second burning truck, he spotted one of the tangos who had been left behind. He moved to the side and fired three round bursts; the man went down. Lyle continued advancing, then a bullet hit him in his pack and bounced off his armor. Lyle stumbled forward, and at the same time, he heard Brett fire. The individual fell just a few feet away from him.

"Eagle here. Area clear to proceed to help Mongoose. It looks like it is not too exposed where he is. From that angle, it will be easier for you to climb back to safety. I have your back."

"Roger that. As soon as you see us clear the area, head to our vehicles."

It took thirty minutes for Lyle and Pat to finally stumbled to safety. The sight of their SUVs was comforting to Lyle who had been assisting the agent with the steep climb with Pat's arm over his left shoulder. Brett had already put away his pack and had the first aid supplies ready for use. When the backpack came off Pat's back, the agents realized there was a flesh wound across the left shoulder. Brett cleaned the area and put on quit clot before placing a dressing and bandage over it. Brett also noted the swelling and bruised areas on the man's back where the rounds had hit his armor. He gave Pat a bottle of water, pain medicine and told him he was in no condition to drive. Then he turned to Lyle.

Lyle had pulled off his backpack and armor. He also had injuries, severe swelling and discoloration from the two rounds that had hit his left and right upper back. Lyle refused the pain medication. Sipping water, he looked at Pat, and then at Brett. "Brett put Pat's extra gear in your rig. Keep his AR-15 and grenades. Shit, you know the drill. Keep him in the back seat. He can still provide some firepower if we need it. I am going to blow and burn his SUV, so there is no evidence of our presence here. We need to hit the road right now."

Nothing more was said as the men rushed to finish loading their gear. They were glad to head back toward the paved road, E50. As they pulled away in the two vehicles, Lyle pushed a button, and Pat SUV exploded and began to burn. They did not worry about noise or dust as they bounced on the dirt road taking them back to the highway.

CHAPTER 64

East of Grozny
Highway 50, next day

A man in a black SUV was speeding toward Grozny on the E50 at one hundred and twenty kilometers per hour. On the passenger seat were an AR-15, a flash-bang, and a grenade. Brett, his partner, was following in another SUV with his injured teammate sitting in the back seat. Lyle spoke into his mike and said, "Eagle, I have not seen any taillights yet from the loaded trucks. They left the waterfront just a few minutes before we did. We have to catch up with them before they get into town where I am sure the nuke will be handed off to someone that we will have to capture, and this could take us all the way to the Black Sea.

"Roger that."

"I am sure Pat planted the tracking device."

When Pat heard his name mentioned, he raised his head in pain, and said, "When I rolled out from under one of the truck, all I could do was to throw the device at the back of the 4 X 4. Tell Lyle to turn on his tracking unit." Brett relayed Pat's statement to the leading SUV,

"Pat asked that you turn on your tracking device. He threw the gizmo at the back of the pickup before it took off."

Lyle slowed his SUV a little, and with one hand on the steering wheel reached between the seats to grab his pack where the tracking unit was. With one hand steering, he was able to get it out of the bag. He pushed the toggle switch forward to activate the instrument. A red light showed, and a familiar beep followed. Lyle called Brett, and said, "It's working. Tell Pat that all the beer he can drink for a month is on me. They are still on the E50 and have just passed the turnoff into Grozny. I have a feeling they are heading for the Black Sea. "Lyle was so happy he was almost singing as he spoke through his mike. "I am going to close the distance to about a mile, be ready for action at any time."

"We are lucky. Pat is looking better and taking in fluids."

"I don't think they know we have a tracking device. If we did not have to rescue the nuke, we could resolve the problem in an instant. You know, I have a feeling the smugglers expect us and are going to set a trap somewhere in the hills up ahead. What's the plan now?"

"I think we might have the edge. When the tangos' vehicles stop to eat or fill with gas, or whatever, let's get as close as possible and continue monitoring their moves."

"Sounds good, but stay back a good distance. Don't forget those damn big 50's that will tear the trees to the size of toothpicks, and us along with them. We will have to hit hard and fast."

"If we could get close enough to throw a grenade or two first, that would even up the odds a little. There are at least eight tangos and only two of us."

It was not long before the two vehicles in front of them stopped near a grove of trees. Both Brett and Lyle pulled over. Lyle handed his binoculars to Brett. After he perused the situation up ahead, he said, "The bastards look cocky and confident, they are filling up with gas from large jerrycans. I am wondering if they are going to get help from some of their friends we ran into coming over the mountain."

"I was thinking the same thing." Someone threw another empty gas can it the back of the truck. Lyle said, "Well, it looks like the Iman and his bunch are leaving. Let's follow and see what happens."

The rooster tail of dust that followed the mini caravan soon vanished into the forest. The rays of the bright sun came from behind allowing Lyle and Brett to pick up a reflection now and then from the side mirrors of the tangos' vehicles.

Over an hour had passed, Lyle continued to watch his tracker, the blip just kept sounding. He was sure they had gone at least fifteen miles or more, and he was confident they were near the ridge top and soon would be dropping down into the valley where the Chechen gang had ambushed them hours earlier. All of a sudden the blip stopped. Lyle gave the signal to come to a halt. "Our friends are taking a nature break or preparing a trap for us. We better fuel up while we have a chance, and take a break our selves." Lyle got out of his SUV and soon had gas pouring from one his jeep cans into his unit. He looked at the monitor and went back to check on Brett and Pat holding the device in his hand.

"Welcome back to the field of action old friend. You look a little pale, but seem to be moving better." Lyle felt like teasing his old friend who had been hammered many times by bullets hitting his body armor.

"I think I prefer this to sitting behind a desk in Paris, listening to that prick of a COS. The arm is a little sore and stiff, but I can hold and shoot a gun if I need to. What's the plan?"

"I am going to pull up our location on the SAT, phone and see what our options are for getting out of the valley in case they try to box us in up ahead."

Lyle handed Brett the tracking monitor and pulled out his NSA phone. Within two minutes he had his location showing on the screen. "It does not look like we have much choice when we leave here. We either go back the way we came or continue straight ahead over the mountains. The second option takes us back into Georgia through the heart of the clan's territory. I wonder what they are doing, and I have a feeling our friends are trying to get help from someone."

Brett looked at Lyle, then Pat. "We have no choice; we have to stop that nuke. Let's push ahead, reduce the distance between us a little and see what happens." Again all the vehicles were moving forward.

Within five minutes, all three men were drinking water and eating as they drove onward. Lyle noticed that the enemy up ahead had slowed their speed again, turned left into a mixed forest of oak and pine. Almost four hours passed before the red button on his tracking device stopped moving. Lyle spoke into his mike. "Our friends have stopped again. Let's back up behind those boulders we just passed. They could be stopping for the night, or waiting for someone."

"Roger that." The two vehicles backed into their protected area, parked so they could pull out on sudden notice.

"Brett, you help Pat get his pack filled with armor, food, water, etc..., you know the drill. We are going to leave him over there, across the field, behind those trees. I have a feeling we are going to have company. You and I are going to take a walk, leave most of your gear with Pat, take what will be needed to give our friends a welcome up ahead. Let's go and see if we can at least blow up that lead." It took some ten minutes to get the supplies and move Pat safely hidden in a defensive area across the open field and behind an outcropping of rocks. "Pat, leave your headset on, we will keep in contact. Don't attempt to take on our friends. They will probably send two men to patrol and leave two behind for cover."

Lyle took the tracking device with him to keep watch on the smugglers' movements. With Brett in the lead, they slipped almost a hundred yards into a forested area, parallel to the road. The mile which normally would take the men about twenty minutes with heavy packs to cover, took nearly thirty-five minutes as they had to stalk their way forward, observe, listen, keep quiet, be vigilant at all times. Then Lyle saw Brett kneel and heard him say. "I think I heard chickens cluck in the distance up ahead. There must be a village or a farmhouse at least."

"Go to your left another hundred feet or so, we are going to move ahead of them, so if they leave, we will try throwing grenades. We have no choice; we must stop that lead pickup."

Silent, the men moved through the trees and brush and soon were looking down on three rock farmhouses, two barns, and a huge yard where the tangos' vehicles were parked. Squatted behind trees for cover, they soon spotted older men with beards, all of them carrying an AK-47 hanging from their shoulder. To their surprise, they soon saw three old women, dressed in black, carrying firewood and water. "It's obvious they have friends here, and God knows how many terrorist friends up ahead. Let's move farther to the left and see if we can work close enough to toss the grenades under the trucks."

The two men worked their way slowly and with stealth to a small rock outcropping. Both of them pulled their field glasses to peruse the buildings. "Lyle, look to my left where those boulders are on the hill. I think one of our friends plans to use us for target practice."

Lyle moved to the left, centered the glasses on the top of the small ridge near the boulders and watched. All of a sudden he saw a man, a sniper, move his tripod forward just a few feet. "I think you have a clear shot; it's no more than four hundred yards. With those new silencers, no one will hear you. Can you make the shot?"

Brett laid his Russian SVD Dragunov sniper rifle across his lap, pulled the pods down. He studied the sniper through the scope on the gun, and said, "What do you make for the wind speed?"

Lyle through a little fine dust in the air, then said, "Two to three klicks."

"That's what I figured also." Brett reached up on his scope with his right fingers and adjusted the settings on his telescope sights. He took several breaths, letting the air out slowly to slow his breathing and relax. Then he put his index finger on the trigger, gave just a little pressure, let his breath out slowly, and fired. There was minimal sound as the 7.62 NATO round sped across space and slammed into the side of the tango's head, just above the ear.

Lyle watched in his field glasses the blood and brain matter spray from the man's head. "Nice shot. He would have cut us down if you had not spotted him. Can you watch me from here as I go down through the trees and chuck a grenade or two?"

"I will move a little to my left, should be no problem. Are you sure you want to go? I can throw further than you."

"You are by far the better shot and will have to cover my ass while I escape back into the woods. If we get separated, let's meet back where Pat is."

"Roger that, and good luck."

Chapter 65

East of Grozny

Old Farmhouses

After making sure he had his ammo, grenades, and a bottle of water, Lyle hid his pack in the bushes and covered it with leaves. He moved like a panther in the night as he slid from bush to bush and tree to tree down toward the old stone buildings. Another man, Patrick, quietly and with painful effort squeezed his injured body between two large boulders when he spotted four tangos stalking their way toward the agents' SUVs. The imminent danger had suddenly restored Pat's mental alertness, and for a few minutes, no pain was felt. With his automatic weapon aimed at the enemy, he was ready to attack.

It had taken Lyle longer than expected to work his way down the hill. The thick grass was dry and made a crunchy noise with each step taken, loud enough, it could attract the attention of possible patrolling guards. Now in the vast and desolate yard, Lyle found refuge behind stacked firewood partially protected with a tarp. He was now about a hundred and fifty feet from the two 4 X 4 pickups and the six-wheelers. He studied the vehicles. They were parked so the 50 calibers machine guns could shoot in the direction of the nearby road and also in the direction of another road, the one where Lyle and Brett's SUVs were parked. Lyle pondered at which vehicle he should throw the first grenade.

A loud explosion broke the silence. Then another one. At the sound of the detonation, Lyle observed two men running back to the farm, they appeared to be returning from where their two SUVs had been hidden. Brett made contact.

"They blew up our wheels. I can see the smoke in the air. If Pat stays put, he should be ok. Blow those units, major and let's get the hell out of here."

As Lyle pulled the pin on the first grenade four tangos with AK 47's came running from the buildings. Lyle counted one, two and threw another grenade, it landed close to the closest pickup and blew. Parts of the truck flew into the air. The right front door was hanging by only one hinge. The windows shattered, sending glass fragments in all directions and cutting several of the men causing them to drop their rifles to be able to cover their facial cuts with their hands. The vehicles began to burn. Lyle threw the fourth grenade as far as he could, it blew up with so much energy that it almost lifted the second 4 X 4 off the ground. Immediately, its gasoline tank exploded, and the fire engulfed the entire unit and the six-wheeler. Full of ammo and explosives, the contents of the huge six wheeler gave place to a spectacular explosion that must have been heard all the way in the valley.

Rapid fire from the terrorist began to hit the wood pile and shed bark from the trees. Lyle pulled himself up the hill, moving from tree to tree. Then he saw a tango fall to the ground, seconds later another man fell. Brett was covering his ass as usual. The screaming and yelling coming from the men in the yard added to the confusion. Then Lyle fell flat on his face, as he had taken a bullet in the armor on his back. He moaned as he tried to catch his breath. He rolled over and over until he was behind a large tree. The tangoes, now aware of Brett and his deadly sniper fire were now hiding in the buildings and shooting out through the small windows in the rock walls. Thank God they can't use those machine guns in the truck, Lyle said out loud to himself. As the deadly fire of the handheld machine guns began to diminish, Lyle pulled himself in behind the rock cover where Brett was.

"I can tell you took a bullet, my friend. How bad, and where?"

"Body armor in the back. Painful, I am ok. Let me get my pack…. we need to get Pat and be moving out of here like hours ago."

As Brett helped Lyle put on his pack he took a last look down toward the burning pickups. He could see four Tangoes running up the road from the direction of their burning SUV's. Then two men begin to move to their left up the road, and two more just to their right, coming up through the woods. "We have company coming and fast. I will throw a grenade toward the two on our right. They will think for a few minutes before they decide what to do." Brett threw the grenade as far as he could, and not waiting for the explosion, he and Lyle moved up the hill. The blast occurred, then the two men started to angle back to the east toward Pat.

They managed to stay ahead of the tangoes and were stalking their way back where Pat was hiding as the sun began to make shady spots from the trees facing east; the two men knew the sun would be setting, and soon providing some cover at least. It would be dark within an hour and the three men needed to be out of the area. As they helped Pat put on his pack, Lyle looked at his two comrades and said, "They will call for help from Grozny, and God only knows where else up ahead. We have no choice but to work our way toward the mountains to the SW into Georgia. How's the shoulder, Pat?"

"I'm fine. That pad you placed on the left shoulder helps a lot. I can shoot fine, don't worry. Let's put some miles between our friends and us."

Lyle, Pat, and Brett worked their way higher into the mountains while trying to keep the road in site. Meanwhile, the Chechen, Aleksey Shamil had called for reinforcements from Grozny and members of a terrorist group living in the valley just over the mountain ahead of them. Aleksey had asked the leader he spoke with to provide support with pickups and men if he could. After being assured of additional trucks, the leader said he would try and send twenty to thirty men. Pleased with the possibility of more help, he then sent a team to go after Lyle, Brett, and Pat.

CHAPTER 66

Next day

Just after one a.m.

Three tired men, two of them moaning at times due to pain, worked their way up and down the slopes long into the night. Even though the air was cold, they were sweating profusely through the bandanas tied around their foreheads. After a while, Lyle called a halt, he sat down on the ground and pulled the straps of his backpack off his shoulders. His face was covered in sweat, and his undershirt was soaked. "It's just after one a.m., men, how far do you figure we have come?"

Brett was the first to answer. "It feels like ten to twelve miles, but it is more like six to eight miles as the crow flies. We have done a lot of climbing."

Brett said, "The packs are slowing us down, but I guess we need everything we are carrying, food, water, and armory, all are necessary if we want to make it across the Caucasus mountains. We won't be in the best of shape to fight off the Iman and his warlords. Can't you call for a chopper to extract us?" Lyle was quick to answer, "I wasn't kidding you when I told you we were on our own. No one can help us unless we are on American controlled soil; even the president must stay out of our problems." There was a long pause before he resumed his thoughts. "Wait a minute; I have an idea. Brett, how about calling sergeant major Jenkins and see if he can get the ball rolling. He could fly to Mosul if we need him. I know it is not next door, probably six hundred miles. One of the two US bases in Turkey would be more logical. I know there is one almost at the eastern border of Turkey and Georgia." Lyle had been searching for a map in his pack.

"Who is Jenkins?" Pat inquired with curiosity.

"An old retired army chopper pilot. He has saved our ass more than once." Brett quickly responded. The agents became almost agitated thinking about getting a hand from Jenkins. They all became quiet when Lyle took out the sat phone. Once he had a connection with the satellite, he pushed the button to connect their old friend who lived in Curaçao, in the Caribbean. After what seemed like an eternity Lyle heard the familiar rough voice of sergeant major Jenkins. Jenkins knew who the caller was. His first words were, "Oh shit, you guys are in trouble. Calling me on this secure phone means you need my services. Where in the hell are you, my friends? Hey, it's so good to hear your voice."

"We need your help again. Dozens and dozens of terrorists and Chechen gang members are on our ass like bees. We are in the Caucasus Mountains, in Chechnya, on our way back to Georgia. We have with us our partner, Pat, who has been injured, as for me, I received a couple of bruises, Brett is intact so far." Lyle giggled as he was staring at Brett. It looks like we have a slim chance of making it back into Georgia simply because we are on foot, the enemy torched our vehicles. We are expecting a horde of assassins to catch up with us."

"I told you, boys, not to go anywhere without Hilda or me. I think you need a Russian helicopter to bring your asses home."

"That would be a relief, dad. For thirty pieces of silver do you think you could use your contacts and head for Iraq soon?"

"As soon as I hang up, I will call Colonel Jackson, then a colonel I know in Iraq. I better get Hilda up, or she will tar and feather me."

"This trip will be more stringent than the last one sarge, are you sure Hilda wants to be part of this suicide mission?"

"You will need her medical and gun skills, so keep your thoughts to your self-whipper snapper. I guess I will be coming in hot again."

"You better be flying ISIS flags all over your bird, have plenty of ammo and rockets, it's super hot in this valley. I have to leave my phone off, no way to charge it as we are in a foot race. One of us will call back in twenty-four hours from now. If no contact, head back home. By the way, when you contact the colonel, tell him we burned the suitcases."

"Will do. I should arrive in Mosul, Iraq, in twenty-four hours, and the bird will be worked on while I am flying there. I know of another closer US base in Incirlik, Turkey. It is very close to Georgia, probably less than two hundred miles from your location. Good luck to you, men."

"Bring up the code 'Vulcan.' The colonel and anyone else will try to move heaven and hell to help you when you mention "Vulcan." Lyle heard a click.

The line had gone dead. Pensive following this call that could solve their problem, Lyle held the phone in his hands for several minutes and remained quiet. He looked up into the sky and could see the Milky Way glowing like burning magnesium. In this remote place, no city lights could hamper the grand view of the galaxy. His mind started to drift; he could not fathom the vastness of this display. Back on earth, Lyle inserted the phone into a pack on his belt, secured the strap, and said, " You heard the conversation, we may get some help if our friend can arrange our rescue. I know he will. He mentioned a US base north-east of Turkey, about two hundred miles from here. Let's rest for four hours and head out. As soon as we can find two narrow ridges coming together into a narrow valley, we will leave plenty of evidence we went through there. We will also plant two of the claymores. That should lower the odds and slow them up."

Brett said, "Sounds good. You were lucky to find Jenkins home. It's going to be like old time when we reunite with both him and Hilda. Those two are one of a kind. If we can hold off the posse, he will get us out of here."

Curaçao

As soon as the phone call ended, Jenkins used a secure phone to contact Colonel Jackson in the States. After informing him that Lyle had burned the suitcases, he described the situation the agents were facing. Jenkins offered his help, and the colonel immediately approved the sergeant's plans to go to Iraq and from there go and rescue the trio.

"Let me know your ETA as soon as you can, and get a list of supplies and anything else you will need to me. I can contact the right people and have your order waiting for you when you land in Mosul. Your country thanks you and Hilda again, sergeant major." Then the line went dead.

Within three hours the two Jenkins were on their way to France where they would change planes to fly to Iraq. Jenkins made contact with his friend, the colonel in Mosul, to let him know what he would need when he and Hilda would be arriving. The sergeant was assured a helicopter in tip-top condition would be ready for him upon his arrival.

CHAPTER 67

Same day

The hue of the morning sun was shining through the trees, and the birds were chirping. If it had not been for the dramatic situation threatening the agents' lives, this resting place could have been ideal for a campground. The three men had spent the night on the edge of a clearing facing a field that looked unreal, every square inch of this meadow was covered with purple flowers in full bloom. All three agents stood there standing, and although not interested in flowers, they were amazed by the heavenly scenery. It was just after five a.m. and the light was partially responsible for the special effect creating this magnificent view.

The spot was serene, Pat and Brett spent some time laying on their back looking up into the blanket of cottony clouds. A third man, Lyle, was standing guard in the trees, listening for unusual sounds and scrutinizing the horizon in all directions. Now joining his friends, Lyle gave some orders before their departure. "Time to piss, hydrate, eat an MRE, and re-pack. We need to leave in less than ten. Although I could not detect any signs of our stalkers, I have a feeling they are getting close. I will take point for a while, Brett. You drop back at least sixty yards or so. Pat, how's the shoulder?"

"Sore as a lady of the night after servicing a load of Marines. No more bleeding." Pat knew that his wound was still oozing and his pain was not going away, but he could not expect his friends to carry any of his load. "I am fine, so let me carry my share."

"Stand down Pat; we have it. If we can find better cover tonight, I will sew your wound closed if I don't detect any infection. Let's go, men." Brett leaned over and helped Pat with his pack. Then Lyle and Brett, in unison, lifted their heavy bags over their shoulder. After Lyle disappeared into the trees, Pat followed, then Brett brought up the rear a few minutes later.

They stopped every hour for a sip of water and to listen and scrutinize the land. So far there had been no unusual human presence, but they sensed the enemy was coming. It was close to eleven a.m. as they approached the top of a small knoll. Lyle Stopped and raised his hand. He waited for the others to catch up. "Look ahead over to the left." Lyle pointed in the direction, and added, "Let's leave our trace over there, where the two ridges come together and then tie strings onto a couple of grenades. To suck them in, I am going to leave a candy wrapper, and also trample the grass as if we had spent time sitting down."

Brett had a better suggestion, "Maybe we should leave Pat's dressing behind instead of candy wrappers, they will be so excited to find out one of us is injured, that will keep them from suspecting a booby trap.

Another hour and a half passed before the men were in the little valley shaped like a trough. As Brett stood guard, Lyle and Patrick left their footprints in the dirt and trampled the grass without overdoing it. Before the men moved on, they dropped a bloody dressing on the dirt. To make sure the assassins would not take this display for a trap, Lyle made the ruse look like a genuine oversight. Since Pat was donating his shoulder dressing, Lyle took that opportunity to apply a clean bandage to his nasty shoulder wound. "I will have to do better than this when we stop for the night." Thirty feet away, Lyle tied a string to two grenades and prepared two traps to go off. Lyle was sure the discovery of this contaminated gauze would give the assassins a buzz that would encourage them to hurry thinking they were on the right track.

Lyle led Pat and Brett around the traps, and they continued their forced march. Surely, after the explosions, the enemy would be less eager to advance without closely keeping an eye on their path, giving the three agents a chance for a headway.

It took over two hours to cross the valley, and another hour to reach the wooded part of the mountain. They filled their water bottles at a spring that was burbling behind grass and dropped purification tablets into them. Lyle decided to take a short break. "Pat, I have some saline, I am going to irrigate your wound and sew it up. Brett, you keep watch."

"Roger that." Brett pulled off his pack, took his sniper rifle, field glasses and faded into the trees. Ten minutes later, he found a small knoll, climbed a tree and looked out into the valley they had crossed earlier. He studied the area closely for several minutes before descending from his perch and returning with his two friends. Once in camp, he noticed that Pat did not grimace with pain when Lyle stuck the needle in and pulled on the suture thread. "Gosh, Pat, how come you don't, at least, bite your lip when Lyle sticks that needle in?"

"He deadened me good first, dummy."

"You're lucky. Lyle never deadened me the few times he had to sew me up; not even a topical numbing medicine was used. Double standard!" Then he laughed. Lyle was quick to put in his word,

"Everybody knows you are tough and brave, Brett. Besides, how many times have you stitched me up, skipping the lidocaine or other deadening agents? You're getting old and becoming a wimp, a big pussy." All three men were now laughing. We better hydrate, eat and move some of Pat's stuff into our rucksacks, Brett. I don't want that wound opening again under tension."

"I can carry everything over my right shoulder. I can carry my share."

"Stand down Pat. Brett, lighten his load, and let's go."

The men had not gone even a hundred yards up the hill when they heard the muffled sound of a grenade exploding across the valley. "That will slow them down," Pat was eager to say. Then a few minutes later the second grenade went off.

"Brett, how far behind do you think they are in terms of time?

"According to the two explosions, I would say we have about two and a half or three-plus hours on them now. It is hard to tell; we did not pay much attention to the time we left the spring. Do you plan on hiking through the night?"

"Roger that. We will stop for five to ten minutes every two hours. Tonight I need to make contact with Jenkins." Then Lyle looked at his watch. "I will contact him in about three hours." Later as the men crested a small ridge, they could see the sun slipping on the horizon and changing rapidly to a blazing orange hue in its final minutes before darkness. Lyle turned and looked back toward the valley. He could see the outline of the moon. The sky being clear, this satellite of the earth would provide the agent some light later.

Before Pat left for guard duty, Lyle asked him if he could have his cell phone battery. "It's yours, but it's down to less than half charge." Pat immediately opened a closed pocket, took out his phone, removed the battery and handed it to Lyle.

"I need to call Jenkins. He is our only hope for possible evac. While researching the area with my binoculars, I found some old ruins across this valley. The walls look to be two feet of rock, and some seem to be three feet thick, maybe more. When we reach them, they will provide good protection for a while, but they will overrun us eventually unless we get help. We also need water if we can find it before we make our stand there. I am going to make contact with Jenkins at ten and see if he can make it by tomorrow night. Let's rest, we're dead tired, out of food and water and running on fumes" Pat had watch duty, Lyle would relieve him in four hours.

"Good night."

Four hours later, Lyle went up to relieve Pat from guard duty. "Seen or heard anything?"

"Been quiet, maybe too quiet. Goodnight, I'm bushed."

Lyle just waved. Lyle then took out his field glasses to look the area over before complete darkness. Lyle checked the coordinates, both latitude, and longitude one more time from the Wikipedia website for the ruins. He would give these readings to Jenkins in a few minutes, and then would get another reading from his sat phone when his men and himself made it to the ruins. Lyle punched in the number of his friend.

"Jenkins here. Man am I glad to hear your voice. I was beginning to worry. We are wrapping things up on the Russian Karmovka Kd-60. Heidi and I will be heading your way in a few hours. We have a site located where we will sit down in Georgia, remove the barrels and refuel. We will have to stop there to refill again after we pick you boys up. Do you have those coordinates for me?"

"Yes. Let me read numbers to you." After Lyle gave Jenkins the latitude and longitude, he had him read them back to him. "If we make it to the site, I will use the satellite phone to make sure they are the same. We all have headsets, so when you are a few klicks out you should be able to talk to us, OK? Also, I can turn my special phone on and maybe you can track the signal, even though there is very little battery left."

"Sounds good. Hilda and I have dreamed up a few extra surprises for those bastards. Give um hell, Lyle, and hold out if at all possible. See you tomorrow, as early as I can."

Then the phone went dead. Lyle turned off his phone and became one with the night.

CHAPTER 68

Next morning

Lyle let Pat and Brett sleep in an extra hour. He awakened them with the good news about his conversation with Jenkins. Lyle said, "According to that map, soon as we come out of the trees today we have a valley to cross and a climb up to some old ruins I mentioned yesterday. With a cliff behind our back, we will be protected on one side. The AD 440 ruins, according to Wikipedia, are all stone. They will provide good solid cover from an AK47, and from the big 50s for a while. Those big guns can tear us to ribbons." Lyle could see the concern on Brett's face. "We're all worn out Brett, but Jenkins should be on his way to Mosul, or here as we speak. We have to make it to the ruins and hold off whoever is on out tail until Jenkins can arrive with the Russian chopper. If at all possible, he will get us the hell out of here."

While the talking was taking place, Lyle asked Pat to uncover his torso so he could look at the shoulder injury and reinforce the dressing if needed. Looking at the wound, Lyle said, "It does not look good, too much redness for my taste, we may be faced with possible infection. As soon as we get to the ruins, we will need you. Once there, I will put you in a sniper position so you can make each shot count." Pat denied having severe pain. Selfless, he wanted to take part in the success of the rescue.

"Our friends have to be here within the next twelve hours or less. Do you think Jenkins can make in that amount of time?" asked Brett.

"It will be close, but if anyone can, Jenkins can. If they have that chopper ready to go, he could make it, and save our ass."

"Have you figured how we are going to position ourselves once at the ruins since it is only the three of us against an unknown number of them. We have no idea from which direction the enemy will be coming. I don't think we have been faced with such a dilemma in the past.

"We will decide when we finally have them in sight. Like you, I wish we knew how large an armada they are bringing. Pat can still shoot, but cannot move fast. I think I will put him at the back of the ruins with plenty of rock in front of him, but still leave him in a position to cover the openings into the ruins on the right side, where I will be, unprotected. I can tell you one thing, when they get here, they are going to go crazy and rush us; those crazy bastards want martyrdom and its reward, those virgins."

"Where are you going to position yourself Lyle? in harm's way, as usual?"

"I have a good stratagem to get rid of a few men and the big 50s. I am going to set up a couple of grenade traps again. Then I am going to place the claymore out where one of the pickups they may be riding could drive over it. Would be nice if we could eliminate one of those pickups with the machine gun. I hope that will buy us some time. We do not know how well equipped they are. They may be on foot, like us. I am planning on moving back and forth, zigzagging, behind a rock wall to try to make them think there are more than just the three of us. Let's I get some shut-eye." Lyle paused before he spoke again. "Wake me in under two."

Brett watched through most of the night; he knew Lyle was giving part of his sleeping time to Pat.

After finishing his boring watch, Brett noticed the dark purple clouds that had gathered on the horizon had started to turn lavender. Soon the sun peeked through, and the sky turned pink and a pale yellow. It was going to be a gorgeous day. Brett Grabbed his binoculars one last time before departure, gave a long and thorough circular survey of the close and distant boundaries, then he awoke

Lyle first, then Pat. After a long stretch, a rubbing of the eyes, and a yawn, Lyle said, "Eat up men, it's the last of the protein bars, take a sip, we need to leave like twenty minutes ago. We will know today if there will be a tomorrow." On this sad note, the three agents started their march to the unknown.

Brett was on point once again, and he picked up the pace as the trio moved down the hill toward a narrow valley. Forty minutes later they stopped under some trees for a breather. Lyle took out his glasses and studied the road which was more of a goat trail than a road and decided to go east. All of a sudden, Lyle who was still observing the land for unwanted presence, shouted, "Oh, shit. There is a dust storm coming our way about twenty klicks or so out. By the amount of dust, I would guess we are dealing with a couple of vehicles with men and guns. Brett and Pat grabbed their binoculars and studiously surveyed the developing invasion. Lyle turned and looked in the opposite direction, "Oh, fuck a duck, there is at least one more vehicle just starting down that ridge to the northwest. I would guess it is also over twenty klicks from here."

"Get into the trees, men, and pick up the pace, we are about three to four miles from those ruins. They don't know for sure we are going there yet, but they will within an hour or so."

Brett dropped back farther than usual, as he knew he would have to buy Lyle time to get Patrick to the ruins. With his sniper rifle, he could keep the terrorists back at least a quarter to a half mile or so. What he wanted to do first was shoot the machine gun operators on the pickups.

As Lyle and Brett moved toward the ruins, they heard two shots, which meant there were two dead tangos. An hour later Brett walked in slowly toward the ruins. He did not know yet whether Lyle and Pat had made it. The two agents had picked up the pace, with Pat using the last of what little energy he had left. They were soaked with sweat, and their muscles were screaming with pain as they moved behind the walls of the ruins.

A few minutes later, Brett heard Pat on his earphone. Area secure, come in, Lyle is working on the grenade traps. I am two rows down from the top where there is a big boulder that is out of place but will provide some cover on my left." Pat stood up and waved at Brett. "I have kept close observation and seen no one come much closer.

As Brett moved to his assigned spot, Lyle dropped his pack behind the row stones where he would make his stand. He left the ruins and went to set the claymore he covered with dry dirt in a passage their vehicles would have to take because of trees and huge boulders blocking off on both sides. The claymore in place, Lyle checked his two trip lines on the way back into the ruins.

Lyle took the time to show Brett where the grenades and trip lines were. "If we can kill three or four with the grenades, or even blow up a pickup, maybe we can buy ourselves another half hour or so."

Brett studied the upper part of the ruins for a few seconds, then pointed toward rocks at the top. "That's the area where I will be, and I can move some back and forth behind the rock wall. In fact, I will be able to cover all of the directions but our back, of course, will not need to, the precipice is there. Let's give them hell old friend and hope we hear rotors turning before long."

"Brett I will be down below moving back and forth hoping to eliminate one or two before I reset myself in another area. I am hoping they will think there are more of us." Lyle reached over, shook hands with his old friend, they hugged each other, and went their separate way.

While Brett was climbing up through the ruins, Lyle finished his last grenade trap. Always so thorough, he checked the other grenade trap once again before taking all his supplies to the low wall, his station. Then Lyle worked his way to where Pat had been posted, hugged him. "I am sorry Pat that our first job had to be one where the odds of getting back are slim."

"I wouldn't want it any other way, Lyle. We have been to hell and back before. Heck, after hearing about the exploits of Jenkins and his wife, my monies are on him and Hilda." Lyle and Pat hugged each other, then Lyle, unusually gloomy, returned to his designated area.

Lyle took out three magazines for his guns, then placed one at each end of the rock barrier and one in the middle. As he moved back and forth, he could eject the empty one, grab another, and be back in action in two or three seconds. Lyle knew that the opponents had a greater advantage over them, and the odds were in their favor. Everything depended on Jenkins arriving in time to evacuate them. His head was swimming with ideas and possible scenarios as he studied all the possibilities that could occur.

After a while, he checked the comm units, once satisfied they were OK, he asked Brett his estimate on the distance to a big dead tree just down from the ruins which he had evaluated to be a thousand feet away. Lyle wanted to make sure of the range so he could fire with better precision. Ammo, like the food and the water, was limited. The men knew they had to kill one of the attackers with each shot. After Brett contacted him with the estimated distance, he then set the scope on his gun. Lyle never contacted Pat, as he had given him orders not to fire until the enemy was closer to their position. Once satisfied with his scope settings, Lyle laid his pack down and took everything out that might be needed. He laid the gear close to the rock wall. Lyle knew it would be cumbersome to try and duck-walk with a heavy pack on his back. He then took the few remaining mags out and placed them in the empty slots on his belts, along with the remaining grenades. Lyle was not worried about Brett and Pat, as the three had worked together so long that they probably had everything set up for what could be their last chance. Little did he know what Brett was thinking.

Brett had done everything that he could do for now. He was sure that this was probably their last mission. Then he said to himself, " I had finally found peace with myself, and something I never thought I would find, love. And now all that happiness was coming to an end. Fuck it, I have served my county and the fellow man well, and I could never have found better friends." Brett then checked the wind and contacted Pat on the comm unit. "Hows the wound treating you, old friend?"

"It's much better since Lyle sewed it up. It's sore of course, but I will be OK, we will be OK. Don't worry about me; we've always made it in the past."

"It doesn't look good Pat. Without help, we're done for."

Then Lyle cut in on the comm unit. "I love both you men; it's been an honor to work with you, but we're not dead yet. For sure Jenkins is probably redlining that motor on the Russian chopper. Let's go out with a dead tangle for each bullet if we can." Then Lyle heard both Pat and Brett double click their mikes, they agreed.

Chapter 69

Same day,

The bright sun had been overhead several hours and was rapidly moving toward the west. Shadows of trees were appearing in front of the men. From their positions in the ruins, they could discern three pickups with, bolted to their beds, 50 caliber machine guns. The trucks had stopped in a curve in the trail about two miles away. Like the three agents, the enemy knew that the ruins, with their walls standing at a different height in most of their perimeter, were an ideal setting for cover. That advantage had been pursued as a godsend, but also as a curse by Lyle. He was conscious the enemy would automatically expect their presence behind those massive walls. Being short of ammo, water and food, Lyle had calculated this place was still the most protected spot for them, and an easy marker for Jenkins. What was left of the old fort was completely detached from any other structure and could not be missed.

With the assassins close by, The trio knew there was nothing much they could do, but lay down behind the walls and hope the old stones would not turn to sand too fast from the pounding of the big guns. There was an eerie silence broken by Pat's message, "A fronte praecipituim a tergo lupi."

Brett who had caught two words, praecipituim and lupi, precipice and wolf gave his own interpretation of the Latin idiom, "Wolves jump in the precipice to die as martyrs and catch the virgins." Then he laughed into his mike.

Lyle knew the meaning, a precipice in front, wolves behind, and had found it very appropriate to their particular situation, the English translation being "between a rock and a hard rock." He was sure his partners, due to fatigue, lack of food, and poor perspectives had reached bottom. He was thinking that Pat's infection was getting worse, and the high fever made him hallucinate in Latin." Then he was reassured when the injured man explained his message. "I never had much to do at the embassy in Paris, so I studied Latin for a while. It means, 'A precipice in back and wolves in front' unless I got it mixed up. But that's what's coming, a pack of hungry wolves and no way to escape."

Although invisible in the darkness, the agents, thanks to their goggles had spotted numerous men appearing between the trees in front of them. Then those same men started firing their Ak-47s and yelling Insha' Allah, Allahu Akbar, over and over. The partners killed the enemy as fast as they could pull the trigger, never missing a shot. Lyle would drop one or two, stay low and duck, walk to a different location, raise and take down another man or two. Pat had an open view also and was killing tango after tango as they tried to move around to the side of the old ruins.

Then all of a sudden the first grenade went flying off, blowing arms, hands and other body parts as three men audaciously rushed through the opening into the ruins. The shooting stopped, and all one could hear was screaming. Within a minute the firing started again as the tangos attempted to move closer to the ruins once more. The pickups were tracking their 50 calibers in a straight line, raising the shots in the direction of Lyle's wall. The big bullets tore into the stone breaking off pieces of rock and sending them like tiny missiles in all directions. Lyle had blood running down his face, and arms from sharp fragments of rock hitting him. Then he heard Brett yell a warning as the other big 50 had got the range on Brett. Thinking someone had been injured, they rushed through an opening in the wall, but they were met by another grenade which exploded, creating more carnage. The screaming and shouting were continuous. The big fifty opened up again as the fanatics continued to yell Allahu Akbar.

Pieces of chipped rock kept on flying and hitting Lyle in more places, his face was bloody as well as Brett's, causing the two men to grimace. The lead pickup started moving closer. As predicted, it drove over the claymore and exploded. Pieces of metal along with body parts flew into the air. The enemy was now conquering the ruins, men were climbing over the walls. Pat was killing tango after tango as they were getting closer to Lyle's location. Pat spoke hurriedly into his mike, "Lyle, two tangos crawling in low on your right, I have to reload."

"Roger that. Lyle dropped down low and fired three round bursts into the menacing tangos creeping toward him, then quickly kneeled again, dropping tango after tango to both Pat and Brett's direction. Just as he emptied the next to his last clip, he heard the sweet sound of rotor blades slapping the air. He retained his breath to savor that sound which was bringing hope.

Brett who was working from a higher wall than Pat could also hear the blades of the chopper slapping the air, wack, wack, wack. For Brett, the sound reminded him of Viet Nam. "Our Angel Gabriel is on his way," Brett said into his mike.

But what came next was not expected. As the big Russian Karmovka-60 began to come into view, they heard the recorded voice of a muezzin calling to prayer over loudspeakers. All of a sudden the ISIS warriors, along with the other terrorists and gang members began to drop their weapons. They were dancing up and down and yelling, Insha' Allah, Allahu Akbar, (God is Great). When the helicopter was in full view, one could see four black ISIS flags flying proudly from the skids of the chopper. As the aircraft began to turn in a circle above the ruins, the writing in Arabic on the doors became visible, "The Prophet has returned."

Many of the ISIS warriors were yelling, "Alhamdulillah," (Praise be to Allah). Others were screaming Ashokrulillah, (Thanks to Allah). Then more of the warriors would point their AK47s, and fire into the air while yelling, "Alhamdulillah," (All praise and thanks to Allah). In the middle of the brouhaha, the assailants had stopped their attack. This unexpected truce brought confusion to the three partners who, to avoid attracting attention, kept hidden and, although ready to fire on the spot, decided to go along with the strange respite. Lyle said, "Maybe they think we are dead."

Once the big Russian helicopter was in full view, a loud cry came from a group of ISIS warriors climbing the wall where Lyle was hiding. They were yelling "Mohammad Raulu Allah," (And Mohammad is his messenger). To the three partners' surprise, the leader of that horde, Aleksey himself, stood upon the pickup with the big 50, and he yelled, "Allahu A'lam," (Allah knows best). Then all of a sudden the warriors laid down their weapons and bowed their heads.

With the arrival of the aircraft and the apparition of the man with a limp, all the activities halted. "Brett, there he is, its the woman and child killer, Aleksey Iman Shamil himself. Can you believe that?"

Brett quickly replied, "I am getting him." Then he started to site the Iman in with his scope.

"Hold it, Brett, let's wait and see what happens."

"You better duck, here comes the wrath of the Lord of fire, 'Vulcan." Abruptly, Jenkins clicked off the sound of the call to prayers and spoke in a cavernous voice into the speaker on the outside of the chopper. "Listen to the wrath Vulcan sent by the United States you assholes." He clicked on the sound of the Star Spangled Banner as he had done on another mission, and let go with the first 9M17 Skorpion missile. Within a split second, it blew the pickup with Iman Shamil standing proudly into millions of bloody pieces. As the body parts and blood rained down from the sky, the second 9M17 took out the second pickup, shocked tangos immediately realized the ruse and began to pick up their AK 47's and started firing at the chopper. For over four minutes the ruins was a cacophony of rocket fire, chips of rock breaking off with the speed of a bullet, blood turning the rocks red. Among the ruins, one could hear the sound of hell. As soon as Jenkins blew up the third pickup, a bullet from an AK 47 hit Jenkins in the left shoulder. He screamed slightly, and said, "I've taken a hit dear, you take over the controls. I will use the Yak-B machine guns on them. Keep rotating the chopper side to side. I want to see more of Allah's boys red blood all over those rocks."

The firing of the guns was deafening, hundreds of rounds a minute were chewing up men, rock, metal and whatever else was in the way. Then it came, all the remaining terrorists had picked up their guns, and while firing began to yell Allah Akbar again and moved forward into the ruins, rushing to their death as they were mowed down by Lyle, Patrick, and Brett. Then Lyle and Brett heard Pat say, "I'm hit, I will be OK, just give me time to stop the bleeding."

Brett had made the mistake of glance where Pat was stationed; he took two rounds on his chest armor. Lyle was throwing the last of his grenades as the wolves began to thin down to only a few. Lyle heard Brett's sniper rifle fire, and someone who was about to pull the trigger and terminate Lyle, had his head chopped off. "Thanks, pard, I owe you again my old friend."

Hilda had moved the chopper to the corner of the ruins and fired a 9M17 missile into a pack of men trying to enter the woods for cover. As she rotated the Chopper back and forth, she tore bodies to hamburger with the Yak-B machine gun. Body parts and blood covered the trees there were bodies scattered in all directions, but the assassins never gave up. A bullet struck Hilda in her chest body armor and another one hit her in the top of the right shoulder, striking the body armor on her back. She needed Jenkins's help, "I took a bullet, old man, can you use your right arm?"

"Good enough to hold you, woman."

"You handle the right control, and I will handle the left. We will have to work in sync now; we are both down to one arm."

Hardly a second had passed when the head of the man that had shot Hilda changed to a bloody mass of flesh. Lyle spoke into his mouthpiece. "It looks like it might be over, thank God for Hilda and you Sargent Major. You showed up to save our asses again, and you got hurt in the melee. As a last humanitarian act, I need to give the coup de grace to any still breathing and suffering. Can you sit that monster down just to the east of the ruins?"

"Roger that, but don't laugh about the landing—Hilda and I are using one arm each to control this monster."

It took Lyle several minutes and more than fifteen rounds to finish off those still fighting for their lives as they screamed in pain. Lyle had said nothing about being hit in the fleshy part of his right leg or about the several rounds that had struck him on the chest part of the body armor. He took a few minutes to take care of the wound of his left leg. Lyle could see a large scrape on Brett's right leg; a bandage was applied to cover the injury. Brett and Lyle, working together were able to get Patrick into the belly of the big chopper. As the two men crawled inside, all they could say was, "Thanks, get us out of this hell hole."

The big chopper lifted off, and dropped down below the edge of the precipice, then moved toward the orange glow of the sun as it began to disappear in the horizon behind the upper Caucauses Mountains, leaving behind devastation. The mission had been arduous and almost disastrous, but Aleksey had finally been eliminated.

CHAPTER 70

Airborne, toward Georgia

Hilda and Sargent Jenkins were doing the best they could to keep the Russian chopper flying straight and smooth. Hilda looked over at her husband who had remained quiet. She could tell he was not well, in fact, he was turning pale. "Lyle you have to reach over the seat and help with Jenkins's right shoulder, he was hit bad back at the site. My stubborn old man would rather die than ask for help. Look at him, his color is bad, see if you can check the bleeding."

The light in the cabin was dim, so Lyle held a small flashlight in his mouth to get a better look at the damage, but first, he had to expose Jenkins's upper back. He kneeled on two superimposed packs so he could reach the patient's back. With surgical scissors, Lyle started cutting away the jumpsuit and ended up removing one bloody sleeve to expose the lesion. He was shocked at the excessive loss of blood; the heavy fabric of the suit was saturated. Brett had been watching the scene, making himself available. "Brett, reach in Hilda's medic kit and get me a hemostat. Also, hand me the disinfectant, and my favorite, the QuikClot gauze. This type of sealant is one of the world's most lifesaving inventions. It increases the rate of clotting, but it needs to touch as much of the wound surface as possible. Right now, I'm more concerned about blood loss than the germs, but let's be as careful as we can." Lyle separated the flesh, opened the hemostat and closed it over the bleeder. After cleansing the wound with saline, he covered it with Quikclot, then placed on a thick sterile dressing, and bandaged the shoulder tight as he could. "Hilda, J needs a fast drip now."

Before Hilda could say anything, Jenkins in his weak voice responded first. "Lyle, my woman, was also hit in the shoulder area. I am OK for a while, patch her up."

As Lyle leaned over to look at Hilda, he could see the dry blood that had run down her right arm. With the end of the small flashlight back in his mouth, Lyle started cutting the top of Hilda's flight suit. Suddenly he stopped. Accidentally, the right strap of Hilda's bra was cut, and the massive, white, and pendulous breast appeared. It had sprung out of its support, and its paleness was contrasting with the dark green flight suit Hilda was wearing.

"What's holding you up, son. Why are you stopping? What you are seeing is a breast, don't tell me you are suddenly prudish. Lyle giggled and said, "I guess I was a little bit too aggressive with my scissors, sorry Hilda." Hilda who was laughing had brought her left arm over her boob. Even Jenkins who was weak and sore managed to laugh too. The only one who didn't find the situation amusing was Pat who, by now, was unconscious. Hilda's right shoulder was no longer bleeding, but the wound was very deep and due to the precarious setting to treat it, prone to infection. "Brett, I need another hemostatic now, disinfectant, and the rest. You know the drill."

As Lyle worked on Hilda, she never moaned, and never told him how to do his job. As he was applying the tight bandage, he said, "Hilda, it's worse then you think. The two Jenkins had kept the helicopter in the air, but the ride was getting hazardous. Lyle with authority ordered Hilda to sit them down as soon as she could, that was an order." Lyle never heard Hilda say, "Yes sir, major."

Hilda was worked the controls of the helicopter while Lyle was checking the work Brett had done on Patrick. "Brett, did you give him any antibiotics yet?"

"Yes sir, maximum load. I also cleansed and dressed his wound. He should be OK until we get him to a field hospital. He is not responding to stimulus, nothing."

"You did a good job. I need to take care of you now."

"I'm OK, let me take care of you first."

"Stand down, Brett." While Lyle was cutting Brett's pant leg past his left knee, he heard Hilda speaking on the radio.

"Mayday, mayday, this is Vulcan to Mosul command. We have five, I repeat, five wounded warriors. Mayday, Mayday, I need you to get a message to Colonel Farnsworth."

"Vulcan, this is Mosul command. Can you give me your location?"

"We just crossed the Chechnya, Georgian border. I will give you our coordinates on a sat phone in a few."

"Mosul to Vulcan, I am sorry, you are out of our district or command area." Hilda never heard anything else. Then all of a sudden the caller continued speaking, "It's Colonel Farnsworth, Hilda. Fuel is our main problem. Can you milk that chopper any further?"

"Negative colonel. Jenkins might bleed out, we are leaking oil, and I see smoke coming from the engine. We are now landing. If you can send help sir, I can give you coordinates to where we stored some fuel."

"I should have known you and that old man of yours would have thought of everything. That's why he saved my ass so many times. I am getting a rescue chopper as we speak." The colonel leaned over to his aide and told him to move his ass. "It will be painted black, no markings. Soon as you are on the ground call me on the Sat phone."

Hilda never answered she was so weak now that the chopper was weaving back and forth. A small and flat opening appeared on the horizon. As the helicopter hit the ground hard, flames began showing inside the engine cowling. "Brett, pull Pat away from the chopper, I will take care of Hilda. When you come back, get Jenkins, and I will rescue the medical supplies and as much else as I can."

The two men stumbled, moaned, and stumbled some more as they pulled the three patients to safety. Just as Lyle was bringing the last box of medical supplies, the helicopter gave a loud bang as fire engulfed it.

In a weak voice, Hilda said, "Lyle, there is whole blood, all our types in that metal box." Then Hilda passed out temporarily from the loss of blood. Brett was opening the refrigerated square box inside which the blood had been stored as Lyle was getting together the medical supplies to start an IV on both Hilda and the sergeant major. Their improvised IV poles were the low branches of a dead oak tree. Lyle searched through his patients' pockets until a found the small sat phone to make contact with the colonel.

Lyle gave Colonel Farnsworth a short sit-rep, then he took time to provide him with the longitude and latitude that Brett had found on Lyle's phone, just before the battery went dead. The colonel still needed one more piece of information, "What about the location of the fuel to get the chopper back to Mosul?"

"I will have that for you by the time your rescue unit gets here colonel. Both the Jenkins are semi-conscious but should be talking within the hour."

"Good enough for me. Hang on the line, and I will give you an ETA." Farnsworth turned to his aide and asked him to contact the rescue chopper and get the info. Another three minutes passed before Lyle's phone rang. "My men will be there in about three hours, give or take. After two hours and forty-five minutes, turn on your sat phone signal." Nothing more was said, and the line went dead.

CHAPTER 71

Next day,

High in the Caucasus Mountains, there were no artificial lights to obstruct the celestial spectacle that the milky way offered to the five warriors who were waiting for their flight. It was pitch dark. Two hours after the rough landing, Sargent Major Jenkins was slowly recovering from his comatose state and was now coherent. As Lyle was checking his vital signs, the now alert patient inquired about his wife Hilda's condition. Lyle immediately reassured J, telling him she was next to him, two feet away, and had responded well to her blood transfusion. Hilda, like the rest of them, was resting on the grass with an army blanket covering her partially bare torso. When she heard Lyle and Jenkins talking, she raised her head and waved at them. Lyle had tried to make everybody comfortable with a minimum. The three blankets he had rescued from the helicopter were cut in half, except for the third one that was kept whole for Pat who was still not responding to stimulus and whose fever, although high, remained stable. Everything was shared, the water, the blankets, and the food rations Hilda had brought along. Lyle told Jenkins that a rescue helicopter was coming from Mosul thanks to his friend, Colonel Farnsworth. Lyle asked J the location of the fuel catch, "Did you or Hilda, write down this information somewhere?"

"Holly shit, whippersnapper. You think this old coot and his lovely lady are antiquated and victims of senility, of course, I have a record of this information. Open either one of our phones and hit the barrel icon." Then he laughed, coughed, and laughed again, as he reached over to caress his wife's head.

After finding Hilda's phone, and making sure they had plenty of battery time left, Lyle called in the fuel location to Colonel Farnsworth. The conversation was short and to the point.

Three hours later the aborted landing of the chopper, Brett tried to sleep, but he heard Pat talking, asking where he was. He now seemed conscious, more talkative. All of sudden a bright light and the rhythmic thump, thump, thump of helicopter blades fully revived all five as it descended toward them. Hilda began to scream with joy. With all the excitement around him, Pat became confused, mumbled a few words, and everybody was reassuring him, telling him everything was going to be OK.

Few words were spoken as two medics jumped out of the helicopter and began doing the job they were trained to do, two men in black, with guns and wearing night goggles set up a controlled perimeter. A soldier helped Lyle and Brett into the chopper; then he returned to pick up their weapons and supplies. Within minutes the medics loaded Hilda and Jenkins in the helicopter on a stretcher, then the guardians of the night followed.

As the chopper lifted off into the air, there was a loud explosion. As Lyle looked out a small window following what seemed to be an explosion, he could see hot orange and yellow flames engulfing the Russian helicopter, and the area around within fifty feet plus. By precaution, the US government was clearing the site where the Russian chopper had landed, leaving no trace of its passage.

The five injured warriors entered the hospital for treatment in Mosul, and later in the day, they were transported to Bagdad. By then, it was afternoon. Three days later they landed in Bergen, Germany. After a few days Lyle, Brett, and Pat were able to walk around the area without too much pain. In Bergen, they had time to play tourists. There they visited the Forestry Museum, north of the city. Jenkins and his wife wanted to get out of their room and join their friends, but because of their age and the nature of their injuries, they were ordered to remain in the hospital. Another four days went by before the quintet was flown home on a private jet sent by POTUS. The plane made a stop in Curaçao to drop off the Jenkins who once again had selflessly risked their lives to come to their friends' rescue. Brett and Lyle had spent very little time with Hilda and Jenkins this time, so to make up for this, they promised to stay in touch as the date of the double wedding was approaching. The Jenkins would be their guests of honor. Then the craft flew on to Washington DC. While on the tarmac, refueling, Colonel Jackson met the group. This unexpected meeting touched Lyle and Brett who were not expecting such a thoughtful gesture from their boss. The colonel spent an hour with the three men. Patrick who was almost back to normal after having dealt with an acute infection followed by an aggressive treatment left with the Colonel while Lyle and Brett continued their flight to New Orleans.

CHAPTER 72

Next day,

If one were to look up, they would see bright stars as far as the eye could see. High in the Caucasus Mountains, there were no human-made lights to take away a view that most in cities never experience, infinity. The quarter moon had passed overhead a few hours earlier, and it was just after two a.m. when Sargent Major Jenkins became coherent. As Lyle was checking his vitals, the first thing he asked about was Hilda's condition. Lyle relaxed J telling him she was doing fine. He gave him her vitals before he could ask. Lyle then made J comfortable as he could, and said, "We have a rescue helicopter coming from Mosul, thanks to your friend Colonel Farnsworth. J, we need the location of the fuel catch, do you or Hilda, have it written down somewhere?"

"Holly shit whippersnapper; I have not finished raising you yet. You think this old coot and his lovely lady are antiquated. Open either one of our phones and hit the barrel icon." Then he laughed, coughed and laughed as he reached over to put his hand on the top of the one he loved.

After finding Hilda's phone, and making sure they had plenty of battery time left, Lyle called in the fuel location to Colonel Farnsworth. The conversation was short and to the point.

Three hours later, as Brett was trying to sleep; Pat was starting to become conscious when all of sudden a bright light and the thump, thump, thump of helicopter blades awakened all five as it descended toward them. Hilda began to scream, but Jenkins reassured his wife everything was going to be ok.

Few words spoken as medics from the helicopter jumped out, and began doing the job they were trained to do, other men in black, with guns and night goggles on set up a controlled perimeter. Another soldier helped Lyle and Brett into the helicopter, then returned to pick up their weapons and supplies. Within minutes the place was sterile. The medics loaded both Hilda and Jenkins in the Helicopter on a stretcher, then the guardians of the night followed.

As the chopper lifted off into the air, there was a loud explosion. As Lyle looked out a small window, he could see the hot orange and yellow flames engulfing the Russian helicopter, and all the area around within a hundred feet plus; the US Government was sterilizing the site where the Russia chopper had landed hard, leaving nothing left for chance.

After hospital treatment in Mosul, the five wounded warriors were transported the following afternoon to Bagdad. After a complete medical checkup and treatment, three days later they were transported to Bergen Germany. After a few days Lyle, Brett, and Pat were able to walk around the area without to much pain. Jenkins and his wife tried to get out of bed several times but were told to rest. Another ten days passed before they were flown home on a private jet sent by POTUS. The plane made a stop in Curacao to drop off the Jenkins, then flew on to Washington DC. While on the tarmac refueling Colonel Jackson met the group. The Colonel met with both Lyle and Brett for almost an hour. After a short greeting on the plane, to thank the Jenkins, Patrick left with the Colonel, and the remaining two wounded warriors continued their flight to New Orleans.

CHAPTER 73

New Orleans

A week later later

Brett taped a protective plastic sleeve over his leg wound to keep it dry while taking a shower. He stepped into the warm water spray, feeling human and alive again now that he had returned to the States in the arms of the woman he loved. Brett feasted momentarily on the news he had received from Hilda in the Russian helicopter when they thought they were going to die. Hilda had hesitated to be the messenger but decided to speak, "I was hoping Fran could give you the news Brett, but I better tell you as it looks like we might not make it. You are going to be a father." Hilda and Jenkins had not wanted to be the ones bringing the news but the situation was so grim, so hopeless, they decided he deserved to know just in case they should all be killed. The announcement had moved Brett so much; he remained mute for a minute. The agent was reliving the happy scene that had taken place at a time of chaotic despair. Now beaming from ear to ear, he stepped quietly from the shower, dried off, and sat down on the edge of the bed.

Brett picked up his wristwatch from the nightstand and placed in on his left wrist. As he looked at the illuminated dial, he noticed it was early, just after four a.m. He slid in under the sheets, put his lips close to Fran's ear and said, "I love you with all my heart, Frannie poo, you and the little one you will give to us." Now awake, Fran said, "You are incorrigible Brett, you just woke me up, but I am glad you did."

Fran vaguely knew that the last mission had been difficult and that everyone had been injured. Brett had presented the nightmare he and his four partners had lived on the mountain just a few days back as an incident. He never mentioning the horrific violence that had taken place in the ruins and the hostile fighting that could have been fatal.

He kissed her softly, then harder, as if to silence her, and she felt his manhood stiffening against her thigh. She wanted him as much as he did her. Fran rolled on her back, and with her arms locked around his neck, being careful not to irritate his recent injury, she pulled him on top of her and let her thighs fall apart. Reaching up with her hips, moaning and gasping for air, still lubricious from their earlier lovemaking, she felt Brett slide deeply into her.

Neither one cared about time or space for a while, but reality soon sat in as the two exhausted and sweaty lovers separated. As Brett held Fran tightly, she whispered into his ear, "We have to get up, I hope you remember we are getting married today."

CHAPTER 74

Wedding day

Lyle and Brett had returned to New Orleans from Germany eight days earlier. Patrick who was doing fine was staying in Washington DC at the small condominium he owned there. He and Colonel Jackson had arrived the day before to attend the double wedding of the two couples, Annie and Lyle, and Brett and Fran. Sergeant Major Jenkins and his wife Hilda, the two wounded warriors injured only three weeks earlier were also in New Orleans. They had arrived three days ahead of time to explore the Big Easy, and of course to attend the wedding which was to be celebrated in the afternoon.

In bed at five a.m., Lyle was running all sorts of thoughts through his mind. He lay their basting in the memories of the night before when they had all gathered at aunt Annette's to go over a few things and share a drink or two. Monique, Lyle's mother, had arrived a week ahead of everyone. At her request, she had been put in charge of planning all aspects of the wedding. She had reserved the hotels for Annie's guests, her two friends, her sister, and Marguerite, her mother. She was the one who had coordinated the church service, wedding reception, all the facets of the festivities. At the restaurant where the wedding reception was to take place, Monique had spent hours selecting the decor of the room and the food items that would be served. She wanted this day to be memorable; her boy, her only child, was getting married.

Lying on his back, Lyle was thinking about his sabotaged wedding in that eight century-old church in Paris, and about the outcome which could have been a lot worse. Annie, little Jennie, and himself had been hit by a sniper and had almost died. This time, they would realize their dream. His friend Brett would be at his side, as he had always been the last ten years, but this time they would be out of harm's way.

The emotion an imminent marriage ceremony brings can generate anxiety, Lyle wanted to relax. He rolled over against Annie, put his hand over her shoulder. She grabbed it gently, squeezed it, brought it to her lips, and gave it a kiss. At her contact Lyle became excited. Everything she did, no matter how innocent and unintentional, enticed him. She could unknowingly seduce him at the drop of a hat and without anticipating the outcome.

Lyle's fingers began to caress her face and body lightly. He kissed her neck, then around her ears. His skillful touch made Annie's body trembled with desire. She rolled over, gently and slowly brushed his torso with the back of her hand, and gave him a multitude of simple, almost chaste, little kisses all over his face and neck. Annie could feel the hardened arousal against her thigh. She could not hold back, she surrendered. The rhythm was slow. The lovers would bring each other to the brink of an orgasm, back off, and then continued until they exploded into one another.

They fell asleep as they had given the maximum to each other. Lyle awakened first, it was almost nine a.m. He remembered Annie had to meet his mother at nine about something to do with the wedding.

With the touch of a master pianist, Lyle awakened his woman. She got up without delay. Annie knew Lyle's mother, but not well enough to be late. After all, the woman had worked hard to make the double wedding a success. She was never sure when Monique was joking or being sarcastic. She called the wedding planner to excuse herself for being late and to let her know she was on her way.

As Annie dressed in a hurry, Lyle made coffee and had croissants and preserves ready for her. She grabbed a croissant and her cup and left the hotel running. At the door, she stepped back to kiss Lyle on the forehead and to say, "I don't know why she has to see me." Then Annie headed for the parking lot.

Later Lyle met up with Brett, Patrick, Colonel Jackson, Sergeant Major Jenkins, and Remi, his favorite uncle. The men had decided to go for brunch then head for the Voodoo shop.